D0680798

CONTENTS

Chasseur à cheval	2
Book 1 in the Napoleonic Horseman Series	4
Copyright	5
Chapter 1	6
Chapter 2	19
Chapter 3	32
Chapter 4	47
Chapter 5	58
Chapter 6	70
Chapter 7	82
Chapter 8	95
Chapter 9	106
Chapter 10	117
Chapter 11	127
Chapter 12	142
Chapter 13	158
Chapter 14	173
Chapter 15	185
Chapter 16	199
Chapter 17	213
Chapter 18	224

Chapter 19   236
Chapter 20   248
The End   257
Glossary   258
Historical note   259
Other books   262
Chapter 1   269

CHASSEUR À CHEVAL

BOOK 1 IN THE NAPOLEONIC HORSEMAN SERIES

By

Griff Hosker

Published by Sword Books Ltd 2013
Copyright © Griff Hosker First Edition

The author has asserted their moral right under the Copyright, Designs and Patents Act, 1988, to be identified as the author of this work.

All Rights reserved. No part of this publication may be reproduced, copied, stored in a retrieval system, or transmitted, in any form or by any means, without the prior written consent of the copyright holder, nor be otherwise circulated in any form of binding or cover other than that in which it is published and without a similar condition being imposed on the subsequent purchaser.

A CIP catalogue record for this title is available from the British Library.

CHAPTER 1

I was born Robbie Macgregor. To many people, I am a traitor. To the French people, I grew up with I certainly was. To the English I fought for, I probably was and to my Scottish relatives? I suppose it depends to whom you spoke. I take no blame for any of this; it was all an accident of birth and of death.

My great grandfather Robert Macgregor left Scotland with Bonnie Prince Charlie after the failed Jacobite rising of 1745. He was loyal to the former king and brought all his family to live in France with the king. His hope was that the Stuarts would be returned to the throne. The Macgregors felt a kinship with the Stuarts and they were loyal. When he died his son Alistair, my grandfather, clung on to the belief that we would prevail and the King of Scotland would be returned to the throne. He married another of the children of the exiles and in 1758 they had my mother, Marie. I suspect had things remained the same I would have been brought up as an exiled Scottish Laird. I would have lived a life of parties, hunting and learning to be a gentleman but fate can be cruel. My grandfather and grandmother were both victims of one of the periodic plagues which swept through France at that time. Bonnie Prince Charlie left France and my mother was taken in by one of my grandfather's friends, the Count de Breteuil. I never knew where the money went. Perhaps it was put in trust with my grandfather's friend. I do not know.

All of this, you understand, was told to me by my mother but she always spoke the truth to me. Those years were good ones for my mother and she was educated as a lady. She was brought up as the daughter the count had never had. Sadly, the old man died and his son, a captain in the Chevau-Légers returned to take the title and the lands.

Count Louis de Breteuil was an arrogant, cold and cruel man and he was my father. My mother was attractive and he made her pregnant. There is no pleasant way to put it. They are the facts. I have no idea why he did not marry her save that he had the option of marrying into another aristocratic French family. My mother had nothing. Her money had gone and she had no title. She was handy and she was pretty. He had been in the army for some years while she had been growing up. If it sounds like I am making excuses then you are probably right. I have to see some good in my father. He was never cruel to her, nor was he kind. He made love to her regularly and then ignored her. She had a room; it was not the best in the house but neither was it the worst. It was large enough for the two of us after I was born. The other women on the estate were also visited by my father but they knew how to prevent children. My mother had been brought up a lady and did not. I was the count's little bastard. A term used by some of those on the estate who disliked my mother.

Once I was born then she became less attractive to the aristocrat and became an unpaid servant in the house. She worked as his secretary. Her penmanship was excellent and she could write a good letter. She also managed the books and finances of the château. He refused to give me his name but he did take an interest in me. Perhaps that was another reason why my mother was kept on. He enjoyed being cruel to me and hurting me but, perversely, he also taught me skills. He had a servant who had served with him in the Chevau-Légers, Jean Bartiaux, and he was charged with teaching me to ride, fence and shoot. As soon as I could walk, I was thrust on the back of a pony. Whenever I fell off, I was told to remount. Jean was no less harsh than his master but at least he didn't beat me when I failed to match his high standards. It made me tough and that has helped me since. Jean was an interesting man. I came to know him much better when I grew up but as a child, I just knew him as a quiet thoughtful man. Looking back, I can now see that he was fond of my mother but at the time I didn't see that. They just laughed a lot together and I liked that. They were the precious times when my mother was happy, they were rare and to be treasured.

The count and Jean would only speak French to me and my accent is that of Northern France, where we lived. Mother could speak French but she only spoke English to me and I grew up speaking that language with a Scottish twang to it. I was fluent in both languages and could shift between them easily. I think that gave me a skill in all languages for I was able to pick up a new language easily. Well more easily than others perhaps.

Once I had mastered the horse, I was taken riding regularly by my father. He was a superb rider and I take it as a compliment that he never made allowances for my youth. The three of us rode everywhere together. I always had to call him sir and he called me boy. I knew where I stood with him. Once Jean taught me to shoot then I accompanied my father as we hunted on his estate. At first, I was just his loader but once he had seen I was competent I was his loader and I also got to shoot. It may sound idyllic, hunting with your father, but he never gave me any sign that I was his blood kin. I was just an unpaid servant who helped Jean. The fact that the three of us shot many animals helped a little in his acceptance of me.

Mother started to become ill about the time I was being taught to fence. She never stopped being beautiful but she just lost more and more weight. I couldn't understand it and nor could anyone else. The old housekeeper, Madame Lefondre loved my mother and she did her best to keep her alive but we all knew that it was hopeless. I was eleven at the time that she passed away. I was taken to her by Madame Lefondre when the priest had given her the last rites. She put her emaciated arm around me and hugged me to her body which was more bones than flesh.

"I'm so sorry bonny laddie but I won't be here to see you grown up. I've done my best but things havna worked out as I would have hoped. You should have had a father who loved you and would care for you. I am sorry that you will be left alone. It makes my journey even harder." She hugged me tighter and I felt her salt tears trickle down my neck. "I have hidden a few things from your father. They were given to me by my mother and father. They're not much but they might come in handy. Madame will give them to you but keep them secret. I hope your father looks after you but I canna be sure about that. Jean is a good man. I know he can be a bit serious at times but he is a good man and you can trust him." She kissed me on the cheek and coughed. Madame Lefondre dabbed away the blood from my cheek.

"If you can, son, get back to Scotland. We should never have left to follow the auld soak, Bonnie Prince Charlie, but your great grandfather was a loyal man, God rest his soul. My father should have gone back when we had the chance but he wanted to go back a success. That's all nonsense. You just get back there to Glen Orchy. There will still be Macgregors who remember your great grandfather." I had had the names of all my ancestors drilled into me as a child and I could go back five generations without thinking and another three with pen and paper. She looked fearfully over my shoulder. "There are some in this house who hate me. I fear that they will hurt you when I am gone. Trust only the two I said." She coughed again and sank back into the pillow.

"Don't die! Please don't die!" I know that I was almost a grown man but the tears came and I fell into my mother's arms.

"Ssh, child. It is just a journey I am going on and I'll be there for you many years from now when you come to me. You are a good lad and I am sorry for the beatings your father gave you. I could do nothing to stop him but I felt every lash of the stick." Her eyes closed. "Come kiss me now and I will sleep for a while."

I kissed her and Madame Lefondre wiped a tear from her eye. "Look after my wee bairn for me."

Madame Lefondre nodded and said, "Oui, ma petite." She led me from the room. Mother lingered on for another day but she never recovered consciousness. The three of us buried her just outside the family plot in the area reserved for the servants. Jean had carved a cross for her. He must have spent her last days working on it. It was beautiful and as we hammered it in it struck me that he must have been working on it for some time. He had known she was dying. I suppose that was the second sign I had that they cared for each other. The first had been when she had said to trust him.

The two of them held me between them. Jean put his hands on my shoulders, "You must be strong for your mother. She would want it. She was a good woman and she was badly used. I will always be there for you but you must tread very carefully around the count. He has a fearful temper. I can do nothing. Do you know that? But I will watch over you as I promised your mother." I nodded and he smiled and left.

Madame Lefondre stroked some stray hair from my face. "He stayed only because of your mother. He loved her but he could do nothing about it. Your mother, I think, loved him." She shook her head, "It was not meant to be. He is right, you must be careful around the count. Now come with me and I will give you the little your mother left for you."

I had no idea what to expect. She led me to her room which was tucked away close to the kitchen. She closed the door and took out a small chest from a large clothing trunk. She opened it, handed me a ring with an emblem on it and said, "This is your family ring. Guard this with your life." I nodded. I looked at the ring handed from grandfather to son and then to daughter. Now it came to a son again. She handed me a small leather pouch. "Open it." Inside were rings and necklaces. "These are valuable. If you need money you can sell them." Her eyes clouded over. "They were your mother's and she loved to look at them." That decided me; I would need to be desperate before I sold them.

Finally, she took out another leather bag. "These are gold Louis. They are worth much money. Each one could feed a poor man for a year. There are ten of them. They are all that your family managed to retain." She closed the box. "I will try to watch over you but there are enemies here."

"Enemies?"

She nodded. There are two women who hated your father for your mother was his favourite; Mama Tusson, the mulatto maid and Anne-Marie, the parlour maid. They made your mother's life a misery and they frequently tried to beat her until the Count stopped them. They resented her beauty. Never be alone with them for they are evil, they are like witches and they will try to hurt you."

I had seen both women and noticed their sour expressions whenever they saw me and now, I knew why. "I will, Madame and thank you for caring for my mother." I suddenly realised how alone I really was, "What will happen to me now?"

She put her arms around me and I noticed that she smelled of lavender. "That depends upon the Count. If he allows it you will work here but if he gets a notion, he may send you on your way. That is why your maman left the gold for you." She shook her head, "She thought you would be a man grown when you needed them."

The day after mother died, I was summoned to the great hall. My father looked up from the papers he was writing. With my mother gone he would have to do them himself. This was not a good start. "Your mother has died. What use are you to me now? Why should I continue to throw good money away and look after you?"

I felt as though someone had slapped me in my face. But I remembered my mother's words. "My lord, I am your son and I will honour your name with my deeds. If you throw me off the estate, I will still be your son and everyone will know I am your son. But it is your decision, my lord. I am powerless."

He gave me a shrewd look. "Jean will find work for you. Can you read and write?" I nodded. "Perhaps there will be some work for you then. When there is no longer any work then you will leave. Is that clear?"

"It is my lord."

I had no choice. I could not get back to Scotland as I had no money save my reserve of coins and I only had two sets of clothes. My shoes would not even get me to the coast and so I would have to find a way to get some money and save.

The next two years saw me grow rapidly. Madame Lefondre could not give me money; she could not buy me clothes but she could feed me and feed me she did. I took over my mother's duties although my penmanship was not of my mother's standard and it took me longer to do the accounts. Jean taught me how to shoe horses and to work the anvil at the smith's. It was hard work but it gave me a skill. Jean said very little but I could see what he was he doing; he was preparing me for a life beyond the estate. That day would come; it was inevitable. If my father ever married then his embarrassing bastard would have to leave. One day, as we repaired some of the farm's tools, I asked him about his life before the estate.

He shrugged. "I came from a poor family but we were horse people and I joined the cavalry to work with horses. It was a hard life but I was paid and I loved the work. When the count joined the regiment, he took me as his servant and I served him. When he left, he asked me to join him and look after the horses on the estate. It seemed like a perfect position." I could tell from his voice that it had not worked out that way.

"You would still be in the cavalry otherwise?"

"Probably."

"What were the Chevau-Légers?"

"Light cavalry. Not the ones who charge in the big battles but the ones who ride ahead to find the enemy. I enjoyed the life." His wistful tones underlined his words.

"Would you go back?"

He shook his head. "If I had stayed then I would now be a brig-adier or even a maréchal-des-logis. They give orders to the officers. I could not take orders from someone younger than me."

He sounded wistful. "Perhaps I should have stayed."

He wondered about his decision when the troubles began in the year 1789. Out at the chateau, many miles from Paris, it seemed far away but in Paris, the king and queen had to make compromises. My father did not like those compromises. He never compromised about anything. He did things his way and he believed that the king and queen had the Divine Right to continue that way. The count became darker and angrier during this time and I kept out of his way. The irony was that I towered over him and could have beaten him to a pulp had I so chosen. If I had done that then my life would have been forfeit. Before the Revolution that would have resulted in my death and so I bit back my retorts and I took the blows. In my heart, I knew that I could fence at least as well as he could and I was a much better shot. When we went hunting it was my bag which returned full.

The count was a man of action and he weeded out all those on the estate who had any revolutionary leanings and threw them from his land. In the final analysis that was a grave mistake but I am looking back with hindsight. It made him even more un-popular in the town. The weeding out of those that the count feared meant that my position was secure and he even began to pay me. I was able to save, at last. I was hopeful that I would soon have enough to fulfil my promise to my dying mother and return home. Events in Paris, however, thwarted my attempts to return to Scotland. The king and then, later, the queen were executed as the Terror took hold. That should have been the warning to the count that he ought to flee to the Vendee, where there were many royalists, or England, where others had fled. He did neither and, in the end, that was his undoing.

One morning he took Jean and me to Paris. I think he was called to a meeting by others of a similar leaning but he con-fided nothing to us. We were his servants and not his peers. We rode along roads which were new to me. He rode ahead of us and was silent and brooding. This allowed me to look at this new land I had never seen before. The France I knew was the estate. Breteuil was a village. Now we passed through bigger towns. They had hotels and inns. There were even some shops. When we stopped, Jean and I would sleep in the stables whilst he would have the finest rooms in the inn. Neither of us minded and we knew no different. It was our place in the scheme of things. The closer we came to Paris the service we received became surlier. It was as though they resented the count because of his position. My father became increasingly angry and I began to fear for our safety. As we entered through the gates of Paris, we saw a different France to the one we knew. It was festooned with the tricolour, much to the anger of the count. Although there was no violence towards him his clothes and demeanour marked him as an aristocrat and the looks, he had to endure were those of hate and loathing. The guards at the northern gate took note of our names and asked the count his address whilst in Paris. When he gave the name of the marquis with whom we would be staying they exchanged a knowing look.

The streets of Paris were not clean and they were crowded. My father must have been angry at the proximity of so many peasants but he did restrain himself from using his crop. Eventually, we halted before a large townhouse. There were guards on the doors which led into the courtyard beyond. Two liveried and armed guards stopped us from entering.

"I am Count Louis de Breteuil. I am a friend of your master the Marquis."

One of them nodded. "You are expected and welcome, my lord, but not your servants. There are many revolutionaries in Paris these days and the Marquis is careful whom he admits."

The count seemed to find that reasonable. He dismounted and handed the reins to Jean. He turned to one of the guards, "My bags are on my horse." As the man unstrapped them the count threw a purse of coins to Jean. "Find a stable close by. Return and tell the guards where you will be staying. I will only be in this," he waved an airy arm around the streets, "rat hole of revolutionaries for the shortest time."

With that, he left us. For the first time, I was glad that I was not dressed in fine clothes as that would have marked us as different from the sans-culottes we encountered while we sought a stable.

Jean drew me to one side. "Do not say that we are servants of the count. It may prove dangerous. I noticed he had many dark looks thrown his way. This revolution appears to be bigger than I thought in Breteuil."

"Who are we then?"

"Say that we are blacksmiths passing through Paris and seeking work."

We found a stable, although the price they charged for our three horses was nothing short of highway robbery. When we asked if we could sleep in the stable, we were refused. "No, I am sorry but I have lost too many horses that way. Yours will be safe here for I keep guards. There is an inn nearby."

The inn we found was little better than a stable and the prices were inflated. Jean seemed philosophical about that. "We have the master's money. I will show him the receipts and he will have his view confirmed that this city is now a sewer filled with rats." We left our bags in our room. We wandered back through the teeming streets to the Marquis' home and told the guards where we were staying. The guards nodded but were reluctant to talk with us and we left.

I was keen to explore the city and we headed north to the bridge which led to Notre Dame. I had heard that it was the finest church in France. I was not disappointed but the priests who were there looked as nervous as the Marquis' guards. There was an air of fear around the city. The Tuileries Palace was surrounded by the National Guard who looked at us suspiciously when we approached. Jean led me away and we headed back to the inn. The food was dreadful. Jean laughed, "Madame Lefondre looks after you too well. This is the normal fare and the normal portions. Get used to it for I think our world is about to change."

And change it did. When we awoke the next day, we both felt a change in the atmosphere. As we left the inn, we noticed that we were closely watched. Jean had not trusted the innkeeper and had told me to keep my valuables about my person. We both had a sword and pistol but they were with our horses. "I think, Robbie that we will see if the count is ready to leave. I hope he is for I most certainly am."

We were a street away when we heard the noise from the house of the Marquis. There was the sound of angry voices and banging. Jean held up his hand for caution and we moved slowly to peer around the end house. There was a mob of sans-culottes and they had manufactured a ram out of a bench. They were trying to break down the door.

"Should we help the master, Jean?"

He shook his head. "Two of us against that mob? I think not. Let us see what happens. These are dangerous times we live in. This is not Breteuil. I just hope that his guards do not make the mistake of using violence. There are too many in that mob."

We saw cracks appear in the door and a face of one of the guards appeared in the window of the first-floor room which overlooked the street. He had a gun and he fired. Two of those holding the bench fell and I saw that one of them was a woman. This enraged the mob even more and they almost hurled the ram through the door causing it to splinter open. They tore inside like ravenous wolves in a sheepfold. We could hear shots and then screams. It seemed an age before anyone emerged. The first we saw was the bodies of the guards thrown, limb by limb from the first-floor window and then we saw a bloodied and wounded marquis and the Count de Breteuil being led, bound and gagged from the residence. I started forwards but Jean restrained me. "Let us follow! We can do nothing to help him yet."

The two aristocrats were led by an ever-growing mob across the Pont-Neuf and towards the palace. They were tethered by the neck and frequently fell to the ground. They were unable to stop themselves as their hands were tied. Their faces became cut and bleeding. They were beaten when they fell. For the count, this must have been the final humiliation. As the crowds grew it became easier for us to follow. Jean saw one inoffensive looking fellow next to us and asked, "Where will they be taken, citizen?" We had quickly learned to use this title as all those in

Paris we had met had spoken of little else.

"Normally they would be taken to be tried but because of the actions of the men's servants, they go directly to the Place de la Revolution. They will be executed." He seemed quite excited at the prospect. "There were no executions planned for today. Isn't it glorious?"

We nodded our agreement but I felt a sick sensation in the pit of my stomach. He had been cruel to me but he was still my father and I was going to stand by and watch him die. Jean sensed my dilemma. "You can do nothing, Robbie. We will follow in case this fellow is wrong but..." I knew what he meant and I steeled myself for what was bound to be a harrowing experience.

Word had spread and there was quite a crowd around the guillotine. I did not wish to be too close and that was as well for we could not get through the press of people eager to see two aristocrats executed. A pompous looking man festooned in tricolours stood. He raised his hands and the crowd fell silent. He had a high piping voice which seemed more fitting for a woman. "These two aristocrats have shown themselves to be beyond the law. This morning they encouraged their servants to murder innocent women and children." The crowd began to bay. I knew that was not true but the truth was immaterial now.

The Marquis had his gag removed and he began to scream as his head was placed in the wicked looking device. The executioner's assistant smacked him on the side of the head with a small cudgel and he was silenced. The executioner pulled a handle and the blade crashed down to sever the head. It landed perfectly in the basket and was so quick that it silenced the scream of the dying aristocrat instantly. His body was removed and the machine was prepared for my father. The blade was slowly raised still dripping with blood.

I wondered if he too would scream for mercy but when I saw the resolute expression on his face, I knew he would not. He had been hard on me and he could be just as hard on himself. My father would die as he lived, without compromise. When his gag was removed, he shouted, "Long live the king. I urge all of you to fight against this terror!"

The crowd booed and hissed. My father calmly put his head in the machine. He was almost smiling when his life was ended. Jean said, "Cheer and smile!" Even though I felt like crying I did as I was told to do otherwise would have marked us out as different. We were now in a most dangerous position. We were trapped in Paris without a friend or employer. Even worse, we had been in the employ of an executed aristocrat. "We will get the horses and leave now before they search for us!"

CHAPTER 2

We reached the stables without anyone taking any interest in us. Wearing the clothes of ordinary people was the safest way to travel. Once on our horses, however, it might be a different matter; the poor did not own horses. The owner of the stables was equally unconcerned, especially as his bill was paid in full. We headed towards the southern gate, just to avoid the crowds at the Place de la Revolution. Events were occurring so quickly that I had not time to think let alone speak. I was in Jean's hands and I trusted my mother's judgement. He would not let me down.

We were stopped by four National Guards at the southern entrance to the city. "Where are you going citizens?"

Jean smiled, "We have heard of work for us at Golfe Juan. They have need of a smith and his assistant there."

"Is that your trade?" Jean nodded. "Where are your tools?"

"The lord of the manor, Count de Breteuil, claimed they were his when he threw us from his land. He said we were revolutionaries."

The sergeant suddenly looked up, "The Count de Breteuil you say?"

My heart sank. He was reading from a piece of paper. Suppose our names were upon that and we were to be captured? I contemplated making a run for it. The men had no horses and, with a horse between my legs, no one could catch me.

"Yes, damn his evil eyes. He used to beat the boy something

terrible."

One of the other guards laughed. "Boy? He has not done badly then. He looks like a man to me."

"Aye and that is the other reason we were thrown out of a job; the count was afraid of my assistant." The guards nodded sympathetically.

The sergeant had not heard a word, he was intently reading. I suspected it was a new skill to him as his lips moved as he followed the words. "It is as I thought. His lands are to be confiscated. If you were to go back you could have your job again. Just see the local committee. The old injustices will now be put right. Long Live the Revolution!"

We all mouthed the words, "Long Live the Revolution!" It was like a chant or a response to a priest in a church.

Jean shook his head. "No thank you, sergeant, we will make a new start in the south." He leaned forward, "And it is a little warmer there too."

"That it is." The sergeant came over to pat me on the leg. "Don't worry son. The days of the aristos are over. It is a new world now and we do not have to bow and scrape any more. Have a safe journey."

Once we were out of earshot and sight Jean reined in the horses. "I thought he had us there Jean."

"If you have to make up a story, always base it on the truth in some way."

I looked around. The world suddenly seemed more dangerous and threatening. "What do we do now?"

"I was going to head home but I do not see the point in that now. If it has been confiscated then we might be jumping out of the frying pan and into the fire." I saw him chew his bottom lip as he debated our quandary. "However, I am worried about Madame Lefondre. We will return but in secret and then…"

"And then what?" I was terrified. My world had been turned upside down and all that I had known, destroyed.

"I know only one job and that is in the army. What say we join my old regiment? You would be around horses and we would be as safe there as anywhere. We will hide in their new army. I fear that someone will get around to asking questions about the two men who entered the northern gate with the count and when they ask at the inn, they will tell them all. We need to ride and ride quickly. We must get as far away from Paris as we can."

I nodded. "My mother said to trust you and I do. Let us join your regiment."

The three horses we had were the best in the count's stables. We kept swapping mounts to avoid tiring them. By dawn the next day we were outside the gates of the estate. I could see the tricolour flying and knew that we were too late but we had to find out what had happened to the only woman we cared for; Madame Lefondre. We knew the land really well and we tied the horses to a tree in a lonely copse and made our way to the wall where we knew we could climb over and enter the chateau unobserved. We managed to get close to the house without being detected; it had been my playground for almost sixteen years. I knew it like the back of my hand. We could hear the house being torn up but we saw no-one. Then we saw old Guiscard the gardener with his sack and spade over his shoulder walking forlornly from the building. We shadowed him until he was out of sight of the house and then Jean said, "Hsst, Guiscard."

The old man turned to look at the hedgerow which spoke. "Is that you Jean?"

"It is. What has happened?"

"The count has been executed as a traitor and the committee has taken over the house. I have been thrown off the land. They said they do not need a gardener any longer."

"And Madame Lefondre?"

"She is dead. That black witch, Mama Tusson, said that she had been putting upon the other servants for years. When the old woman argued Mama Tusson screamed that Madame Lefondre had a knife and the guards shot her."

Jean shook his head. He had known the old woman too well. "She didn't have a knife, did she?"

"No Jean. She was a kind old lady and she did not deserve to be shot like a dog. That witch has much to answer for." He shot me a strange look and then shook his head. "You had better run. The witch named you and Master Robbie as royalist sympathisers. There is a price on your head and you are earmarked for the courts. That means the guillotine. It was the first thing they did once the news came that the estate had been confiscated. She now lives in the master's bedroom with the fat pig from the committee."

"Thank you, Guiscard. Where will you go?"

"My son, Julian, has a farm. I will go there to die. God bless you both."

Jean's face was white with anger as we recovered our horses. "I swear that I will cut that witch's heart out. She made your mother's life a misery and now she has killed the kindest woman in the world. She deserves to die." It was a sacred oath and I knew that Jean would keep it and I would help him.

We headed north using the quietest roads that Jean knew of. He was familiar with the roads having grown up in that region. We reached Sedan at dusk. The town was the home to the Chevau-Légers of West-Flandre, my father's and Jean's old regiment. "It is too late to enlist tonight. We will stay at the inn nearby; it used to serve fine ale and I could do with a bed."

This far north we felt safer than we had for some time. The landlord was pleased to have paying guests for we still had plenty of money left over from the count's purse. We sat in a quiet corner and had the best meal and ale I had had since leaving the estate. It seemed a lifetime ago now.

Suddenly the peace and quiet were broken as ten soldiers came in. I felt a sudden chill of fear but Jean smiled. One of the soldiers, who seemed to have a lot of stripes on his arms, suddenly left his friends and charged over to us. "Jean Bartiaux! You are still alive! Good to see you old friend."

"And to see you." He pointed to the sleeve of the uniform, "Maréchal-des-logis-chef I see."

"Bring some ale over here and your young friend can meet a real soldier. You would have had the same promotions if you had stayed in; maybe more you were always a good soldier. How many years ago was it now?"

"Seventeen!"

The grey-haired soldier shook his head. "Who would have believed it? And who is this?"

"I was a friend of his mother. After she died, I looked after him. Robbie Macgregor. Robbie this is Albert Aristide. He and I joined on the same day."

"Good to meet you and I think there is a story here but that can wait until we have some ale."

We moved over to their table and Jean poured the beer. "What brings you to Sedan?"

"We are thinking of joining up."

The other soldiers brought his ale and Albert swallowed half of it without even pausing. "Well you can join of course but the boy, he is a little young and I do not know if he has any skills."

Jean laughed. "I'll tell you what. If any of these men with you can ride, fence or shoot better than he does we will leave tomorrow."

"You are that confident."

"I am that confident and we have our own horses too."

I could see that the old soldier was working out how he could profit from this. "Bring him and the horses along tomorrow. I will see if you are telling the truth."

The rest of the evening was spent pleasantly enough. I listened more than I spoke but I learned much. It seemed that many of the officers had been aristocrats and had deserted to the royalist cause. They were badly under strength. Albert told us that he expected to be given a commission. Jean was delighted to hear that the old colonel was still in command and Jean felt positive about that.

After they had returned to their barracks, I asked Jean about his boast. "Are you sure I can do all that you said?"

He laughed. "Just do what you did every day with the count and you will. Believe me; I was not building you up for a fall."

The barracks was not far from the inn. We did not take our

horses and we left our weapons in the inn. "We are as safe here as anywhere.

Albert was waiting for us and he had a wicked gleam in his eye. "I hope that you were not exaggerating last night Jean? Perhaps the beer was talking?"

"No, I am confident."

"Come then let us go to the stables first. We have a horse for him to ride there."

When we reached the stables there were four of the men, I had met the previous night. They too were all grinning. I heard a banging coming from one of the stalls. Jean's face creased into a frown. "That is not the horse that Robbie will have to ride is it?"

Albert shrugged. "You said he was a better rider than any of my men. Well here is his chance to prove it. None of them can ride this beast. It took four of us to get his saddle on him."

Jean started to shake his head. I said, "No Jean, I will try. The count used me to break in horses remember?"

I took off my jacket and went to the stall. It was a jet-black horse. He was magnificent but I could see fear in his eyes. He stamped his hoof belligerently. He flared his nostrils and bared his teeth. I approached him with my head down and I stroked his mane with my left hand while holding his nose with my right. I just spoke gently to him. "Ssh. There's a good horse." I began to hum a nursery tune my mother had used with me and then I breathed into his nose. At first, he tried to break away from me but I had a firm grip on him. All the work in the smiths had built up my strength. Gradually he began to calm down. "That's a good boy. Now I am going to get on your back." I was not even aware of the others watching me. I only had eyes for the horse. I took the reins in my left hand, put my foot in the stirrup and I hauled myself up. I felt a slight movement as he made a half-hearted attempt to throw me but I leaned forward and hummed my tune close to his ear. I clicked my tongue and touched his flanks with my heels. "Walk on." He walked out of the stalls and the stable on to the parade ground. I walked him until I was happy that he was under my control and then asked him to trot. He was a beautiful horse to ride. He had an easy action and was responsive to the reins. I saw the troopers and Jean standing close to the stables watching me. I turned the horse and then urged him on. He began to gallop. I saw the fear on the faces of the troopers. They ran. Jean was smiling and he restrained Albert. I jerked the beast to a snorting halt, less than four feet from the sergeant.

I sprang from his back. "That's a good horse. He just needs a careful rider."

Albert began to get some colour back into his cheeks and he laughed. "Well, you can ride I'll say that for you. Let us go to the practice range. Pierre put Killer back in his stall."

Jean looked at Albert, "Killer?"

This was the first time I had met Pierre. He was a few years older than me but he always had a retort or a quip. "Aye, the lads nicknamed him that. He seemed to fit the bill until you came along!" He grabbed the halter and led the horse back to the stalls.

As we neared the range Jean said, "I hope they all get to use the same weapon Albert. No trick guns eh?"

Albert laughed. "It will be a fair test."

The weapon was a musketoon. I had never fired one before but a gun was a gun. Albert gave the weapon to a tall man next to him. "Claude, you go first." Claude looked to be an experienced soldier and was much older than Pierre had been.

The targets were a hundred yards away and I suspected it was a long range for such a weapon. The trooper grinned at me as he carefully loaded his weapon. Claude seemed at ease with the weapon. He loaded and fired. It was not a bad shot and it hit the target. Grinning he handed the weapon to me. I cleaned the pan and went to the musket balls. I discarded four before I found the one which was the roundest. I carefully measured the powder and then I lay on the ground.

Claude said, "I didn't lie on the ground."

Without looking up I said, "The more fool you."

With my arms supported by the ground, I looked down the

barrel. There was a very crude sight at the end and I lined it up. I took a breath and then fired. The smoke obscured my vision. When I stood and looked at the target, Jean clapped me on the back, "Dead centre!"

Albert gave me a grudging smile, "In the cavalry, we cannot always lie down."

Jean said, "In the cavalry, you know your own gun. This is yours is it not, Claude?" A shamefaced Claude nodded and took his gun back.

Pierre had joined us and he had two sabres. "And now Jean let us see what he is like with a sword. I will be honest with you..."

"That will be a first."

"I will be honest with you; Pierre is the best swordsman in the squadron."

"Good, then this is a fair test."

I chose my sword and felt it. It was not as balanced as the ones I had used with the count and Jean but it was not a butcher's knife. I faced Pierre. He had not seen me shoot and he had a confident look about him. That was his first mistake. He thought he could beat me. He was smaller than I was but that could prove to be an advantage with the curved cavalry sabres we were using. I was taking nothing for granted and I did what I had been taught to do. I assessed my opponent to find his weakness.

We touched blades and I saw in his eyes that he would try to disarm me. He gave a flick of his wrist to try to throw the sword from my grip. I knocked his blade away. He shrugged. His first ploy had failed. He was a fast fencer. He tried tricks to defeat me instead of technique. Having seen the way, he fought I knew how to beat him. After he had tried to get inside my guard twice, I feinted to the right, spun to my left and had the tip of my blade pointed at his middle before he knew what was happening. His face showed his shock but he smiled and held out his hand. "Very good."

Jean clapped me on the back and Albert said, "Well you were right Jean. So, do you still wish to join?"

I looked at Jean and we both nodded.

Albert took us to the colonel. Colonel Armande was a professional soldier. Although he had aristocratic blood in his veins, he had been one of the younger sons and joined the cavalry as a lieutenant when he was just sixteen. He had only ever known the Chevau-Légers and the regiment was his life. He recognised Jean as soon as he entered.

"Ah, Bartiaux, how has life treated you?"

"Well, sir."

"And the count, how is he?"

"He is dead sir." Jean left it at that and the silence which followed was eloquent.

"I see and I understand that you would now like to rejoin the regiment along with this young man."

"Yes, sir."

The colonel stroked his waxed grey moustache. "You were always a good trooper and I was sorry to see you leave us. You would by now have had a number of promotions. I am delighted to have you rejoin us. And as for this young man... I enjoyed his performance on Killer." The colonel had been watching. He smiled. "I like a good horseman. Sergeant Major, how did he do with the shooting and the fencing?"

"He defeated our two best men."

The colonel's eyebrows came up a notch. "Really? Then I think we can accept you both. Sadly, we have lost a number of officers... well, we all know the reason and we can do little about that. As I am short of them, I would like you to accept a commission as a sous-lieutenant." I saw Albert's face fall. "And you sergeant major will become a lieutenant. I need all the officers I can muster. See the quartermaster for your uniforms and then Trooper Macgregor you can join your troop while I brief my two new officers."

And with that, I joined the French Army. The times were difficult ones, I know that. Had I have tried to join a couple of years earlier then I would have been rejected but the regiment had lost so many officers and men that they were in danger of not being able to muster more than a handful of men. There was a war with Britain and the Low Countries and this regiment was as close to the border as any. They would have to fight and fight soon. I discovered all of this within an hour of joining. Pierre was garrulous.

Jean, or Sous Lieutenant Bartiaux as I had to address him, came to see how I was settling in. "It seems Robbie, that we are down to one squadron. When I was in the regiment, we had four. Many of the officers who defected to the royalists took some of the men with them. I would not be an officer otherwise. You are to be in my troop. Here." He handed me a handful of coins.

"What are these?"

"The quartermaster took the horses off our hands. This is your share. I know that we did not get their worth but it is in lieu of payment from the count eh? And I am afraid that from now on I am no longer Jean, but Sous-lieutenant Bartiaux."

I grinned, "That's alright sir. I shall just have to get promoted."

He smiled back at me. "That may come sooner rather than later. We go to war. We have come at a propitious time. It seems we go north to fight the British and the Dutch. War brings rapid promotion for all." He nodded to my small box of treasures given to me by my mother on her deathbed. I always kept the box close to me and it had been in my saddlebags until we sold the horses. "The troopers here are good men and would not steal but you have temptation in that box." He took out a canvas belt. "I have two of these. This is my gift to you."

"What is it?"

"There are many pockets in the belt. You put in your treasures and wear it around your body. It goes under your garments and uniform. You will be sure that, so long as you are alive, then your treasures are safe."

"And if I am dead?"

"Then you care not and, if you are lucky, your comrades share the treasure amongst them and remember you with a drink." He saw my look and added, "Life is harsh and, in the cavalry, you may be alive one moment and dead the next; live life to the full, Robbie. It is what your mother would have wished."

He was right of course. That had been my mother's intention as Madame Lefondre had told me.

I had no time to get used to my new surroundings or to spend any of my newly acquired money. We headed north. I also discovered, as I trotted next to Pierre and we looked at our new standard, that we had had our name changed to the 17th Chasseurs à Cheval. Pierre had shrugged. "We have the same uniform, the same weapons and the same horses. The name makes no difference to us. We do what we always do."

I liked Pierre. He and I got on well. Although a little older than me he had some similarities in terms of background. He had been brought up on a large estate and had practised his fencing with the son of the aristocrat. His former master had left the country early on which explained Pierre joining the cavalry.

"Where will we be going then?"

"It will probably be north into the Low Countries. Our job is to find the enemy and then the infantry fights them."

I was disappointed. "Don't we fight then? I thought it would be all cavalry charges and the like."

Pierre laughed. "When I fenced with you that was the first time this year, I have had my weapon out of its scabbard. I have never fired my weapon in anger yet and this," he patted the horse pistol on his saddle, "only ever gets cleaned. We rarely get to fire them. This is not a glorious regiment but we get paid and the officers aren't as bad as some. Now that Albert has been promoted it is even better. He knows what the score is and we will all be much safer now."

The journey north was a new experience to me. We were on campaign and we were given a flimsy piece of canvas which two men shared. I shared mine with Louis, a dour, brooding and almost silent Frenchman, from Alsace. I did not learn much from him. I think in all the time I knew him he never said more than a dozen words. He was the opposite of Pierre. We cooked our own food in sections of five tents. Luckily, I was with Pierre and the others I knew so my silent companion was not a problem. When we reached our camp area, we lit our fires and tended to our horses. Once that was done, we cooked. The time of year meant that the camp soon became a muddy morass which sucked at your boots. Our breeches were splattered with mud and were soon brown rather than green.

I also learned picket duty. We all had a two-hour watch each night. If you were lucky you were the first or you were the last. If you were unlucky then you were in the middle watch. You would just have managed to get off to a lumpy sleep and the sergeant would wake you and you would either freeze in the cold night air or try to find shelter from the incessant rain of those parts. Campaigning was anything but glorious, even for the cavalry.

We soon caught up with the main body of the army. But life became no better. I was shocked. They looked to be a rabble in blue. Some men had no shoes. Some appeared to have blue jackets which had been hastily dyed. They ran alarmingly in the rain leaving them a sort of streaky grey. There was little sense of order and organisation. I could see no ranks and none of the officers rode horses. The officers looked to be young men who had also been drafted. Some carried muskets and most had no swords.

Pierre leaned over to me when I asked him about them, "These poor sods have just been drafted. If you had not joined then you would have been drafted into the infantry. You made a wise decision." He was wrong of course. If I had stayed at home then I would have likely as not ended up on the guillotine. "I bet they have never even fired their weapons yet."

As we rode in the fields next to the road, they all cheered the flag we carried and shouted, "Vive La France!" They waved their guns in the air. They were enthusiastic but I wondered how they would stand up against the British. My mother had told me how the British army had managed to defeat a passionate and enthusiastic Highland army by their discipline and drills. This looked to be an ill-equipped Highland Army. I wondered how I would stand up to such discipline. In the chasseurs, it appeared to be quite casual. You said sir and sergeant but it did not seem important to the likes of Albert and the colonel.

You could see the puzzled looks on their faces as we rode along the side of the roads. They equated horses with the aristocrats. Added to that was the fact that we appeared to be comfortable and we were riding to war while they were trudging in the mud. They did not know of the work we all had to do each day with our horses and our equipment. One advantage the infantry had was that they had so little equipment it would not need much care. We had to look after our own and the horses.

We did, however, have swords and all of us had a musketoon. When I saw the infantry muskets, I realised that even though I had not been happy with the weapon when I first handled it, it was better than the infantry musket. The range of both weapons was abysmal. I longed for the fine muskets of my father's estate. Even the powder we had was poor. We had already experienced many misfires when we practised. The ammunition was of uneven quality too. I wished I had brought my moulds from the chateau to make musket balls. When you made your own you knew their quality. The ones we had were rarely round and therefore rarely accurate.

I looked to the north and the land of our enemies and thought about the life I would soon be leading. I would be fighting soldiers who were more experienced and led by officers who knew what they were doing. Our regiment was well led but I would see the infantry officers and knew that they had neither knowledge nor experience, just courage.

CHAPTER 3

We camped, that night, close to Liege. It was the beginning of many uncomfortable nights until my body adjusted to the rigours of the campaign. I had to learn how to be on duty for four hours a night and then still ride for ten hours a day. The hard life at Breteuil stood me in good stead. The next morning Jean and the sergeant took us out on our first patrol. There were twenty men in our troop which was the smallest in the regiment. I didn't mind that for it meant that I knew my comrades well. Claude had been promoted to sergeant and we had to salute the new Sergeant Claude Alain. He took our smiles in good part. Until the day before our arrival, he had been one of the boys but the new regiment meant that many men had to be promoted.

We were the only cavalry available and we were spread very thinly. We headed towards the coast. We had seen no signs of the British or the Dutch but they were likely to be nearer to the coast. Anyone we met would be an enemy. There were Austrians as well as Brunswickers and Hanoverians and they were all looking to bring the rabble that was the French Army to battle.

The flat land we were travelling through made scouting difficult. The roads were lined with hedgerows and they twisted and turned this way and that. It was after just such a twist that we encountered the enemy for the first time. I was in the middle of the small column and the first I knew was when there was the pop of muskets. I heard Sergeant Alain shout, "Draw sabres! Forward!"

I drew my weapon and kicked hard into Killer's sides. I had not renamed the beast for he didn't seem to mind his name. He responded instantly. As I turned the corner, I saw the red uniforms of the British cavalry disappearing along the road. There were two men lying on the ground. One was dead but the other was wounded. We galloped for a couple of hundred yards but it was unlikely that we would be able to catch the rest of the horsemen. The trumpeter sounded recall and we gathered around the two soldiers. They were English. Jean waved me over, "Trooper Macgregor, come and question this man." I dismounted and gave my reins to Pierre.

"Sir. What do I ask him?"

"Find out all you can. Your English will be better than mine and he might tell you more than he would me. We need to know where their army is."

I saw that he had been struck in the leg with a sabre and he was bleeding. I tore the shirt from his dead companion into strips and bound his wound. He was staring at the horsemen around him. I suspected he was worried for his life. "What is your name?"

He almost jumped into the air and I suppressed a smile. "You're Scottish! What are you doing in a French uniform?"

"No, I am half Scottish and half French and as you can see from the uniform I am fighting for my French half. What is your name and what is your unit?"

"Trooper Davy Brown of the 7th Queen's Own Hussars." He did not sound like my mother. Some of his words were hard to understand but I managed to decipher them.

"Where is your regiment?"

He looked confused as he pointed west. "Near Charleroi."

"Are there any infantry there?"

He suddenly seemed to realise that I was not a fellow Briton but an enemy. "Bugger off frog!" I had never come across that swear word before but his meaning was obvious. He spat at me. I did not blame him. I could understand his emotions. To him, I was a traitor.

I stood. "They are close to Charleroi, sir."

"Damn that means they are threatening our lines of communication. Put him on his horse and let us return to the colonel. He needs to know this." We tied the prisoner's hands and mounted him on a horse. Louis led him.

As we rode back Pierre asked, "You speak good English."

I nodded. "I am half Scottish and my mother only ever spoke English to me."

"That is handy; especially as we will be fighting the English."

I looked at the trooper we had captured. His horse was not in good condition and I noticed that his uniform was a red hue. It was tighter fitting than ours. On his head, he wore a helmet. It looked like it could take a blow. Our mirliton caps, a sort of early shako, would crumple when struck by anything. The turban which surrounded ours could, at least, be used as a sort of scarf in the cold. On the whole, I preferred our uniform. The green uniforms afforded us more chance of avoiding detection as we could blend into vegetation. He did, however, have a look of grim determination about him, even when captured which I found I admired. He had not given up just because he had been captured. I was lulled into a false sense of security by our first encounter with the English. I thought all our enemies would be as easy to defeat. The next few would not be as successful.

The colonel and our captain were delighted to find they had an English speaker in the regiment. Rather than making me a figure of suspicion, as I would have expected, it gave me a status I was not used to. On the estate, I had been little more than a serf but in this new French Army, I was held in some esteem. I liked the experience.

Once the news was sent back to the general the whole regiment was ordered south-west towards Charleroi. It was vital that we find the bulk of the enemy. We were assigned the area to the west of the town. We divided into troops once more but this time we were less than a mile from any of our comrades. We could summon aid if it was needed. It was our troop who, once again, found the enemy. This time it was not the British we found but a column of Austrian infantry protected by cavalry. Their white uniforms were a little less than smart after tramping along the sodden roads of the Low Countries but they marched with purpose. We came upon them suddenly. They were coming along one road as we crossed theirs from a minor track. The difference was, this time it was we who were outnumbered.

Jean roared, "Fall back! Retreat!

I saw the Musketeers quickly loading their weapons but they were not the main danger. Before we could turn our horses, the Austrian Light Dragoons thundered into us. I managed to draw my sabre just as an Austrian tried to split my head open. I desperately blocked his thrust with my sword. Unfortunately, the poor metal bent alarmingly. Killer suddenly turned to try to bite the grey horse of my opponent. As the horseman struggled to control his horse, I hacked at him with my sabre. I felt it bite into the flesh of his arm before grinding into the bone. He screamed as the sword fell from his hand. I managed to wheel Killer around and found myself next to Jean who was fighting against two horsemen. I jabbed forward with my sword and it sank into the back of one of his opponents. It pierced his back and dark blood began to stain the grey and white jacket. He threw his arms in the air and then fell dead to the ground. I had killed my first enemy. It would not be my last. As Jean finished off his adversary he turned and saluted me with his sword. "Now let's get out of here."

As we turned, three Austrians barrelled towards us. Louis and Pierre had seen off their opponents and came to our aid. I parried the sword of one trooper as Pierre speared him. The officer who was fighting Louis brought his sword down with a crash. It shattered Louis' sword in two and split his face open to his skull. He did not even have time to scream. He just crumpled to the ground. Jean whipped out his pistol and fired at almost pointblank range. The officer fell in a bloody heap to the ground.

The three of us were the only living Frenchmen in the lane and the death of the officer halted the leaderless dragoons. We urged our mounts forward and soon outdistanced the pursuing Austrians. The lane was filled with riderless horses and wounded men. We left many of our comrades there in that unnamed crossroads close to Charleroi.

We halted a mile down the road. The trumpeter was dead and we had no way of sounding recall. The men gradually joined us one by one. Many were sporting wounds. As our horses recovered, we counted our losses. Eight men were missing. I knew there were at least five dead in the lane, including my tent mate Louis, the others were probably with him. Many of our men had wounds but the sergeant and Pierre were, like me, unscathed. As I discovered, the blades we used could catch a face, hand or arm easily and cuts were common in the cavalry. The difference was those wounds did not kill, they just scarred and many cavalrymen enjoyed a scar on the face as a mark of their bravery. I preferred to avoid wounds altogether.

Jean shouted, "Load your pistols. If they come again, we may have to discourage them."

As we did so Pierre shook his head. "We were lucky then Robbie. That was a full squadron we faced. If we had been in open country we would have been slaughtered. The Austrians have good cavalry. We were helped by the narrow lane and the fact that we have some good soldiers who can fight. You did well there especially as it was your first combat."

"I didn't even think when I killed them. I was just fighting for my life and defending myself."

"That is war. It is rare to be able to chase men who cannot fight back. The ones we meet will be just as keen to live as we are."

Just then we heard one of our trumpets sounding recall to the east. Jean nodded, "Well some of our boys are there. Let's join them."

Half an hour later we found Lieutenant Aristide and the remnants of his troop. He gave Jean a rueful smile as we approached. "I see you met horsemen too. The Austrians?"

"The Austrians. We lost eight men."

"We lost five." He looked around. "I think the front line has moved. God knows where the rest of the regiment is."

"How about we head south? Even if we come across the enemy, they will be heading in the same direction so we will probably strike their baggage train first."

"Sounds like a plan to me." He turned to the rest of us. "Keep your weapons primed and your ears open. We may not have time for orders. You see a white uniform then shoot first and ask questions later."

I had yet to use my horse pistol and I had no idea what effect it would have. I knew that once I had used it then it would be useless and I would have to rely on my sword again. The range of the pistol would be ridiculously short although the ball was so big that if it struck it could make a hole big enough to put your fist in. Jean suddenly shouted, "Robbie and Pierre, the two of you ride a quarter of a mile ahead of us. You both have young eyes and ears. Perhaps you can give us some early warning."

We kicked on and soon the column was out of sight. I knew it made sense to only risk two troopers but I felt sick to my stomach as we headed down the lonely little lane. I did not want to end as Louis had with my head split open or cut in two by a musket.

It was a dismal day; it was not raining but it felt as though it was and the air was heavy with damp. The trees were not moving at all in the still air. I wondered if my mind and hearing were playing tricks. I thought I heard a whinny. I was about to ignore it when Killer's ears flicked and he snorted. "Stop!"

Pierre stopped his horse too and we listened. Then we heard the sound of men marching. We gingerly moved forwards as slowly as we dared. The road rose a little ahead of us and hid the rest of the highway. I dismounted and edged my way up to the crest of the road. I crouched and kept as low as I could. I wanted to avoid being seen. There, just ahead of me, was the baggage train of the Austrian army and a squadron of dragoons guarding it. I turned and mounted. "The Austrian Army."

Pierre turned too and we rode swiftly back down the road towards the rest of the troop. "Sir, the whole of the Austrian army is just ahead."

I don't know what had alerted them but two of the dragoons who had been guarding the baggage train suddenly appeared, like wraiths, at the top of the road we had just vacated. They ineffectively popped their guns at us. "We will have to go across country. Head east!" Lieutenant Aristide pointed with his sword and we headed for the open gate. The field had had some sort of crop in it and was uneven but it was safer than the Austrian filled road. The gunfire had brought the rest of the dragoons and they were trying to reach us. The hedgerows were not tall as they had been coppiced ready for winter and Killer leapt over them easily. He was a powerful horse and took everything in his stride. I saw one of Lieutenant Aristide's men take a tumble but we had no time to recover any lost men. If you fell you were either dead or doomed to be a prisoner.

Pierre and I were at the fore still and I began to think that we would escape when eight dragoons suddenly emerged from some woods to our right. They had obviously taken a short cut. I grabbed my pistol and fired. Pierre did the same. We hit nothing but the sudden crack and smoke made the Austrian horses veer away from their line. I holstered my pistol and took out my sabre. Two of the troopers were clinging on to their mounts which had been frightened. I slashed wildly at the first man who came close to me and managed to strike him across the face. The blade ripped across his nose and barely missed his eyes. He reacted by jerking his reins and his mount away from the danger.

"Robbie! Ride left!"

As I turned left the rest of the troop fired their pistols and the dragoons halted as the pistol balls headed their way. Killer cleared the wall easily and I followed Pierre and the others. It started to become dark and we were forced to slow down. Our horses had galloped almost all day. Jean had been at the rear and he told us that we were no longer pursued.

"We need somewhere to rest. The horses can go no further." Lieutenant Aristide pointed to two of his troopers. "Find us a deserted building." As the two men rode off, he turned to me and Pierre. "You did well there and that was bravely done."

Jean nodded his approval too. "Even if we do find somewhere to rest where will we go in the morning? The rest of the regiment could be anywhere."

"True but we were the furthest west of the troops. We were closer to the coast and that is where the enemy will have larger numbers. It may be that they did not find the enemy and they are safe."

I wondered at that. I was new to the art of war but there appeared to be a large number of the enemy behind what we had thought was our lines. Our army was marching north and yet the British, the Dutch and Austrians were to the west of our army. I had thought that war would be simple but obviously, it was not. If we were the eyes of the army then we were in trouble for we had no idea where the enemy was. What hope for the barefoot recruits who would have to stand up to this disciplined and well-trained army?

One of the scouts returned and saluted. "Lieutenant, there is a barn over the hill and the farmhouse is burnt out. We should be safe there."

When we found the barn and saw the burnt building, I wondered which army had destroyed the livelihood of the farmers. This was the border country and the existence of the civilian population could not be guaranteed. Anyone of five armies could have decided to fire upon the house. We set pickets up and the lieutenant sent men to forage for food. I did not have high hopes as the house was almost destroyed and was now a mere blackened shell. However, when they returned, we discovered that they had been successful.

The six men had four chickens and a shako full of eggs. They were laughing. "Whoever set fire to the farm forgot to round up the chickens. They flew to the trees and carried on laying! We eat well tonight." I quickly learned that the older soldiers were past masters at finding food in the most unlikely of spots. It was a skill I acquired over the next few months. Rations and pay were in short supply at this period of the war. The chicken cooked over an open fire and a mass omelette made in a kettle, we found, augmented our dried meat well and we slept better than we might have hoped.

The next day was foggy. That helped us and put us in danger at the same time. It would be harder to see us but the fog would muffle sounds and make it hard for us to identify potential enemies. Sergeant Alain led us. Pierre confided in me that Claude had the sharpest ears in the regiment and an almost sixth sense of where the enemy was. We were fresher, after food and a good night's sleep, as we headed east. When the fog began to lift, we started to recognise the land through which we had travelled a few days earlier. We started to relax and then we all heard the whinny of a horse and our nervous hands went to our weapons. It was with some relief that we heard Claude shout. "It is the regiment. We have found the rest of the troopers."

The colonel looked worried as he trotted over to greet us. "When you did not return, we feared the worst."

The lieutenant pointed to the west. "There is an Austrian army heading south. They have artillery, cavalry and a large baggage train. We barely escaped with our lives."

The colonel might have been the oldest man in the regiment but he was decisive. "Captain Roux, break camp. We must find the general."

The rest of the regiment had not suffered any casualties and the colonel insisted that we be spared any more losses. "Lieutenant Aristide, take your men and head back to the barracks. The general said that we had some new recruits who would be arriving soon. They are the new draft. It looks like we will need them."

I felt cheated and disappointed. We had done nothing but run from the enemy. If it had not been for the capture of the single English cavalryman it would have all been a total disaster. Now we were running home with our tails between our legs. It did not bode well for my career in the cavalry. Would my father be disappointed in me? Probably.

The journey back was not without incident. We were travelling through the country patrolled by Hanoverians and Brunswickers. These allies of the British were almost professional troops and, as we discovered, were not to be underestimated. We emerged from a tree-lined lane and heard the crack of muskets followed by the boom of cannon. To our left were a battalion of infantry and a battery of cannons on a low hill. The cannon balls cracked through the trees beyond us, the smoke from their barrels spiralling smoke rings into the sky.

Albert yelled, "Ride before they load with grapeshot!"

I had heard of grapeshot. It was a shell filled with small metal balls. We were lucky they had not loaded with them already. If they had then we would already be dead. The muskets were too far away to be effective but the cannons could fire for a mile or more. We kicked hard. The next crack we heard was followed by a rippling like the sound of paper being torn. They had used grapeshot. The hedges disappeared in a metal filled storm which cut the two troopers at the back in two. Then the road dropped and turned to a hollow and we were beyond the death-dealing guns. Even Pierre was shaken by the losses. The enemy was less than three hours from our barracks and our home. I could not see the recruits from the road stopping them.

The barracks seemed oddly deserted as we rode through the gates. The skeleton staff we had left behind was nowhere to be seen. As Pierre said, "They would have taken the opportunity to slope off and earn a little extra money on the side. They would not have expected us back so soon." Many of the older troopers who were unfit for active duty continued to work in ancillary roles. If there were not soldiers in the barracks then they would take part-time jobs to make more money for drink. It was the old soldiers' Nemesis. The adjutant was an old drunk who rarely left his office. He had been in the regiment almost as long as the colonel but he had just enjoyed the life of an officer rather than the life of a soldier. Too indolent to leave with the other officers he had drowned his sorrows in a bottle. He was largely ignored by the rest of us. With the adjutant incapacitated it was Lieutenant Aristide who was in command. His recent promotion had not taken away his need for order and we were soon given a series of tasks. Pierre and I were given the job of sharpening the swords and bayonets. It was mind-numbingly boring but in light of our last skirmish one not to be taken lightly.

Pierre tapped the sword he was sharpening. "These are very poor quality. Every time I use mine, I half expect it to shatter."

"You are right. You feel every vibration right up your arm. I saw poor Louis' shattered in two when that Austrians struck it. Does no one have a decent blade?"

"The officers buy their own if they can afford it. It is a good investment but they are not cheap. A decent one can set you back six months' pay." I thought about the money in my money belt and wondered if it was worth spending it to get a good sword. "Your best bet is to get one from a dead enemy officer on the battlefield. The Austrians have some good ones."

"What about the British and the Dutch?"

He shrugged, "Those ones we met the other week were the first ones I have seen. I think they only came over to help their Dutch allies. They should be good though. They still have aristos in England, don't they? They must have the money to buy a good sword."

As we were working Pierre suddenly stopped and looked at me. "Do you mind if I say something about your appearance?"

I wondered what he was going to say. He sounded quite serious. "Of course. Is there something wrong?"

"Well, your hair and your face. If you look at the rest of us, we all have a fine moustache and our hair is in pigtails with a queue. It marks us as light cavalrymen. We have élan and we have style. I am afraid that you look like a country bumpkin." He gave an apologetic grin, "No offence meant."

My face must have fallen for he laughed. "I am sorry it..."

He waved his arm airily. "I can sort this out in a moment." He placed the last sword in the rack and wiped his hands on a cloth. "We have finished here. Come to the barbershop. He is not there at the moment and I will use his equipment."

I had never been shaved by someone else before and my

mother had always cut my hair. Since she had died, I had just let it grow. I knew that it was untidy but I rarely looked in a mirror so what difference did it make? By the time he had finished, my hair looked much tidier and the pigtails and queue made me look more like all the other troopers. I did not have much of a moustache as I had been shaving regularly but the last few days campaigning meant that I did have a little growth on my top lip and it was the start of my moustache.

"Now you need to decide how it will look. Will you twist the end? Perhaps make it droop. It is your decision but you must choose for yourself. While it grows you can look around the regiment and find whose you admire." Pierre's had a flourish at each end and his beard was pointed. It did look dashing.

"I will, Pierre, and thank you."

"We are now comrades and we have fought together. That makes us brothers."

The lieutenant had organised a rough meal at noon. As we ate, he singled out Sergeant Alain. "Sergeant, take four men and a wagon and go to the depot in Paris. There should be uniforms for the new draft we are expecting." He shrugged, "Although if those recruits, we saw the other day are anything to go by you may come back empty handed."

Claude nodded, happily. I knew from my conversations with the others that a trip to Paris was always worthwhile. He came over to me. "Well young Robbie, do you wish to come to Paris with me?"

I had a sudden chill. I did want to go but I was too afraid. They might still be looking for me, yet I did not want to offend Claude. Jean's voice rescued me from my dilemma. "I am afraid that Trooper Macgregor still has paperwork to do for his enlistment. We left so quickly for the north that we did not complete it."

"Sorry sergeant."

"No matter. I know you will come, Pierre."

"Of course. Do you wish anything bringing Robbie?"

I grinned. "Some wax for my new moustache?"

He laughed. "Now you are thinking like a cavalryman. It will be my pleasure." They asked the others and soon had their money and a list of things we could not buy here.

After they had gone, I sought out Jean. "Thank you for that sir."

"I knew that it would cause a problem for you besides we do have paperwork to do. You have to be enlisted properly so that you can be paid. I was already on their books and I was just re-instated. You are new."

The afternoon flew by and then, towards dusk, the colonel and the rest of the regiment returned. They did not look happy. The only one of my new comrades who returned was Jean-Michel. The others were either in Paris, dead or in the sick bay. He leaned over as we ate. "It is like a morgue in here."

"What is the matter?"

"Apparently the allies have completely thrown us out of the Low Countries. We were the last Frenchmen on the wrong side of the border. All the gains we made last year have been lost. And I heard that the Royalists have landed in the Vendee. The only place still holding out is Dunkirk. If that falls then we will be surrounded."

"Is there no good news then?"

He shrugged as he mopped up the last of his onion soup. "We are doing better in the south. There is supposed to be a good general of artillery there. I would like to serve in the south. It is warmer."

"I am used to the cold. I lived in the north."

"Well I come from Bordeaux and there it is warm and we have decent wine. We have to drink beer up here." He made a face. "I hope Pierre managed to pick up some decent bottles in Paris. I cannot survive the northern winter on beer alone."

The mood was lightened a few days later when the sergeant and his party returned with the new equipment. More importantly, the troopers had spent wisely and all the items we had requested were supplied. I was really happy until Claude and Pierre drew me to one side. They looked very serious.

"What is the matter with you two? Have I done something

44

wrong?"

"There are posters in Paris. They have the names of those the National Committee wish to question for crimes against the state. The lieutenant's name was on the list."

A shudder ran down my spine. "Jean?" They nodded, "Is he wanted for anything in particular?"

"No. But they are looking for someone called Robert de Breteuil. He is the son of an executed count."

I am no actor and my face fell. Pierre nodded. "I thought that it was you. Are you the son of an aristocrat?"

"I was the illegitimate son and I was treated like a slave. I suppose that doesn't matter to the committee." I told them of my background and how I came to join with Jean.

"We are your comrades and your secret is safe with us. We will not betray you. You are Trooper Macgregor and you are one of us. You are the lieutenant's friend, you had better warn him."

"I will do and thank you."

"It is nothing." Pierre grinned. "It is fortunate that I changed your appearance is it not?"

"Oh yes, and I shall grow the largest moustache that I can." I realised how lucky Pierre's intervention had been. Each time I looked in the mirror to see how my moustache was coming along it was like looking into the face of a stranger.

Jean was phlegmatic about the news. "It is a five-day wonder. They will soon become bored with looking for me. Bartiaux is a common name in these parts. The Terror cannot last forever and they will find someone else to persecute. Besides we have so many enemies that France needs every soldier it can get. They have announced that every man over the age of sixteen has been called to arms. The rabble we saw the other day is the future. That is the new French army."

I did not have any time to worry about my prospects as we were thrown into an autumn of training new troopers and preparing to go to war. Pierre was promoted to Brigadier. It did not change things much for he liked me. The corporals were the workhorses of any regiment and Pierre was popular already.

Jean was also promoted to full lieutenant and Albert to captain. We did not know why until we were gathered with full kit one icy cold January morning.

The colonel sat stiffly on his horse. "Chasseurs, we are going to war again. We lost many good men last year and today we begin to avenge their deaths. We will regain the honour of the regiment. We are the spear point for the army. We are going to drive the Austrians back to Vienna."

We all cheered, of course, but I wondered just how ready we were to fight such a huge army. It was the middle of winter and our uniforms were not the best. Would the rabble Jean had spoken of be able to stand up to the bayonets of the Austrians? We had not defeated them last year. Indeed, we had not even dented their numbers. The British, the Dutch and the Hanoverians all had huge armies to call upon and the Royal Navy could supply any British army on the continent. I did not feel confident.

CHAPTER 4

The army was all moving north and we were the eyes and ears of that army. The Austrians must have thought that no-one would be insane enough to fight in the depths of winter when the rivers were frozen solid and you could see your breath freezing before you but it was a masterstroke. We crossed the border, one foggy morning, without being seen. We slipped across like burglars entering a house. Our scouts were successful and Jean-Michel took us to a crossroads where we found four Austrian soldiers huddled around a brazier. They barely looked up as we approached. The cold was so severe that our uniforms looked white with the hoar frost. They smiled as we clattered towards them. As soon as we spoke, they realised their mistake for we were not the Austrian cavalry they had thought and they meekly surrendered. They were the sentries for a squadron of cavalry. The colonel brought the rest of the regiment up. We surrounded the camp and, with muskets at the ready captured the whole camp of sleeping Austrians. It sounds simple and it was. The thing about a camp of cavalry is that they rely on their sentries. It was so cold that they were all huddled beneath blankets and greatcoats. When we appeared at their tents with muskets pointed at them, they had little choice but to surrender. Our guns might not have much of a range but they would have made a mess of ten men sleeping in a tent. We took the surrender of over two hundred Austrian horsemen. I could not believe how easy it was. We escorted them back to the army the next day but not until those of the troopers who had less than perfect equipment had taken it from the Austrians. They could not object as they were under our muskets when it was done. The officers took the swords and I wished, just for a moment, that I was an officer for I so wanted a good blade. We were all in good spirits as most of us had taken the money and other equipment from the well-equipped squadron. I managed to get some coins and a good working knife which I found useful when cleaning Killer's hooves.

I found out on the next patrol that not all Austrians were as placid as the ones we had met. Sergeant Alain led a patrol of ten of us as we pushed towards the Texel River. All rivers are important in war but this one was even more important as the Dutch Fleet was sheltering there. We were so keen to get to it first that we rode headfirst into an ambush. The company of light infantrymen we encountered were hunkered down in a farmhouse. They must have been about to march down the road for they heard us as we clattered along the cobbles. There were some of the men lined up in front of the farmhouse in the farmyard as we suddenly appeared. They tried to fire as soon as we hove into view but it turned out to be a ragged volley from the twenty men who loosed their muskets. That saved our lives. Even though the balls were badly fired we were so close to them that three men fell from their saddles and I saw Claude clutch at his arm.

Pierre suddenly shouted, "Charge them, they have not fitted bayonets!" Once you had fired your musket the only defence for an infantryman was his bayonet and these had failed to fit them. I could understand that they were so long and heavy that they made aiming a gun almost impossible. Lady Luck was on our side again.

We whirled our horses and charged them. There were only seven of us but the horses we rode made us look more intimidating. We do not ride small horses and we towered over the tiny light infantrymen. I slashed down with my sabre at the nearest soldier. The Austrian tried to deflect the blade with his musket

48

but he merely succeeded in directing the edge of my sabre into his neck. My blade jarred in my hand as it struck his skull. I felt the vibrations right up to my shoulder. Killer trampled another soldier who tried to roll beneath the horse. It was a foolish thing to do and I suspect they had not faced cavalry before. His death was mercifully swift.

The action was so fast and furious that I found it difficult to react to all that was going on. A tall officer raced towards me, his sword raised to strike either at my horse or me, I had no idea which. I dropped my right shoulder to enable me to lean to one side of Killer and make a more difficult target for his long sword. It also helped me to lean forward and to use my longer arms to my advantage. The officer was committed to his stroke. It slashed through fresh air where my head had been and I thrust my blade forward to stab him in the neck. As I jerked forwards, I felt his blade slicing through my cape as it continued on its downward, dying swing; luckily it snagged on the metal chain which held the cape around my neck. As I withdrew the sabre, I saw that it was covered in his lifeblood.

I was in no mood to stop and I charged the next soldier. He had obviously emptied his musket and without a bayonet fitted was defenceless. He held his musket like a club and swung it at me, trying to knock me from my horse. The poor quality of my blade was shown when the stock of the musket shattered my sabre in two. I threw the half I held at him like a knife. Spinning through the air it stuck grotesquely in his cheek and he fell to the floor screaming. I grabbed my pistol and fired at the infantryman next to him who was levelling his musket to fire at me. He was leaning against the farmhouse wall and when he saw the pistol rising he turned to climb through the window and escape. My ball struck him in the top of the leg and he crashed through the window spoiling the aim of the men within. The soldiers in the farmhouse now began to fire at us. Although it was still a ragged volley they might hit us and we had done enough. I heard Claude yell, "Fall back!" and I gratefully obeyed the order.

As I wheeled Killer around and headed away from the farmhouse, I saw the dead officer I had just killed. His body lay at an unnatural angle. His sword was still in his handheld there by a cord. I remembered what Pierre had said about the officer's swords and I stopped. I leapt from Killer and, despite the balls buzzing around my head, tugged it from his dead hand.

"What the hell are you doing?" Pierre's voice was incredulous.

"I am just getting a new sword, Brigadier!" As I lifted my head a flurry of musket balls, sounding like a swarm of wasps, filled the space where my head had been. "Come on Killer. We have outstayed our welcome." I laid flat against his back as we galloped away. That was the day I realised that the only danger from musket balls is when there is a regiment firing at you and even then, you have to be ridiculously close to be in danger of getting wounded. My horse and I left without a scratch despite the attention of every musketeer in the farmhouse.

We halted some way down the road to dress Claude's arm and to assess the damage to our patrol. We had lost four troopers. As we were dressing his arm the sergeant said, "We were lucky to get out of there alive. Well done corporal, that charge saved the day."

Pierre laughed and slapped me on the back, "What about our mad Scotsman; he stops in the middle of a battle to get a sword."

"Well I had to, mine was broken!" It sounded pathetic even as I said it.

They all burst out laughing at that. "Here let me see that blade." Pierre knew swords. I looked at the weapon for the first time as I handed it over. It was longer and straighter than the sabre I had been using. "Phew! This is from Toledo. You have got a superb weapon. Do you want to sell it?"

"No thank you. At least this one won't break." All the way back Pierre kept offering me more and more money for the sword. He was normally parsimonious which made the blade even more valuable in my eyes.

When we reached the colonel with our news, we found he had with him the colonel of a newly formed French infantry regiment. The infantry officer looked to be a little older than I was. "We are to form a flying brigade with this regiment of foot who have just arrived from Paris. It is a pity they weren't with you today. They might have lessened your losses."

On closer inspection, I could see that the young colonel of the infantry regiment was older than I had first thought, possibly a little older than Pierre. He nodded vigorously. "My men are desperate to get to grips with these enemies of France. Together we will write a glorious chapter in the history of our new young country." He was obviously an idealist.

The colonel was too much of a gentleman to comment and he just nodded. "Sergeant, get that wound seen to. We will be riding first thing in the morning so make sure you are fully prepared."

Jean was also impressed by my sword. "Some of these Austrian officers have Spanish connections, you are very lucky to have acquired such a good sword. This will give you a greater chance of survival than using that piece of tin they equipped us with. I suspect that we will not be fighting the Austrians much longer. We heard today that they are pulling their troops out to defend the Rhine. Our armies are doing slightly better there. We are going to take on the Dutch."

I knew nothing about the Dutch or the Belgians and I asked Pierre about them. The corporal was dismissive. "They are not real nations or soldiers; they are like a mongrel with little bits of many little countries. They will not stand when we charge. Trust me on this."

I was not convinced. We left camp the following morning and we formed two lines alongside the infantry who trotted between our horses. It gave them protection. If we found the enemy and had to move out quickly, they would grab the stirrups of the nearest chasseur. I noticed that they were all young men and most looked to be my age. I had little experience but these appeared to have none at all. They were the conscripted youth of France. I knew then that things must be desperate to throw them into the fray so quickly. They had patently had little training; you could see that by the clumsy way they held their weapons and their confusion when given even the simplest of orders. I had yet to see infantry fight. I had been on the receiving end of Austrian muskets but I did not know how our young warriors would do. I knew that they were patriotic but would that make up for a lack of training?

Jean's voice rang out in the crisply cold morning air, "Brigadier Boucher, take Macgregor and find the river. We need to find somewhere safe to cross."

We kicked on, pleased to be let off the leash. Travelling at the speed of marching men is no fun. The air that morning was so cold that we could see our breath and that of our horses but we soon warmed up as we galloped across the flat, monotonous landscape. One advantage of the Low Countries is that they are flat and largely featureless. The only features are rivers and canals. In winter the water is normally frozen which means there are no obstacles to a good horseman. I suddenly spied pennants in the distance "Look Pierre, masts. The river must be close by!"

We slowed down and we made towards the forests of masts which appeared to rise mysteriously from the mist-shrouded river. When we saw the flags at the stern of a huge three-decker we knew we had found the Dutch fleet. "Now Robbie, we just need to find a crossing place." He peered along the river looking for a sign of a ford or a bridge.

Killer walked to the edge and I could see that the river was frozen. "Why not go across the ice?"

He laughed. "You can try it. I am not risking a soaking."

It looked thick enough and I dismounted to lead Killer across. It felt firm enough. There was neither ominous creaking nor cracking. I walked twenty yards across and then risked mounting Killer. The ice held; it was thick enough and safe enough. "It seems able to take me and my horse." I pointed to the ships. "The ships look to be trapped by the ice. They aren't going anywhere soon."

"Then let's report to the colonel."

The journey back was quicker as we knew the way back and

also realised that we had no time to waste. The enemy had left the fleet unprotected and we could do some damage to them.

"The Dutch fleet?"

"Yes, sir."

"You have found them close by? And the river is frozen?"

"Yes sir, Trooper Macgregor rode out on the ice and it showed no signs of cracking. It is very cold out there."

The colonel might be the oldest soldier I had met so far but he had the sharp mind of a youngster. "Colonel, assign one man from your regiment to each trooper. They can ride on the back of the horses until we get to the Dutch fleet. We can get a large number of men there much quicker. Let us try to capture these ships."

A young nervous conscript called Alan hoisted himself behind me. He smelled of sour ale and damp breeches but he was game enough. "Are you on?"

He nodded, "Ready to fight for France sir."

He clung on grimly as we trotted across the frozen ground. I was pleased that he was light. I noticed that he held his musket awkwardly, almost as though he had only just been given the weapon. "Have you ever fired your weapon before?"

"No, sir! We were only issued them yesterday but I have seen one fired."

I smiled. He assumed because I had a horse, that I was an officer. "Robbie will do, I am not an officer. Well make sure you don't leave your ramrod in the barrel or this could be a short engagement."

"Thank you. I will remember that." I was suddenly grateful to my father and Jean for the drills with the muskets. To me it was second nature; to poor Alan, it was a nightmare.

Pierre and I led the way. We followed our own tracks and reached it quicker than we had on our first journey. Once we reached the frozen ice, I did not let Alan dismount even though the others did. I thought I could get him further across the river and save him getting cold quickly. His shoes appeared to be made from canvas. He would freeze on the river. I was pleased that there were no alarming cracks appearing as Killer, with a double load, stepped on to it. It creaked and groaned a little but there was no sign of a crack or fissure of any description. The others dropped their infantry and joined me. Lieutenant Aristide was at my side. "Why do you still have the passenger?"

"He is only light sir and Killer has been across here before."

"Son, you can dismount now and join your comrades."

"Thank you, sir, er Robbie." The youth tried to run on the slippery ice but he lost his footing and fell flat on his face. I said nothing but I knew my expression showed the lieutenant that I still thought I had acted correctly.

"I want every trooper to head for the ship at the front of the line. Have your muskets ready in case they decide to fight."

Our muskets hung from a metal clip on our saddles. As far as I knew none were loaded and I hoped that I would have enough feeling in my hands to enable me to do so if we had to fire them. As we clattered along the frozen river, we heard the alarm being sounded on each of the ships as we passed. I wondered what they would do. Each ship seemed to have many cannons peering from their gun ports. I saw faces appearing along the rails and some of the crew looked to have muskets and pistols too.

I took out my horse pistol, which was loaded, just in case. Killer's stride had taken her ahead of the others and I saw the puff of smoke and then heard the crack as a musket was fired from the ship nearest to me. The ball struck the ice some thirty paces in front of me. I wheeled Killer around. He found it difficult to find purchase and his hooves slid a little until he regained his footing. He was soon hurtling towards the wooden wall of the huge Dutch man of war. I headed straight for the ship. I was too big a target beam on. I knew that head on I would be harder to hit. The crew who had guns kept firing at me but the smoke from their guns and the fact that I was a moving target made it hard, if not impossible, to hit me. When I was thirty yards from the ship, I raised my pistol and aimed at the officer in the blue uniform who was shouting orders. I aimed at his middle. The pistol cracked and the ball struck the rail just in front of him. The effect was the same as if the ball had hit him; it kicked up splinters of wood from the rail as it gouged into the oak and drove them directly into his face. It must have been like being struck by ten arrows at once. He fell screaming to the deck and the rest of the men around him ducked down to safety.

I suddenly felt foolish. I didn't want to run away and so I halted and took my musket from its sling. I shouted up in French and then English. "Surrender or we will fire!"

The crew looked at each other and I heard a hurried conversation. Amazingly, the flag on the jackstaff was lowered in surrender and the crew raised their arms. Pierre rode next to me. "You are a mad little Scotsman, you know that. Look. The whole fleet is surrendering!"

I saw the rest of the ships gradually lowering their flags. This one must have been the flagship. I don't think that I made them surrender but I helped. The line of horsemen and infantry all levelling their muskets at the ships had the desired effect. We took the whole of the Dutch Texel fleet without a casualty! The colonel himself rode up to me and clasped my arm. "Trooper you are a true cavalryman and very brave." He lowered his voice, "Your father would be proud of you and if he were here now, he would acknowledge you as his son. For this, I promote you to Brigadier. Well done Corporal Macgregor!"

Pierre was close enough to hear and after the colonel had left to accept the formal surrender, he clapped me on the back. "You have luck on your side. I am in this army for years waiting for advancement and you have been in for five minutes and yet you get promoted."

"Sorry!"

"Don't apologise. I am pleased with you. I will stay close to you in future. You can't beat luck in a battle."

Rather than resting on our laurels we just waited until the rest of the army caught up with us and the brigade moved on. The commanding general praised us but I knew that he would take all the credit for the surrender. We were all buoyed by our success and the troopers of our squadron enjoyed making fun of my foolish, yet heroic act. Jean's sudden appearance made them stop and his smile, which was rare, showed me that he approved. "What made you do it?"

I shrugged, "I thought I would be hard to hit if I moved towards them and then when I was there…"

"You didn't know what else to do. You are like your father. You are a natural horseman with the instincts which every great cavalryman has. I salute you and I am happy that you have been promoted. It shows that we took the right decision to join the chasseurs. Well done but remember now the men will look to you. Your youth will cut no ice with them."

I suddenly laughed and he looked hurt. "I am sorry sir but that is the first time I have ever heard you crack a joke and I don't even think you know you have, 'cut no ice.'"

He suddenly laughed. "You are as quick and clever as your mother, Robbie, and she would be proud of you. Your great grandfather was known as a brave and reckless warrior. You are taking after him and your father was not a man to back down from a fight. That is probably why he lost his life. You have chosen the right profession. Being a soldier is in your blood."

Our ride did not stop until we reached the sea. In one gloriously short campaign, we had captured a whole country. We spent a month in Ghent while the French Government announced the new Batavian Republic. We enjoyed the joys of victory and paraded around the town in our fine new uniforms. We no longer looked like tramps. We were all heroes and we looked like heroes. The young conscripts who had ridden into battle with us were now seen as veterans and yet few of them had even fired their guns in anger. When we celebrated in the inns of Ghent, we met some of them and I saw young Alan. He was so proud that he had ridden on the back of my horse. He brought the others up to speak with me and to shake my hand. I was a sort of good luck charm for them; the cavalryman who made a fleet surrender. It was as though he had helped to make the ships surrender just by being on the back of my horse. I was happy for them all. I only had a month or so more experience than they did but I knew that death was just around the corner. I had ridden into enough ambushes to know that. I just hoped that they would have some of the luck that I had. I would hate to stand in a line of men less than a hundred yards from an enemy and blast away. I preferred being on a horse where you had, at least, speed on your side. I also liked having a sword. One bad one had nearly cost me my life and I hoped that my new one would bring me a better fortune.

As spring came, we were sent back to Sedan and the barracks. The conquering heroes of the Texel were being given a short rest. We were in high spirits as we headed home. We had avoided losing any more men and every trooper was far more confident. Capturing a fleet without a casualty does that to a regiment. Our fame had made the Paris newspapers and a young French General called Napoleon Bonaparte had heard of us. We were to join the Army of Italy and Pierre would get his way. We would be in the south of France where it was warm and they had wine. The days of icy patrols would be a thing of the past. "You see Robbie, you are lucky!"

CHAPTER 5

Although I was excited to be travelling to the South of France and Italy, I was more than a little nervous as I thought we might be travelling close to Paris and Breteuil. Suppose someone recognised me? Pierre had come to know me well and he laughed when I told him what was bothering me.

"You are a fool! You look like every other one of the troopers. With your shako and your uniform, no one will recognise you. Do not look at anyone. The ladies love a haughty look so look aloof as you ride by. Besides, you have more to worry about with your new troopers. The colonel promoted you but there will be troopers who wish to see you fall flat on your face. I know that they did when I was promoted."

Our newly found friend, General Bonaparte, decided to have us parade through the streets of Paris. It was my worst nightmare. I had hoped to slip through quietly and remained unobserved. Now we were lauded as the heroes of the Texel and there would be no hiding place. One benefit was that we were all issued new equipment and uniforms. The general wanted us paraded through the streets of Paris as heroes and not as tramps. The new uniform was brighter and better fitting. We received the new model shako. We received the latest musketoon and my damaged cape and dolman could be stored in my chest as a backup. That was the only bright spot. We did look smart. The uniforms were bright and bold and the sky-blue trim stood out on the cuffs. I knew that within a few weeks the sky blue would have faded and run into the green of the jacket. The green would have become duller. That was a good thing as it helped to hide us when fighting in woodland. For the moment we looked as though we were brand new toy soldiers, freshly painted in a box.

As we prepared to ride through the streets Pierre shook his head and walked over to me. He cocked his head to one side and with his hands on his hips said, "The shako should be worn at a slight angle." He carefully adjusted it to get just the right jaunty look. "We are going for style. That is better. That is how the hero of the Texel should look." My moustache had come on and Pierre gave the end an extra flourish. "There. You are a chasseur." He checked that my queue and pigtails were even and clean. When satisfied he nodded. "Now check your men."

The troopers were all smart although I did have to make two of them adjust the saddle girths on their mounts. Some of the new recruits were not as good on horses as we would have liked. The draft had given us the best of what was left but those in authority had not deemed riding as a necessary skill! Bureaucrats! We had to spend the whole of the journey turning them into horsemen. A cavalry battle does not favour the incompetent horseman.

Officially it was not a parade but the executions had lessened lately and the fickle crowds wanted entertainment. A parade was almost as good as seeing heads roll into a basket. The fact that we had lost so much land the year before made this victory even more special. We were directed to travel through the centre. This meant that we passed through the Place de La Revolution and the sombre sight of the guillotine. I kept my head straight so that I would not have to see it. The crowds there were huge and they were cheering fervently and patriotically as we approached in a column of twos. It made our numbers look greater. The previous year had seen France threatened and within a couple of months, we were secure to the north and the east. It was nothing short of a miracle. Our horses behaved impeccably but I identified a couple of troopers in Bombardier

Boucher's section who were not sitting straight. I would have a word with them later on. A good posture was important for the horse and the trooper. I was desperate to look over my shoulder and watch my men but that would have been a grave indiscretion. The crowds were just as big at the palace where the National Guard saluted us. They too had smart uniforms but I would not like to rely on them in a battle. Pierre and Claude had told me that they were nothing more than armed thugs. They had no discipline and little intelligence. They were useful for keeping the Paris mob under control.

I kept my head looking forwards and I was careful not to smile. My face was impassive and I hoped that no one would remember me. I fervently prayed that no-one from the inn or the stable would turn out. They would be the ones who might recognise me. Once we passed the cathedral, strangely empty, we could relax a little more. We still had the southern gate to negotiate and then we would be on the road to Nice. Annoyingly the colonel decided to halt just inside the southern gate to allow the horses to drink from the troughs there. To my horror, I saw the sergeant who had allowed us to exit when Jean and I had fled Paris. I kept my head down and hidden behind Killer as I took my turn at the trough. The sergeant chose that moment to wander over and speak to me and Pierre.

"You lads are an inspiration to us all you know that. We were worried that the Austrians and the Dutch would attack Paris." He shook his head. "Of course, we would have sent them packing but we were glad that you did such a good job. Can I shake you by the hand?" He shook Pierre's hand and then mine. "If you ever return to Paris just ask for me Sergeant Major Desnottes. I'll stand you a pichon of wine."

As we mounted and headed south, I was grateful that Sergeant Major Desnottes had not recognised me. Perhaps my disguise was effective after all. The journey through the heart of France proved to be both pleasant and illuminating. It seemed to be made of tiny hamlets and villages. There was little of the Revolutionary fervour we had witnessed further north. It was almost like a holiday as the weather improved and we were feted as heroes all the way down to the warm Blue Cost of the Mediterranean.

The new troopers who had been less than acceptable at the start of the march gradually became better as they were chivvied by all the non-commissioned officers. We had plenty of time to look for flaws and we did just that. Our increased numbers meant that we had promotions. Claude was promoted to Sergeant Major and Pierre to sergeant. I was happy with my rank. In fact, I thought I didn't deserve the promotion I had received. I was just in the right place at the right time.

Lieutenant Bartiaux rode next to me for a while as we were passing close by Avignon. "I saw that you were worried on the bridge at St Marcel. You needn't have worried. The National Guard would not take on a chasseur, especially not the hero of Texel."

I shook my head, "I am not sure that I believe that."

"Look around you. These are the most dashing soldiers in the whole French Army and you are one of them. All the men in the Place de La Revolution would have traded places with you in an instant."

"You weren't worried?"

He shook his head, "Not I."

"The thing is sir. I found it hard that first day when we found those Englishmen. Until then I thought that our enemies were the Austrians. I know I didn't have to fight the English or the Scots but I am not sure I could. They speak the same language as my mother. I know that my great grandfather hated the English but they are now the British. I keep hearing about the British. That means they are my own people."

"I see. Well, the good news is that there are no British soldiers where we are going to in Italy and that will not be a problem. But if you think there might be a problem then you will need to think about leaving the chasseurs. You cannot let your comrades down when in action."

"I couldn't leave them, sir. They are like my brothers."

"Then you will have to resolve this little problem yourself. Although there are no British in Italy, they are a little like the itch you cannot scratch. They never go away and they never know when they are beaten. France will have to fight them someday and that means that you will have to decide where your loyalty lies."

We reached the fortress of Antibes. It was there we were to be assembled before we began our advance into Italy. I could not believe how unbelievably beautiful the land in the south of France was. The sea was a blue which appeared to have been painted. The buildings with the white walls and terracotta roofs seemed to dance in the reflections of the sea. It was warm and there were the most wonderful smells of herbs and flowers drifting down from the mountains. The fortress of Antibes had a commanding position above the town and looked to be the most secure fort we had seen during our travels from the north.

The only disappointment for Pierre was that the wine of the region was rosé and he preferred red. He was convinced we would find some. However, the olives and the fish more than made up for the deficit in the wine. Claude did have a cautionary message for us. He pointed ahead to the east and the mountains which seemed to rise directly from the sea. "That is the country in which we will be fighting. It is not a cavalry country. It is light infantry ambush country. Your men will be using their muskets more than their swords. "Although the others poured scorn on his ideas, he was proved correct.

Another reason for our delay in Antibes was that our general, Napoleon Bonaparte, was busy ridding Paris of the dissidents who were attempting to halt the revolution. He was gaining power by giving the crowd a whiff of grapeshot. It endeared him to the Directory and those in power. It was his first step on the ladder to the top. The colonel was ordered to provide the escort for the mercurial general when he finally reached us. Whatever the cause for the delay we did not mind.

It was also in Antibes that I discovered just how close the British were. Frigates and sloops constantly patrolled the waters of our southern coast. They travelled in squadrons of three of four and always stayed out of range of the guns in the fort. However, if any soldiers were foolish enough to be caught on the cornice then the Royal Navy vessels hurtled in to unleash a fierce bombardment. A whole company of recruits was wiped out while we were there. We had the advantage that we travelled in small groups, we wore green and the moment we saw the ships we could head inland very quickly. The infantry also learned to take cover quickly. In battle, there are two types of men, the quick and the dead. If you are not quick to learn then you die.

When the general finally arrived, I was slightly disappointed. He was tiny. I had expected, from the comments about him, that he would be a giant of a man but he was small. He was also very difficult to understand as he had the accent of a Corsican which I found hard to understand. It was almost like a foreign language. Over the next couple of years either his French got better or my ear became attuned to his words for I understood him more as time went on.

He insisted on inspecting us. We stood next to our horses. He seemed a little wary of them. When he reached me, the colonel introduced me as the trooper who had ordered the fleet to surrender. He was impressed but then said. "He is a little young is he not?"

The colonel gave a cough and said, "Bravery does not come from age General Bonaparte, it comes from the heart."

"Quite so; and your name, Macgregor, it is not French?"

I answered, "No, General Bonaparte, my mother's family came from Scotland."

"Ah, so you can speak English?"

"Yes, sir."

The general turned to his secretary, "Make a note of that it may come in useful." He looked up at Killer. "A fine-looking horse. What is his name?"

"Killer."

He looked surprised, "You gave him that name? Why?"

I smiled and spread my arms, "The men named him that as a

joke. None of them could ride him and they gave him to me to see if he would throw me."

"Did he?"

"No, sir."

He laughed. "I like your spirit. When I was a cadet, they tried all sorts of tricks me with. They learned that I am not a man to be trifled with. You will go far in this army."

Pierre made fun of me for the next couple of days. As he said, "Hobnobbing with the generals eh! Whatever next? Captain Macgregor perhaps?"

I think he was a little jealous of the interest shown in me by the general. Little did I know, at the time, the effect it would have on my life.

Bonaparte was even more famous than us and the crowds lined the small fishing villages we passed through. He was the hero of Toulon; the man who had sent the British passing. Once we reached Nice, I saw that he had been planning this invasion for some time. There were camps set up all around the fishing village. There were hundreds of infantries. I counted twenty battalions. There was just a squadron of dragoons, the 5th, as well as the artillery so beloved of our little general. I had no idea what to expect for the cannons were small calibre and mountain guns. The infantry looked as though they could manage without the help of a regiment of chasseurs.

As soon as we arrived, we received news which made Napoleon explode with anger. A French brigade had been defeated by the Austrians in Voltri which was just along the coast. Jean, who was briefed by the colonel, told us that the general was annoyed that the French had been caught by a much larger force of Austrians. He did not blame the colonel of the brigade but the lack of scout cavalry which would have warned the infantry of the presence of an enemy. As soon as Jean told us that I knew what our role would be.

The next day we were divided into our eight troops and sent to find the enemy. Out orders from the colonel were quite rclear; we had to keep headquarters informed of events as they changed and yet not lose touch with the ones we were shadowing. I was glad that I was with Jean. He seemed to know what he was doing. Claude was still recovering from his wound and stayed at headquarters with the colonel. Pierre was more than happy about that arrangement. "We will get the best billets, my friend. Claude will see to that. This will be simple. Find the enemy, tell the general and then sit by the sea drinking wine."

He had a hard lesson to learn, for the general in question liked headquarters to be wherever he was. Normally that was just ten miles from where we were. Claude and the colonel had a much harder job than we did.

Our sector to patrol was in the mountains. The whole regiment used the coast road to reach it riding quickly through Monaco, now in our hands, Menton and Ventimiglia and the other smaller coastal towns of the Gulf of Genoa. Once we reached San Remo, Jean led us northeast towards the high mountain passes. I was not sure of the geography of the land and I could not see much reason to fight for it. I turned to the lieutenant, "I mean, sir, it isn't as though there is a big river bringing a lot of trade down here. They are tiny villages and hamlets of a few houses. It is a waste of time."

"When we stop, I will show you the map, young Robbie and then you will see. Next time look at the maps before we leave. If Pierre or I are killed then you will be in charge. Think on that."

It was a rebuke and a well-deserved one. I hadn't done enough preparation. I was responsible for the lives of others. That morning in April, riding along the narrow mountain roads I began to change.

Badalucco was a small collection of six houses some ten miles from San Remo. We halted there to allow the horses to drink. I joined Pierre and Jean around the map. "The general needs to strike at the northern heart of Italy. That is Milan. At the same time, if we can force a way over the mountain passes of the Tyrol then we can close with Vienna. The problem he has is that the enemy can block his route at any of these narrow places." He pointed to some key towns which lay ahead of us. "We have to find out which ones are unguarded and then he can use those."

"What if they are guarded, sir?"

"Then we try to winkle out the enemy and send for help."

I looked at the troopers all taking advantage of the rest to eat, drink and stretch their legs. "But we haven't even got a full troop. There are just fifty of us."

Pierre smiled, "Then, my friend the forty-nine will have to do the job while someone goes for help."

I smiled, "Yes I see that sergeant but we are horsemen."

"Ah, the horse. You notice Robbie, that on the horse you have a pistol and a musket. We will get off the horses and fight on foot."

Jean spoke to me slowly as though I was an imbecile. He was right; I was behaving like a fool. "Sorry, sir and the next chance I get I am going to fill my second holster with another gun."

"That's better. Now you are thinking like a soldier."

The column headed off. We were now under Bonaparte's orders and that meant living off the land where we could. We had our blankets with us; hopefully, we would find a building in which to shelter. The April nights were cold in the mountains.

Jean stopped us when we were above the town of Altara. It was one of the bigger towns we had seen and it nestled next to the river beneath the mountains. We were in the tree line just off the road which meant we could see but not be seen. Our green uniforms came in handy again. Jean gestured me forwards. "Robbie, take five men and work your way down to the outskirts of the town. I can't see any flags but this looks to be big enough to have a garrison of some description." He pointed to the church tower. "If the town is clear then wave from the top of the tower."

"And if it is not clear?"

"Then get back here. Choose your own men."

I was pleased about that. There were some of the men I trusted implicitly and we had worked together well before. "Jean-Michel, Guillaume, Francois, Charles and Richard, come with me." We made our way through the trees which bordered the road. I remembered the ambush in the Netherlands. "Make sure your pistol is primed."

There were still pockets of snow in the trees but Killer was sure-footed and we negotiated the slope easily. I could smell the town before I saw it. There was a smell of wood smoke and cows. I held up my hand to stop the others and I moved forward to peer through the thinning trees. I could see the buildings and the people. It looked to be a farming community but at this end of the town, there was a slaughterhouse which explained the smell of cows. I could see that we would be hidden from the road if we rode around the rear of it.

I took out my pistol and led them across the open ground and then behind the building. Any noise from our hooves was masked by the sound of the animals in the abattoir and the noise and chatter of the workers. There was an old barn and we rode into it. "Charles, keep watch. The rest of you dismount."

I had decided that riding the horses around the town would make us more visible. I replaced my pistol in my holster and began to load my musketoon. "We will take the muskets. Trooper Blanc, you guard the horses. If you hear firing then we might have to leave in a hurry."

I located the church tower as we left the barn and headed for the centre of the small town. It was important that we were not seen. This was Piedmont and there were no French troops ahead of us. Any soldiers we saw would be the enemy. I peered around the corner close to the main square. It was not a large town but it had a square with a statue in it. I suddenly saw uniforms. They were neither blue nor green. They were an enemy. I could have returned with the news of our find there and then but I felt responsible. Who were they and how many of them?

"Have your weapons ready but do not fire unless we have to."

I decided that boldness would be the best tactic. We stepped into the street and walked purposefully towards the square. I was assessing the soldiers as I walked up. There were eight of them that I could see. They appeared to have swords and bayonets only. They were smoking pipes and cigars and were drinking outside the small inn. The uniforms suggested infantry or artillery as they had neither pelisse nor dolman. That worked in our favour; it meant that we could outrun them on our horses if we had to. As we neared them one of them glanced around and saw us. He did not react straightaway, which allowed us to close a couple more steps. Then he did and he crashed his chair to the floor as he leapt to his feet. He grabbed his sword and I fired the musket from waist height. They were only thirty yards from us and I knew that I could not miss. The others all fired at the same time and I drew my sword and raced towards the survivors.

There was pandemonium as people ran for cover. One officer raced towards me with his sword aloft. I still held my musket in my left hand and I blocked his sword thrust and stabbed him with my sword. It went right through him carried there by our joint momentum. I withdrew the blade. As the others arrived, I could see that, as Francois despatched the last man, we had eliminated them. There were no survivors which meant that we had no prisoners to take back. "Jean-Michel, get the horses. The rest of you reload."

I searched the six men and took any papers I could. They appeared to be written in Italian, which I could not read, and I pocketed them. Remembering my own sword, I said, "If there are any nice swords you might want one." They retrieved the weapons which were all better than ours.

Francois found money which he jingled. He grinned, "We'll share this later."

When the horses arrived, we mounted. "We have made enough noise to waken any more soldiers. Let's ride through the town to see if these had any comrades and then send the signal to the lieutenant."

The whole place was like a ghost town as people cowered in their homes and we rode through empty streets. We found their horses in a stable. The stable owner looked petrified. Trooper Blanc spoke a little of the local language and he calmed the man down. It confirmed what I had deduced. These were officers out for a little pleasure which meant there was a regiment, at least, close by. We rode back to the church with the horses in tow. I was about to race up to the top of the tower when I heard the clattering of hooves. Our hands went to our guns but we relaxed when we saw it was the rest of the troop.

Jean shook his head, "We heard the firing. What happened to the orders? You were supposed to return if it was occupied."

"It wasn't occupied. There was just a handful of them. Besides it, all happened too quickly to do anything else."

"One day you will push your luck a little too far you know!"

CHAPTER 6

One effect of our sudden action was that the people of the town were more than happy to accommodate us. Jean made sure that we paid for everything. The fact that it was Austrian money we used was irrelevant. He sent a messenger back to the colonel and we enjoyed a night under shelter having eaten and drunk well. My little squad were delighted. They all had a decent sword and we had sold the other three and shared the profits. I was the favourite Brigadier in the troop.

Pierre gave me a sour look. "You could have saved one for me."

"You know the way it works sergeant. The men who are there when we capture things share in the profits. You could have bought one. Francois would have done a good deal with you."

"If you think I am spending my hard-earned money..."

I laughed, "Then you had better ask to be the next leader of the scouts. I was just in the right place at the right time."

Pierre did lead the next patrol but it brought him nothing. He found where the Austrians had travelled from, Montenotte. "Sir, there look to be about ten thousand men there. They have artillery but no cavalry."

"Well done." After he had sent a messenger back to the general, we took the whole troop to watch the town and to make sure that we knew their dispositions well.

Captain Bessières brought the rest of the regiment up. I was close by Jean when he arrived and overheard their conversation between Captain Bessières and Captain Aristide. "The colonel is not well. The general advised him to stay at headquarters. I am to command until he returns to service."

Captain Bessières had recently transferred to us from the 18th Chasseurs which had been disbanded. I had little to do with him as Captain Aristide commanded our troop and squadron. The newcomer seemed affable enough. He was younger than Jean but then almost all of the officers were. "We have been ordered to the other side of the town to prevent the enemy escaping."

Albert had served with the colonel for many years. "I hope he is receiving medical help."

"He is. The general's own doctor is seeing to him."

"He has his own doctor?"

"But of course. General Bonaparte is an important man. It is rumoured they are selecting horsemen to be his personal escort to replace us. "I could tell from his words that the captain hoped to be one of them. For myself, I wanted to get back to doing what we had been doing.

Captain Bessières took out a map. "Captain Aristide, take your squadron and cover this road which leads to Milano. I will take the rest and prevent them from reaching Genoa."

Getting around the town was easier said than done. If we took the main road, we would struggle to pass by the town without being seen and fired upon. I was new to war but even I knew that it was imperative that the general achieve surprise. Jean pointed to the map. "Sir, if we head north, here, then we can travel up to this road and approach from the other side. It will add five miles to our journey but…"

"But we will achieve surprise. Good. Your troop can lead." With so many soldiers around we saw few signs of life. Every farmhouse we passed was shuttered although the tendrils of smoke from their chimneys showed that there were people within.

"Robbie, take Tiny and scout out the road ahead."

I gestured at the seventeen-year-old recruit who had recently joined us. He was the youngest trooper we had and I suspect that Jean was giving me the chance to get to know him and to train him at the same time. He was as tall as me and I wondered at the use of a nickname.

"How come they call you Tiny? What is your real name?"

He looked embarrassed. "My father served the old king and he named me Louis. He was killed a year after I was born. Mother thought that Louis was not a good name in light of the Revolution. She said to use my nickname." He shrugged, "And I am a big lad so..."

"I understand. Well Louis, when you are scouting you need to keep both eyes watching. Look for movement. It could be a bush or a branch or even something which you only half see. Trust your instincts. If you think you have seen something then look carefully. We are lucky, most of the soldiers who fight us wear bright uniforms and find it hard to hide but, in these mountains, they have Jaegers who wear green. This is their home so watch out for them."

He nodded and we rode until we came to the road junction. We took the right side and circled the small mountain to our right. Its slopes were covered in small scrubby trees. They would stop an avalanche in winter but, fortunately for us, would afford no enemy a place to hide. As we reached the other side, we saw the town and the valley below us. The road ran along a small ridge and would afford us a good view of the town and the battle.

"Let us find some cover. We may not be against the skyline but Killer is a little too black against the hills."

As we waited for the rest of the squadron I asked, "Have you loaded your gun yet?"

"I thought the ball would fall out as we rode?"

"Not if you make sure you ram it down well. You don't prime it but that it the matter of a moment." As he took out a ball from his cartridge pouch, I said, "Try to use a round ball. The first shot is the only one you are likely to aim so you might as well make sure it is a good shot." I smiled to myself as he earnestly followed my advice. It was the same advice given to me by Jean some ten years earlier with my father impatiently drumming his fingers on his own weapon as he waited to fire.

We heard the drumming of hooves as Albert brought the rest of the squadron to join us. "Lieutenant Bartiaux's troop, dismount. One in four men to act as horse holders. Form a skirmish line there." He pointed to the wall which abutted the road. There was a steep drop the other side and was obviously intended to prevent animals from falling. The captain sent half of his troop to the other side of the road leading from the town so that we had crossfire. He retained half of his troop mounted in case they were needed. When you had twenty years' experience of the cavalry such things were second nature. When Captain Aristide was in command you knew that every contingency was catered for.

Suddenly Jean-Michael pointed as he shouted, "Look, sir. The infantry, they are advancing."

We could see the battle unfolding before us. Our general was outnumbered but I suspected that he would not worry about that. We heard the bugles and could see the Austrian regiments racing to form three deep lines before the town. From our lofty position, we could see that the cannons were behind the walls and would fire over the heads of the regiments before them. There were also battalions behind the wall. I hoped the general knew his business.

We would see the blue columns as they approached. Suddenly the light infantry battalions left the column and began to spread out to head up the slope. They scurried like ants disturbed from an anthill. They moved in ones and twos and not in great solid lines. The Austrians opened fire and Jean laughed. "They are wasting powder and ball. Look, not one man has been hit."

I could see what he said was true. The range was too far anyway. They fired again. I could see the problem immediately. The soldiers of the light infantry were not standing but running and ducking when the order to fire was given. The light infantry waited until they were less than a hundred paces and then began to fire from a kneeling position. They did take casualties but I could see that they were causing more amongst the tightly packed ranks of Austrians. They were firing into solid blocks of men and even a bad shot was bound to hit something. I saw Austrians begin to fall. The Austrian cannons were firing at the distant columns that were slowly approaching but the slope was not helping them and the smoke from their own infantry meant they could not see fall of shot.

The firing from the Austrians slowed and I saw men peeing down the barrels of their guns. "Sergeant Boucher," I asked quietly, "why are they doing that?"

"The powder cakes in the barrel and the barrel gets hot. It is the quickest way to clear your barrel and cool it. If they had not fired so early, they would not have had to do that."

I stored that information. I could now see why a ragged volley would not hurt us when in skirmish order and it would take battalion fire at a solid line to cause casualties. The light infantry were advancing again and causing more casualties amongst the Austrians. Suddenly we heard the pas de charge as the columns of line infantry began their attack. The Austrian cannons still had no target and were firing blind and the light infantrymen were now targeting the artillerymen. The battle was mesmerising to watch. The French columns did not halt when they neared the Austrian lines. They charged. There was a small volley from the men at the head of the column but the main musket attack still came from the light infantry who were picking off the Austrian officers and sergeants. When the three columns struck the white line, the Austrians broke and ran.

Jean shouted, "Ready muskets!"

I looked down my men and saw Tiny grinning as he pointed to his musket. I shook my head. He was young. The Austrians did not take long to reach Captain Aristide's men. There was a volley which sounded like the popping of corks. It slowed down the exodus but did not stop it. Captain Aristide and his mounted men took off after those who escaped down the road while we began to fire at those who attempted to cross in our direction. After I had fired my first ball the enemy were hidden by a pall of smoke. I reloaded and peered through the gloom.

There was little point in firing blind and I waited until I saw a shape loom up ten yards away. I fired and the body fell to the ground.

"Cease fire!"

When the smoke cleared, we could see that the Austrians had surrendered. The soldier I had shot had been so close that I had completely destroyed his face. His mother would not have recognised him.

"Disarm them and line up on the road over there." Jean pointed to the road leading from the town. All the way back into the town we could see Austrian and Piedmontese surrendering. We had won.

Captain Aristide returned with some prisoners. "We had better take them into the town and see what the general has in mind for us next."

Bonaparte was delighted with our victory and with our role in it. Captain Bessières took it all as though it was a compliment personally directed to him. His squadron had had little action and they had captured only four prisoners. Pierre was phlegmatic about it. "The ones who do all the hard work, the ordinary soldiers never get any credit so what difference does it make which officer is praised. It doesn't help us." He gestured at the prisoners. "This lot were piss poor." He held out a handful of coins. "This won't even buy a pichon of wine. Not that you could get one up here." Pierre had this ability to bring every military action down to the basics of food, drink and money. It was much later that I realised the wisdom of such a philosophy. In those days I was still a naïve idealist and not the cynic I became.

We had no time to rest on our laurels. The general had no sooner given us praise than he ordered us to head west. I found out from Captain Aristide that the general intended to destroy the army of Piedmont and Sardinia so that he could concentrate on the Austrians. What we did not discover until much later was that there were two other armies attacking the Austrians from the north and the west but they were being trounced. We were the only force which was having any success.

Once again Jean and our troop were given the honour of scouting. We passed through Ferrania and Carcare without seeing anyone. Pierre was delighted when we reached Carcare as he was able to use the coins, he had acquired from our prisoners to buy some olives, cheese, bread and wine. He was a happy man once more. I had been spared the scouting duties until the midday break but I was sent, with Charles and Francois this time to look for a billet for the night. "I don't think there are any more soldiers in these parts. The general looks to have cleared them all out."

He was wrong. We had passed the ruined castle of Cosseria and were approaching the tiny mountain hamlet of Millesimo when the troopers following the three of us were subjected to a fierce fusillade. The hidden soldiers had allowed us to pass by. I was furious with myself. As soon as the fusillade began, I could see where they were. There was a low wall halfway towards a farm and there must have been a company of light infantry, at least, there. As I drew my musket to fire, musket balls came from the town ahead. The walls of the town gave them shelter and enabled them to fire down on us. A chip of rock from the wall flew up and gouged Charles on the cheek. I shouted my command, "Right boys back to the lieutenant." We galloped through a gunpowder shrouded storm of lead but we reached them unscathed. I saw two dead troopers as I rode along the scene of the attack. "Sorry sir, we didn't see them. There are a lot more in the town ahead. I couldn't estimate numbers."

"Don't worry Brigadier. That was probably my fault. I was complacent and these men died because of it. I have sent a rider back to the general. Let's form a skirmish line. We might be able to shift those men ahead. Dismount!"

Captains Bessières and Aristide arrived. Captain Bessières did not look happy at the delay. "Can we not just charge them Lieutenant Bartiaux?"

Captain Aristide rolled his eyes as Jean explained. "They have cover behind a wall and the slope is steep and rock covered. We would lose too many men. I am sending the men up on foot."

His arrogant sniff told us of his view. "Very well they are your men. Take command, Captain Aristide, I will report to the general."

Once he had gone, I heard Albert say to Jean, "Arrogant little prick. I'll use my men as well. Troop, dismount."

I reloaded my musketoon and turned to my men. "Make sure you have the best ball you can." I saw someone fiddling with his bayonet. "Don't bother with that. It pulls the barrel down too much. If we get close use your sabre."

"Then why do we get issued bayonets?"

"It's handy for digging holes," I heard one old soldier say that and it had stuck. I chuckled, he was right. I had never used my bayonet for anything as yet.

"Forward!"

Rather like the light infantry at Montenotte we walked crouched over and with a healthy space between us. The puff of smoke and the rippled cracks told me that they had fired their muskets at our movement. The balls flew around us but I only heard one trooper cry out. "Hold your fire until I say. Do you hear me?"

I heard my section shout, "Yes Brigadier." The smoke of their guns hid us from the enemy but they showed us where they were. When we were eighty yards away, I shouted, "Drop and crawl!" The slope and the wall meant that we would be safe from their fire. I waited until we were forty yards away when even our musketoons would be accurate and I said, "Kneel! Find a target and fire!" I could hear the others ordering their men to fire too. I lifted up my musket and aimed at the line of smoke. I fired and then shouted. "Charge!"

I dropped my gun and drew my sword. A musket ball plucked at my sleeve and then I saw a ramrod, hurtling like a spear through the air. One soldier was not going to be able to fire again soon. The smoke had thinned and I saw a soldier aiming his gun at me. I knocked the barrel up with my left hand and stabbed him with my sword. I quickly clambered over the wall. A Sardinian officer raced at me with sword raised. I parried his blow and then, with a deft flick of the wrist, disarmed him and held the point of my blade at his throat. He threw his arms in the air and shouted, "Quarter! Quarter!"

I gestured for him to kneel. As I looked around for any others, I could see the remnants of the outpost fleeing back to the hamlet.

The general arrived soon afterwards. He dismounted close to where we were guarding the prisoners. He gestured to me to approach. I wondered what he was going to say but he merely rested his telescope on my shoulder so that he could view the town. He turned to the general of brigade next to him. "Joubert take the light infantry and Banel's brigade. I cannot see guns. You can take the town."

He nodded curtly to me and then said to Albert, "Captain, take your men and scout the area around Dego. One of the prisoners from Montenotte told me that there was an army there." He suddenly grinned. "We should be able to finish off these Sardinians sooner rather than later eh?"

"Yes, General Bonaparte." Had he been a dog then Captain Bessières would have wagged his tail! He promised the general that the area would be sealed off tightly.

Pierre, of course, was delighted. He had noted that there was a bakery in Carcare and he was sure that we would find some wine too. I was more concerned with the men we had lost. Although the enemy had lost more, we still had five wounded troopers and four dead ones. The war was proving expensive.

I rode next to Charles as we headed east. I still felt guilty that my lack of attention had caused him to be wounded. "How is the cheek?"

He beamed at me and then winced. "It still hurts but this will become a wonderful scar. The women will all believe I earned it duelling. I will still have my moustache and it will add a certain elegance and style to my looks."

I shook my head. Many of the chasseurs were so vain that they cared more about their appearance than their health. "Well make sure you keep the wound clean. You don't want to get an infection."

He suddenly looked serious. "Thank you, Brigadier. That is sound advice and I will heed it."

We halted in Carcare to allow the horses to be watered. Jean and I wandered the streets to pick up any gossip we could. This was the heartland of Piedmont. If these people felt like peace then we might stand a chance of achieving what we had in the Low Countries; a relatively bloodless victory. The people we met were friendly and did not seem at all belligerent. In fact, they appeared to welcome us. The Ligurian Republic along the coast was seen as a better form of government and they were hoping that our little general would do the same.

We reported the facts to Captain Aristide who just shook his head. "This young general appears to have the luck."

"But sir, isn't he a good general?"

"The soldiers we have been fighting are not very good soldiers. Remember the Austrian cavalry that we fought in the Low Countries? They were real soldiers. This is the soft underbelly of the Empire. Wait until he meets some real soldiers and then you can judge." Albert was a wise man. He was the sort of soldier who had made France great for so many years. He was solid and dependable. I suppose he was one of the success stories of the revolution. If there had not been a revolution he would just have served as a sergeant major. As a captain, he could put his experience and knowledge to real use.

The prisoner had been correct about Dego. There was a mixture of Sardinian and Austrian uniforms which lined its defences. The large hill next to the town had been heavily fortified with ditches but I could see no artillery and nor could I see any cavalry. We placed ourselves across the main road into Dego and awaited the arrival of the rest of the army. We did not expect them before the next day. Captain Aristide chose a campsite which was on the other side of the river and also on an elevated piece of ground. To Captain Bessières this was not important. When Captain Aristide announced that he would put vedettes out, the temporary commanding officer, Captain Bessières, laughed in his face.

"I think you over-estimate these Piedmontese soldiers. Why I am certain that we could take all of them with just our two squadrons."

"Nevertheless, Captain Bessières I feel we ought to put sentries out. It is what the colonel would have done."

"Pah! An old man still fighting old wars but if it makes you happy then so be it."

I could see the anger on Albert's face. His beloved colonel had been insulted but the old sergeant major kept his voice under control as he ordered Jean to set sentries.

The next day Captain Bessières had a superior look on his face as no one had attempted to breach our lines. He had the good grace not to say anything but you could see he felt vindicated.

When Bonaparte arrived, he had General Massena with him. This was the first time I saw the little general who was so successful. He struck me as a greedy little man but the general thought highly enough of him to have him as his subordinate. This time he gave us a real role rather than just watching. He was determined to break the will of the Austrian allies and we were placed in a three-deep line to the north of the town. Our orders were quite simple, as soon as we received our orders we were to charge and break the enemy.

Captain Bessières was delighted with the new role while Albert was sceptical. "There are very few of us who have ever charged. It is not an easy skill."

"They are cavalrymen and this is what they were born to do."

He led the first line, Albert the second and we were with Jean, in the third line. Some of the younger troopers were unhappy at this but I was delighted. I had never charged boot to boot before and the chance to do it without anyone firing at me seemed eminently preferable to being in the front rank.

Captain Bessières was correct about one thing, however, the enemy were not the best soldiers we had ever fought and they soon began to retreat from the relentless attack of light infantry and heavy columns of determined men. As soon as the signal was given the captain ordered the bugle to sound the charge and two hundred troopers began to trot, then canter and finally gallop towards the fleeing enemy. It was not as easy as one might think to keep to the same speed as the other horsemen. I had to keep shouting at my troopers to hold their horses back a little. The point of a cavalry charge was that you hit the enemy as a solid unbroken line. When we hit them, the captain was well ahead of the rest and the Piedmontese were struck piecemeal. They were still slaughtered but had it been a more disciplined army then things might have ended differently. The third rank had nothing to do as the enemy all surrendered. It was the end of the armies of Sardinia and Piedmont. General Bonaparte was delighted.

He slapped Captain Bessières heartily on the back. "You and your chasseurs have done well. I will take a squadron with me now to accept the surrender of the Savoyards." I could see the eager anticipation on Bessières face. "You have done enough today my friend. I will take Captain Aristide and the other squadron. You and your brave men can celebrate your victory. General Massena is in command during my absence."

He put on a brave face but we could all see that the ambitious horseman wanted to be as close to this mercurial comet called Bonaparte as possible. For our squadron, it was just a job. Not one of us was under the spell of Bonaparte. He was a good general but as Albert had said, the proof would be when he faced a better enemy than the poor Sardinians and Savoyards.

We left the celebrating army and headed north to the old capital of Savoy, Turin.

CHAPTER 7

It was a long ride. The staff, which accompanied Bonaparte, was used to quick decisions and his equipment was ready on pack-horses just as soon as we were. The general, to be fair to him, was a hard man on himself and he was just as hard on us. He just kept going. We had two stops for food but none for sleep. Ten hours after we left Dego we entered Turin. For a little man, he had a great deal of presence. While we kept guard outside the palace he and his advisers strode in as though they owned the place. I was exhausted and just wanted to sleep but that was out of the question until the general gave us permission.

Eventually, one of his aides came out and told the captain that we just needed to leave ten men on guard and the rest could sleep. Jean arranged the rota and my section had the midnight stint. I didn't mind after all, mine had the youngest troopers and the ones best able to cope with sleep deprivation. When Pierre woke me and my men, I was more than a little worried. I had never guarded such an important person before. I was deter-mined to do a good job. I wondered where he was sleeping.

We found the troopers we were to replace and they were, thankfully, inside the building for it was exceptionally cold. I placed my men in their assigned positions. I would not be able to relax until we were relieved in two hours. I walked all around the sentry posts until I was almost dizzy. Suddenly the door opened and the general stood there. I had been convinced that he would be asleep.

"Ah Brigadier, I have an urge for some bread and cheese…"

I waved over Francois. "Fetch some cheese and bread. Would you like wine as well sir?"

"Thank you but no I need a clear head." He started to go back in and then stopped. "You may be able to help me, come and join me."

The room was devoid of people but the table was covered in maps and jottings. He saw my look of surprise and smiled. "We concluded the treaty hours ago. I am planning my next moves in this game of chess. Tell me, Brigadier, you have fought the Austrians before; what do you think of them?"

"They fight well enough and they have good equipment but they seem a little rigid."

"Rigid?"

"Yes, sir, like when they fought the other day at Montenotte. We were watching and you could see that they had never fought with light infantry flitting like flies before them. They couldn't cope."

He nodded, "And how would you have coped?"

"I would have had my own light infantry in front of the lines but armed with a weapon which had a longer range and then we could pick them off before they reached us. Our light infantry suffered few casualties in their attack. Had they done so then they might not have been so resolute."

"Is there a weapon with a longer range?"

"Oh yes there are muskets with longer barrels but Jean, the man who taught me to shoot, used a rifle sometimes. A little fiddly to load but you can hit someone at four hundred yards with one of those."

"And are you a good shot?"

There was little point in false modesty. "Yes, sir."

"Good. I like honesty." He looked up as there was a knock on the door. I went to open it and Francois stood there with a tray filled with bread and cheese. I took it from him and placed it on a chair; there was no space on the table. "Would you care to join me?"

"No thank you, sir. It will only make my comrades jealous and I am still on duty."

"You know I am forming a company of guides. They will be chasseurs in all but name. Their function is to be my personal guards." He shrugged, "The Directory thinks it is necessary. When they are formed you might be useful. Think about it."

I had thought about it and my answer would be no but I couldn't insult him. I lied. "That would be an exciting prospect."

He smiled, "But you are not enthusiastic about it."

"I like my comrades in the regiment."

"Esprit de corps. I admire that. Still, if you ever change your mind there will be a place for you on my staff. And now I will get back to my plans. Thank you for the conversation Scotsman. It was most illuminating."

The next day we escorted him back to Dego to rejoin the army. This was a more leisurely ride but it still took us all day. The messengers reached us from Captain Bessières when we were halfway there. The Austrians had attacked Dego and come close to capturing the town from Massena. The general was furious and we had to whip our horses on. The courier who had been sent was Jean-Noel and he was one of the older troopers. He rode next to Jean and Pierre and I had his conversation. "It was Captain Bessières fault. He didn't bother putting any sentries out and the first we knew was when the camp was filled with Austrians. Luckily General Massena is calm and cool. He organised the men and we defeated them. We lost thirty troopers though." Even though he lowered his voice I heard the next comment, "The captain is saying he ordered Lieutenant Laborde to put vedettes out which is convenient as the lieutenant died. "

When we reached Dego some semblance of order had been introduced. I noticed that our glorious captain made sure that he spoke to Bonaparte along with Massena; I dare say he was getting his story straight. We spent two days there while we gathered our reinforcements. Napoleon returned to Turin to conclude his negotiations. This time he took Captain Bessières and twenty troopers chosen by the captain as well as General Massena and a hundred grenadiers.

He came to see us before he left and he had a smug expression on his face. "I am to serve the general as one of his permanent escorts. The troopers I am taking with me are also leaving the regiment. Until the colonel recovers, Captain Aristide, you are in command."

He did not know that I had been offered a place with his guides and that we were delighted to be commanded by an officer we trusted. We all gave him false smiles as he left us. As Albert gathered us together to tell us the news, I noticed that there were just one hundred and forty of us left now that Bessières had selected his men. He smiled as he said, "And now we will just be the scouts! No more charging up hills! The new general is Serrurier. I know nothing about him save that he served as a sergeant major too so he can't be all bad, can he?"

We were heading west to mop up the last resistance to French rule in Piedmont. We were joined, as the huge column lumbered along the roads which clung precariously to the hillsides, by two regiments of Dragoons. Albert was pleased. There were now medium cavalry to act as skirmishers and to charge when necessary. We were the light horse once again.

We camped that night close to the other troops. Jean, Pierre and I went to the town to see if we could buy some bread. It was unlikely but we had money and Jean suspected that if we offered above the asking price then some might be miraculously found. We had to pass through the infantry camps. Suddenly a voice shouted, "Jean Bartiaux! Is that you?"

A chill seemed to grip my heart. Who had recognised the lieutenant? We didn't know any infantry. Jean never panicked he looked in the direction of the voice and his face screwed up as he tried to recognise the soldier who walked towards us with his hand extended. "It is me, Guiscard's son, Julian. The last time you saw me I was a boy."

I felt relief and Jean smiled as he grasped the soldier's hand. "Of course. How is your father?"

Julian's face fell. "He died."

"I am sorry. He was old though."

He shook his head. "It was her; Mama Tusson. The black witch hounded him. She hounded him about someone called Robert Macgregor. It gradually wore him down and he just seemed to give up and die."

My fears rushed back. Jean surreptitiously restrained me. "Do you know why?"

He shook his head. "No, but she is a powerful woman now. She owns the old place at Breteuil and my farm. She has connections with the local committee. It wasn't much of a farm but it was all we had. She threw us off when my father couldn't tell what she wanted to know."

"I am sorry to hear of your loss. She was always an evil young woman but I thought that she would have been happy just to have the house. Your father said her heart was set upon it."

"Aye, but she is ambitious." He gestured for Jean to come closer. I could still hear what they said, "My father said that she had murdered a couple of people on the estate, a parlour maid and the count's woman. Poisoned them apparently." My heart went cold. My mother was the count's woman. "I am glad to be clear of her." He suddenly seemed to see that Jean was an officer. "Oh, I didn't see you were an officer. Sorry, sir."

Jean shook his head and handed Julian a coin. "It doesn't matter. Have a drink for your father on me. I liked the old man and do not worry, justice will catch up with the witch eventually."

As we continued on our way Pierre asked, "So why is this woman still looking for you Robbie?"

"I have no idea. She murdered my mother but I would have thought that would make her steer clear of me."

"There is something else here, Robbie, but we can do nothing while we are here. When we return to the north we will investigate."

Sergeant Major Alain was waiting back at the camp when we arrived. "Finished skiving at headquarters, have we? Come to join the real soldiers?" Pierre and Claude were old friends and often made fun of each other.

"The colonel is dead. His heart gave out yesterday. He was ill for some days and I stayed with him."

I could see that Pierre regretted his words and there was no way he could take them back. It was our way, we bantered.

"He was a good man and a good officer. We will not find another like that." We all nodded agreement at Jean's words.

Albert wandered over. He too looked sad. "I see that you have told them." He nodded. "It seems I am in temporary command still but I do not enjoy the promotion. The colonel was like a father to me and I didn't even get the chance to say goodbye."

Jean shook his head. "Saying goodbye is a luxury which soldiers do not have. We just bury our comrades and get on with it."

Albert took out the sword he carried. It was the colonel's. It was a superb blade and I had envied it each time I had seen it. My sword was a good one but it was put to shame by the colonel's. He held it to Jean. "He wished you to have it. He knew you were the best fencer in the regiment and he wanted it to go to a good owner. There is a pair of boots too for someone with the same size feet." He gave a sad smile, "He left me his uniforms."

Claude nodded, "He thought it might make him a smarter soldier. He had no family and the regiment is his heir and beneficiary. The regimental fund is healthy now." The fund was what we used when soldiers were invalided out. There was little employment for one-armed soldiers. Each time we relieved money from the enemy we put a tenth in the regimental fund. Some put in more. If you put money in then you were still healthy and above ground. "I brought some decent wine with me. I thought his old comrades could drink to the memory of a fine old soldier.

When we reached our tents, I started to go to mine. Albert said, "Brigadier Macgregor. Where are you going?"

"I am not an old comrade. I have only served with him for two years."

"And he thought highly of you. You will drink with us and that is an order."

As the five of us drank I realised that we were the last of the original soldiers. We were the last of those who had set off from Sedan when France's back was to the wall. It had bonded us into a band of brothers. Although I was new many of the older men had died or gone with Captain Bessières. I was almost a veteran. It gave me pause for thought.

We had thick heads as we headed west the next day towards Millesimo. Our orders were to find the enemy who were reported to be beyond Cosseria. The battlefield was still a raw wound and the crosses marked where both sides had buried their dead. We had not invested it after our victory for the general believed in lightning strikes. As we reached Millesimo Albert saw that the bodies were being dug up by the locals. I had heard of this practice but never seen it. They would strip the corpses and even take out the teeth of the dead and cut the hair to sell.

Albert did not like it and he roared. "Sergeant Boucher, take ten men and scatter those carrion."

He turned to me. "Brigadier, bring your section. Use the flat of your sword. Don't kill them!"

We charged up the hill towards them and the men took off like seagulls from a rubbish heap. I saw a huge bull of a man and I turned Killer towards him. He tried to twist and turn but Killer thought it was a good game and followed him relentlessly. I drew my pistol as I neared him and swung the handle towards the back of his head. There was a satisfying crack and he fell unconscious. When I reached the others, they were beginning to rebury the dead under the supervision of our section.

Pierre glared at them when they had finished. "When we come back through here, I want these graves to be well tended and undamaged. If not, we burn your town to the ground. Do you understand me?" There was a great deal of venom in his words and they nodded fearfully.

As we rode back to the squadron, he shook his head, "Civilians! Sometimes I think they are the worst enemy."

We reached Mondovi in the early afternoon and we found the

enemy. They had cannons covering the bridge into the town and we could see the flags of the battalions within its walls. "Well, out little general won't find this so easy a nut to crack." Pierre had this ability to forget that we were all in the same army. He despised generals and senior officers. The only one he had had any respect for had been the colonel and now he was dead.

"The bridge you mean?"

"Yes. If you look at the river you will see it is a torrent. The snow has melted in the mountains and the only way across is by that bridge. I can see at least three cannons facing the bridge. If they fire canister, they will kill anyone who tries to get over. Even the light infantry will be no use. They want to stop us here and it is a good defensive site." He gave a happy smile. "At least we won't have to do it."

The messenger returned after Albert had sent the report. He summoned the officers and the non-commissioned officers. "The general wants us to find some fords."

Jean looked surprised, "He is back with the army? Does he never sleep?"

"No!" I said. They all looked at me and laughed. I was, of course being serious.

"Take your sections and find a ford. Go ten miles in each direction. I think he wants this war over quickly and then he can get to Vienna."

"Well I like a patisserie as much as the next man but..." Pierre brought things down to their most basic level.

The roads in this part of the world were little more than tracks and I lead my twelve men in single file. Francois rode behind me with Tiny following him while Charles brought up the rear. I still smarted over the ambush which had nearly ended in disaster. This time I would watch and keep my men close. I scanned the skyline constantly for signs of movement or colour. It paid off as I caught the glint of sunlight on metal. There was someone above us in the rocks.

"Dismount! Muskets. One in four of you hold the horses." My men had learned to obey instantly. I had watched Pierre and saw how he did it. "Keep the horses at the side where they are safe from random musket balls." I pointed to the rocks. "In pairs make your way up there. One of you moves across the hillside and the other one covers. I want no casualties. Be careful. Tiny, you are with me."

I squatted behind a rock and looked up at the skyline. I knew where I would hide to ambush those on the road and I headed in that direction. "Cover me."

I sprinted to the next rock on my left and peered over with my gun at the ready. "Now, Tiny!" Tiny soon joined me. "Good lad." While I had been waiting, I had seen my next cover just fifty yards to the right and slightly up the hill. I was halfway across when I heard the crack of Tiny's musket. A second later a stone flew up just ahead of me. I reached the rock and tried to work out where the shot had come from. I saw a bush moving slightly. There was no breeze. "Now Tiny." As he started to run, I saw a barrel followed by a gun appear. I fired. There was a scream and the barrel disappeared.

When Tiny joined me he puffed, "He's a sneaky one, corporal. He is listening for the shouts."

"Then this time I will wave my hand when I want you to move. Have you reloaded?"

He looked shamefaced. "Not yet."

"Then do it and I will watch. I reloaded as soon as I had fired." There was criticism in my voice; I thought I had taught them better than that.

I could hear the pop of the other muskets further along the hill. I estimated that we had fifty yards to go to the skyline. There was a rock thirty yards away. "Do you see that rock up there?" He nodded. "That is our target. When you reach it don't stop. You go right and I will go left. I don't know how many will be on the other side but it doesn't matter we will be better than they are. Understand?"

He grinned his reply, "Yes Brigadier Macgregor!"

This time I kept my eye on the spot where I thought he was hiding. He did not appear. When I reached the rock, I waved my hand and a few moments later Tiny reached me. I immediately ran the last ten yards to the top. There were four Austrian Jaegers and one was wounded. I fired from the hip as soon as I saw the first one. I saw one of the muskets turning to shoot at me and I leapt on the man. He was below me and I am a big man. I knocked the wind from him. I clubbed him with my musket and then, as I turned, drew my sword. I saw Tiny struggling with two men, the wounded Jaeger and his comrade. I stabbed the one nearest me through the back and Tiny overcame the wounded Jaeger. "Are you hurt?"

"No corporal. I shot one and then these two grabbed me. Thanks."

"Don't mention it, you did the same for me on the way up. Load your weapon. I will keep these pair covered." I hoped they wouldn't remember that my gun was empty. Just then there was a skitter of rocks and Francois appeared. "There were four more around the other side. They are dead." He looked at the bodies around us. "Looks like you two didn't need any help."

"Search the bodies for papers and then get two troopers to take the prisoners back to the general for questioning." As he did that I peered around. What had they been guarding? They were too far from the town to be part of those defences and they were facing the town so they weren't stopping reinforcements. There had to be something along the road.

When the prisoners had been escorted back, we carried on along the road. I noticed that it began to drop towards the river. It was still a torrent and looked perilously close to the road in places. Then I found a small waterfall and when we reached the far side, I noticed the river was quieter and slower.

I turned to Charles. "This could be the ford. It looks safe enough."

Charles looked dubious. "With that waterfall on the other side do you want to take the chance?"

"It is safer than riding boot to boot against Austrians so let's try it. Tiny, you come with me. Charles, just in case I go over the edge, you are in command."

I rode Killer to the edge of the water. It was covered in white bubbles making it difficult to estimate the depth. It looked to be about thirty yards across. The danger would be slipping on the larger stones and rocks. If the ford was going to be usable then it had to be shallow enough for infantry. I slipped from Killer and led him by the reins. I turned and saw Tiny about to dismount. "You stay on your horse Tiny. If I fall over then you will be the one to rescue me."

I stepped into the river and it was icy cold. Killer seemed reluctant to enter. "Get in there you a big soft thing!" He snorted and stepped into the water behind me. I tested each step as I went. I didn't put the weight on my foot until I was sure the river bed was beneath it. The water came to my knees when I was a third of the way across. It stayed that way until I was halfway through my journey. I glanced behind me to make sure Tiny was still close. At the halfway point, the water came up to my groin. It was a painful experience. I realised that I could not feel my legs. As I walked further towards the other bank the river bed began to rise and soon the water was at my knees again. I became overconfident as I saw that the other bank was just ten yards away. It was like stepping off a cliff. Suddenly I was up to my armpits in the water. Had I not had Killer's reins I would have fallen. I did not know what to do. Which direction should I go? Straight ahead or off to the side?

"Tiny, ride across to the other bank of the river. See if this is the deepest part."

I heard him splashing behind me and then he was next to me. The water was deep on his mount but, as he took another step forward, he began to rise and within two yards the water was knee deep again. He turned and grinned. "Looks like just a deep hole. I'll ride left and right of you to see."

I clambered back on to Killer. There was little point in me getting even colder. As Tiny rode upstream I rode downstream. It was just a hole in the riverbed. I shouted over the river. "Charles ride back and tell the general we have his ford. Francois, keep two men there and send the rest over. We will scout the other side. You can watch the ford in case there are other guards we missed."

They both waved their acknowledgement. When my men were across, I headed in the direction of the town. I could hear the distant crack and pop of artillery and muskets. I wanted to make sure that there were no more surprises waiting for us. We rode two miles down the valley until we could see the smoke-shrouded town. "I think that we will secure this bank and await our soldiers."

When we reached the ford, I saw that Pierre and his section had joined us. I waved him over. He was shivering when he emerged from the water. "They told me that you walked across on foot?" He seemed incredulous.

"I wanted to make sure that infantry could get across and they can. There is just one hole which is deep enough to cause problems and they can get over that."

"I don't know some of these light infantrymen are midgets you know."

"Well, we can fish them out then."

We set the men to collecting firewood while others filled a kettle with water. The easiest food for us would be a soup of some kind. Tiny wandered over. "I'll try and catch something corporal. Fish or something." He pointed to the river. "There might be something in there."

Pierre shook his head. "Your lads are very keen. Mine would have sat on their backsides and watched others work."

"Tiny is a good lad if a little lonely. I know what it is like I grew up alone."

"Well, you are lucky. I had two brothers and four sisters. I couldn't wait to leave home."

"Ah, but you had a home. I just lived in a big house."

"Did you share one bedroom with your brothers, sisters, mother father and two grandmothers who smelled of cat pee?"

"Well no."

"Then don't complain."

It was quite pleasant eating by the side of the bubbling mountain river. We could still hear the occasional crack of small arms fire from lower down the valley. If it were not for that we could have been having a peaceful ride in the country. We sent food for the boys on the other bank and set sentries. We would not be caught out as Bessières was at Dego.

CHAPTER 8

It was late morning when the troops came to cross the ford. We were acknowledged but that was all. Captain Aristide signalled for us to return to the other bank. He nodded his approval. "You did well. The prisoners gave us some useful information. General Bonaparte was pleased."

I gestured at the departing General Augereau, "He didn't look very happy."

Albert laughed sardonically. "That is because the soldiers were so hungry when they finally captured the town that they pillaged food and ransacked shops. We lost more men than we should have and the general has chewed him out. Some Swiss Grenadiers recaptured it and he lost six hundred men."

"So, we captured the ford for no good reason."

"No, the general is chasing General Colli, who is trying to get the remains of the army away to safety. The ford will save time as our forces can go around the town."

Jean shook his head, "I would have thought that was a perfect role of us."

"We are considered too few. Besides Captain Bessières arrived with the new Guides who are to protect the general. They have fine new uniforms and I believe our former colleague is trying to impress the general. They have much dash and élan!" He shrugged. "Let them chase Colli all over the mountains. We have been ordered to Alessandria where we will meet the general. We are then to scout around Milan. We will be travelling for some time, my friends."

One of the first things Albert did, when we reached the captured town of Mondovi, was to requisition as many pack horses as he could. The wagons we had been using were no use at all in the mountains. It also meant that the farriers and cooks could keep up with us. Of course, the cooks complained that they would not have their ovens to use but the captain promised them that they would have the best kitchens in whatever town we were in. They were mollified. He had been with the regiment so long now that no one would argue with him anyway.

With only a hundred and thirty troopers in the squadron now we were able to move much quicker. We were a compact force. It may sound silly but I preferred being a small regiment. Since the departure of Captain Bessières, I felt as though I was now in a real family and I liked that family. With so few officers left Claude was promoted to Sous Lieutenant and Pierre to Sergeant Major. When I was made up to sergeant, I was amazed. Pierre put it all in context. "When you joined up Napoleon Bonaparte was a lieutenant and now, he is the most important general in the French Army and one of the three most powerful men in France. The Revolution has meant we all have the chance to shine. You deserve your promotion." He grinned mischievously, "And of course, I certainly do. If we ever get paid then we might be able to afford to eat!"

The two main issues every soldier had was the lack of food and money. We were no different although we managed to acquire money through the taking of prisoners. So long as I was being fed, I was happy and I still had the money Jean and I had received from the count as well as my treasures from my mother. I had not spent them yet and I knew that someday I might need them. I was young and enjoyed life, worries about money did not even enter my head.

Alessandria was a pleasant little town and we managed to obtain a nice piece of land close to an inn. I suspect the man who let us have the land at such a low price was doing so to ingratiate himself with us, the victors. It was one advantage of being the first ones in a captured town. We took advantage of it, of course. I was no longer a boy. I had grown wiser and less naïve. The last couple of years had seen me grow into a man. I did not drink to excess and I still exercised each day as I had with Jean on the estate. I was keen to be the best that I could be. Now that I was sergeant, I felt I had more responsibility. It had all come so fast and yet everyone seemed to think that I had deserved such a rapid promotion. I was the only one who did not.

When General Bonaparte arrived, he made a point of coming to speak with the captain. We were all waiting outside when his secretary, a fussy little man, even smaller than the general, came out to us. "The general would like all the officers and sergeants to hear the briefing."

It was still a small group even with all of us present. "You are my lucky charm gentlemen. When others let me down and fail to do what I demand of them, you go beyond what I ask. It has not gone unnoticed. Captain Aristide, despite having such small numbers in your regiment I believe you warrant the rank of colonel. It may help when you have to work with other colonels." He smiled impishly. "At least you will not be outranked. Now as to your duties; I need a detailed break down of where the Austrians are in relation to Milan. I want every ford and river crossing finding." He sat in a chair but still leaned forwards, his eyes bright with enthusiasm. "They think I will take time to secure Piedmont and Sardinia." He waved an impatient hand, "I have concluded my peace treaty already and that is thanks to you and our little excursion to Turin. I want daily reports as to what you find."

"Where will you be general?"

He smirked, "I will be in the saddle colonel. You will have to find me."

The next week was hectic. We lived in our saddles as we traversed the land around Milan. At least the roads were wider than they had been further west in the mountains of Piedmont but we still found pockets of Austrians and remnants of the Sardinian army.

We had four columns of thirty men. I rode with Jean. We had enough numbers so that we did not fear the enemy but we were in danger of being seen by the enemy. If we were spotted then the enemy might ambush us. I still remembered the two ambushes I had walked into and I did not wish a third. On the first day, Jean put my mind at rest about that. "The general is using us. We are fast and can move around a great deal. The Austrians will think that there are more of us than there actually are. He is keeping them guessing as to where he will strike. He will keep moving troops around when he hears the chasseurs are close by. Albert is helping the illusion by splitting us into four. It is very clever."

We had found out a great deal of information. Every day we sent riders back to the general with the new maps and lists of troops. On the third day, we ran into the rearguard of the retreating Austrian Army. We had seen the column snaking away towards Lodi and wondered if it was a column of refugees. As soon as we approached and heard the popping of individual muskets, we knew we had not. We reined in. "Robbie, send a rider back to the column and tell the general that we have found the Austrians."

Tiny was next to me and it saved me repeating the order. "Tiny, you heard. Go!"

Jean said, "Form line." Even as I repeated the order, I looked at him. He pointed towards the infantry who had halted and were speculating what to do. "If they think we are about to charge then they will form a square. That means they can't move. It gives the general more chance to catch up with them."

"But surely that only works for a short time unless we charge."

"That is, it, Robbie, we are going to charge. At least we are going to make them think that we are about to charge. Draw pistols!"

Thanks to our recent victories I now had two pistols. They did not match but that mattered not.

When he was sure that every trooper held his pistol Jean shouted, "Charge!"

We had no bugler but the Austrians got the message quickly and began to form a square. They were not as fast as they should have been and we were within forty yards when Jean shouted, "Halt! Fire! Fall back!" in quick succession. The pistols sounded feeble and I had no idea of the effect but the smoke helped to hide us as we turned and retreated. We heard a ragged volley and I felt some musket balls flying through the air above our heads. We halted a hundred and twenty paces from them. They could still fire at us but we knew they would be wasting ammunition. I checked the line. Jean Claude had been struck on the leg but I could see that it was superficial and he waved at me as Charles bound it. He was in no difficulties. As the smoke from the two volleys cleared, I could see that only one man had been struck but they were in square. Further ahead I could see that other battalions were now in square.

Jean rode to our front and the Austrians would assume he was exhorting us to charge again. "Well done. This time we ride forwards when I say halt take out your muskets and fire. Aim low, they are inaccurate guns anyway and will buck up. Then we retreat." He returned to the centre of the line. "Forward!"

We lumbered forwards and I could see the infantry bracing themselves for a charge. The front two ranks now had a solid wall of bayonets facing us and the third rank had levelled muskets. That suited us for it meant they had fewer muskets aimed at us. "Halt! Fire!" This time the muskets sounded louder. "Fall back!"

As we rode away, we heard another volley but we were out of range by then. As I checked the line, waiting for the smoke to clear I saw that the horse of Alphonse had been nicked. He was stamping his hooves in anger. Once again there was but one casualty. Then I heard a bugle from the Austrian lines. The call sounded like our cavalry call. Sure enough, we saw a column of brightly dressed cavalry approaching. After the battle, we discovered they were Neapolitan cavalry.

Jean shouted, "Reload." To me he said. "They will charge us. One volley and we retreat."

The cavalry formed themselves into two lines before the relieved square. I saw them draw sabres. As soon as they charged Jean shouted, "Aim, fire!" As the muskets cracked out, he shouted, "Retreat!"

We wheeled and went into a column of twos. I stayed at the rear with Francois. I could hear the cavalry as they roared their charge behind us. As I clipped my musketoon to my saddle I glanced under my arm and saw that they were an ill-disciplined lot. They had not kept a straight line. That meant that some of the eager riders were closer to us. "Francois, get your sword out." I drew my sword and deliberately slowed Killer down. The Neapolitan who was closest suddenly saw the black hindquarters of my horse approaching. He tried to jink his reins to come around us. I slashed at his face and watched as he plunged to the ground. His horse veered away. I urged Killer on and Francois and I rejoined the column. The Neapolitans soon gave up the chase. Their horses did not look as good as ours.

We soon found Albert and the rest of the squadron. "You have done well but the general wants to bring this army to battle. He doesn't want it to get inside Milan and its walls. We have to slow them down."

"They halted when they saw us. Perhaps we can continue to do that."

He nodded in agreement. "It is the only option we have until the dragoons catch up with us. Let us ride."

Jean led the way and my section formed the rear. By the time we had caught up with the Austrian column, they had begun to move again. The cavalry had left the rearguard. I would guess they thought they had chased off the handful of scouts. As soon as we formed line again, they formed square. We just waited and they didn't move. After a short standoff the rear-guard commander obviously thought we were bluffing and they began to form a column. As soon as they did so the bugler ordered the charge and we rode in two lines. As we neared them each section loosed his pistol and then rode to the rear. They began to form square again but we had killed a handful of men. We retreated to our original position and waited. Every moment bought Bonaparte more time to bring up the army. I could see the column ahead had halted while they waited to see what we would do. Inevitably they sent the Neapolitans back to discourage us.

They were similarly armed cavalry to us, they were Chevaulegers but I did not see any muskets on their saddles. That gave us an advantage although they outnumbered us by three to one. I could not see Albert indulging them by charging at them. It was not to our advantage. He saw them forming a line to charge. "Front rank muskets! The rest ready your swords for a charge."

The bugle sounded their charge. When they were fifty yards away, we fired and our bugle sounded the charge. The smoke made it difficult to see the effect of our volley and we were only trotting when we struck them but we must have thinned them out because they were no longer boot to boot. I held my sword forwards. It was an infantry sword and longer than the cavalry ones. I saw a blur through the smoke and felt the tip of my blade strike something. When the trooper rolled backwards from his horse, I knew that I had struck a man. A sword came at my left-hand side and I quickly parried it and then I was through their lines and facing their infantry. I was relieved to hear the recall and I turned before the infantry could fire at me. I was the last trooper to reach our lines and I saw the worried look on Jean's face as I galloped up.

Albert smiled, "Killer is always a little eager to get you into a fight, my reckless young friend. Haul back on his reins next time."

We had a standoff for an hour while the Neapolitans and Austrians worked out what we already knew; we were too few to harm them and the infantry went into column and marched away leaving the Neapolitans guarding the road and preventing us from pursuing. Albert was not put out by this he shouted. "Load!"

"Captain Bartiaux, take Second Troop forwards and form a skirmish line. First Troop. Dismount. Horse holders remain here. First Troop forwards."

While we sat astride our horses with musketoons at the ready the rest of the squadron came forwards and knelt in front of us. Our weapons were notoriously inaccurate on the back of a horse but when kneeling they were a serviceable weapon. The Second Troop all had musketoons at the ready. Sergeant Major Alain shouted, "Choose your targets and fire at will!"

There was no volley. Every man chose an enemy to fire at. The range was fifty yards and more musket balls struck than missed. A man on a horse was a big target. The Neapolitans became annoyed at this and started forwards. Jean roared, "Second Troop fire!"

The combined firepower of the squadron did the trick and they turned tail and galloped off to join the column. Once we were all remounted, we followed. This was repeated many times for the rest of the afternoon and the following morning. It was not glorious but it was relentless. We were wearing them down. We saw the town of Lodi grow closer and then we heard the thunder of hooves behind us. Two squadrons of Dragoons had come to relieve us. General Bonaparte had arrived. His flashily dressed Guides announced his arrival.

He leaned over to shake Albert's hand. "Well done colonel. You have stopped them from fleeing to Milan. Tomorrow we will end the Austrian presence in Italy! You and your men may retire and rest." He smiled, "Until I need you again!"

We were able to watch the battle of Lodi, the battle which made Napoleon Bonaparte's reputation, from the hills overlooking the town. Once again, his men had to force a bridge and, once again a ford was used to outflank the enemy. At the end of the battle, the general was careful to control the troops and prevent the mayhem of Mondovi. We did not mind missing out for it was an infantry battle. Bessières and the Guides sat like a protective cloak around their leader and any messages to the generals and brigade commanders were delivered by the green and red clad horsemen.

The victory finally forced the Sardinians to sue for peace and the surviving Austrians took refuge in Mantua. We marched across Italy to join the army besieging that ancient town. When we reached Mantua, we were assigned a piece of ground well away from the entrenchments. It seems our role was to give advance warning of enemy incursions. If the general could capture Mantua then the rest of Northern Italy would fall to France.

The next few months saw us playing cat and mouse with the enemy. We did not know the general's plan at the time. I do not think anyone did. He kept those things to himself but he was planning to bleed the Austrians dry. He had no intention of attacking Mantua. It would be too expensive in terms of men but we had almost twenty thousand men trapped there and the Austrians had to attempt to relieve them. The general kept the poorer troops, the ones without the shoes and the ones with barely any training, surrounding the walls of the ancient town. The good troops, like the 17th Chasseur a Cheval, were used to defeat every army the Austrians sent down to relieve Mantua.

We came to know the hills to the north of Mantua like the back of our hand. We were stationed along the front, just ten men in an isolated patrol but the moment we saw the enemy a message would be sent to the general and by the time the army was close to Mantua, there would be a French army to defeat it. General Bonaparte began to station our light infantry in the hills and defiles so that when we were chased by the enemy they could be ambushed. Jean told me the term for this kind of warfare. It was a war of attrition. We lost a few and they lost many. Occasionally one of our chasseurs died but we killed more than we buried. We were never called on to fight in the battles, it was not cavalry country and we were too few anyway but the colonel was happy with our role. As he told us it was what we were trained for and no one did it better than we did.

At the end of November, I was summoned along with the colonel and Jean to the general's quarters. Captain Bessières met us there and he actually smiled in a pleasant way. I think that he was an ambitious man and had hitched his horse to the general's wagon. He could now afford to be genial with us.

"Welcome gentlemen. I am pleased to see that my old regiment is still performing as well as when I commanded it." We all bit back our retorts and smiled at the man who had been a brief and forgettable interruption in a well-run regiment. "If you would wait a moment the general is just briefing General Murat."

That was the first time that I met the flamboyant cavalry general who was so mercurial. He never walked anywhere he always strode dramatically. He was like an actor on a stage, always striking a pose. When he came out, he stood to allow us to admire his uniform which had more braid, buttons and gilt on it than a drum major's uniform.

Captain Bessières said, "General. This is the colonel of the 17th Chasseurs and two of his men."

He beamed a smile at us. "You are cavalrymen after my own heart! I heard what you did at Lodi and since. You took on a whole regiment with a squadron. Well done! Well done! I look forward to our times together." He strode away with a purposeful stride.

"Quite a leader eh? Now if you would follow me."

The general was seated at his table with maps and papers all around him. "Thank you Bessières. You may leave us now."

I enjoyed the look of disappointment on his face as he had to leave the meeting. When the door had closed General Bonaparte waved us over. He cleared the papers until there was just the map. "I have a little task for your men colonel. I would like Captain Bartiaux and the sergeant to lead a small mission for me. It is quite a delicate affair and there will be a high degree of danger. I would like you to be part of the planning. I am aware that I am taking some of your best men away from you." Albert said nothing but nodded his agreement.

Bonaparte pointed. "Here is Naples. They are allies of the Austrians. But you know that you have been trouncing their horsemen for some time." He laughed at his own joke. "As a nation, they are not important and we shall conquer them in the fullness of time but the British have a mission there and a naval presence. I want you to go to the port and use your scouting skills to discover how much influence the English actually have. I need to know how many British ships are using the port." He smiled, "I have something in mind."

He sat back and smiled as though he had asked us to bring him a plate of food from the kitchens. Albert looked at the map. "Could a ship not do this easier, quicker and safer sir?"

His face became a grimace. "The navy? They are incompetent and besides they would not be able to get close to the British Legation." He pointed at me. "Besides we have someone here who can pass for an Englishman. I am not asking you to fight merely to count. It is simple enough."

Jean coughed and drew a line with his finger on the map. "We have to go from here to here. This is not French territory."

"No, but the first part will be simplicity itself. The Pope and his armies never leave Rome. Once you are close to Naples there will be few soldiers there for, they will either be guarding the palace or the fortresses of the kingdom. You can have civilian clothes for when you are close."

I could see that his mind was made up. "How many men will we have, sir, apart from the captain and myself?"

The general rubbed his hands together, "Good that is what I like to hear, intelligent questions. No more than four others. You are to be like ghosts sneaking through their land. I know you have the courage and I believe you have the wit to do what I ask. There will be promotions in this," he added slyly. Our faces told him that we would do as he wished. "Good. I will send a man with some money and some civilian clothes." He pointed to the upstairs. "This belonged to a Neapolitan merchant and his family. They left rather hurriedly and I am sure there are clothes here to fit you. If not then use your natural ingenuity." He stood and, one by one shook us all by the hand. "In serving me you are serving France."

CHAPTER 9

Albert shook his head as we walked back to our camp. "I think this is wrong. You will be shot as spies if you are caught."

"Then we will have to make sure that we are not caught. Do not worry old friend. With Robbie's good fortune we will end up rich men after this."

"Rich men? How so?"

"I do not know but this young man has a habit of falling in a pile of horse muck and coming up smelling of roses!"

"You are probably right. Who will you take?"

Jean looked at me, "We don't want to take your best men and I think Robbie knows his section better than any. Who do you think?"

Three of them were obvious, "Charles, Francois and Tiny are obvious ones. As for the fourth," I shrugged.

Albert stroked his moustache, "Then if I can suggest Michael. He comes from near Nice and he can speak Italian. He also looks a little more like an Italian than you do." He looked at me. "You, my friend, stand out like a sore thumb. You can never pass for an Italian."

"You were not listening, colonel. I only need to pass for an Englishman and my colouring will do that perfectly!"

The four men were delighted to be chosen. "The general has promised promotion if it is a successful operation." I could see the obvious pleasure when they heard that.

"I would do it anyway colonel." Tiny was impetuous but he

had found his home in the regiment and would do anything to please the colonel and me.

The clothes and money arrived after dark. We did not need to be told that we had to leave the camp as though we were going on patrol. It would be a secret mission after all. The colonel ensured that we all had two pistols. I already had a pair but the young troopers did not. He also gave us two spare horses to carry clothes and supplies. We had no idea how long the journey would take.

Albert came along at dawn the next day to see us off. "Do not take risks, Jean. Our little general is ambitious. I am not sure what benefit this information will have for France. Bring the boys back safely. This war is almost over and we want to enjoy the fruits of peace eh?"

"Do not worry about me. Worry about yourself. I have heard that this General Murat craves glory more than Bonaparte! Watch yourself. I think you will be charging more than you like, old friend."

Our uniforms were enough to secure our passage south of the lines of trenches which surrounded Mantua. They were filled with the raw recruits. They had numbers but that was all. There would be no assault for that would risk the threadbare confidence of the infantry. It was an attempt to starve the enemy into submission. It was now well into early winter. General Bonaparte had managed to gather every morsel of food for our men who were besieging. The cold and the hunger would do what lead and iron could not. He would starve the enemy into submission and, if they were foolish enough to attack then they would bleed in the cold northern Italian winter.

I rode next to Michael. The two of us would have a crucial role to play. We would be the ones who would have to speak with the enemy. "Is there any difference in the accents in Italy?"

He nodded, "Yes sergeant. Where we are going, in Naples, they speak quite uncouthly. I interrogated one of the Neapolitan prisoners and he was hard to understand. However, the more I speak with them the easier it will become. And you, will there be a difference in British accents?"

I nodded. "My mother spoke with a Scottish accent and I have learned that when I interrogated an English prisoner, I noticed he used some different words to the ones I knew." I shrugged. "I will have to play the wandering Scotsman."

We headed for the east coast and Ferrara. The mountains were too much of a risk as there were still bandits and brigands. It was bad enough avoiding the military but we could not afford to be fighting off the men of the mountains. "Sir, how long will it take us to get there?"

Jean had studied the maps along with me and we had estimated time but that did not take into account unforeseen events. "It will be the better part of a week."

Tiny looked at the threatening December skies. "I thought the weather was warmer further south."

Michael shook his head. "Not at this time of year and be grateful we are not in the mountains for there they get snow. At least this way we will not freeze."

When we reached the outskirts of Ferrara we changed into our civilian clothes. We had left our musketoons at the camp with the colonel for there was no way we could explain those away. Our swords and pistols were understandable for travellers in such dangerous times. We split into three groups and approached the town from three different directions. "Remember your story. You two," he pointed at Charles and Tiny, "are heading to Naples to seek employment with the king. If anyone asks why you are Frenchmen doing this then say you fought for the king's army in the Vendee." The last royalist uprising had been cruelly put down and there would be many royalist sympathisers fleeing. "Michael and Francois, you are travelling to Naples for the same reason but you are from Piedmont. The sergeant and I will be travelling to seek passage on a Royal Navy ship and escape back to England. You have the money for the inn. Use it wisely and keep a low profile. Haggle, if you were soldiers fleeing, it is what you would do."

I thought that our stories were a little thin. I felt even more nervous when we came to a gate where there were two armed men. They looked at us suspiciously as we approached the gate. Michael had taught us a little basic Italian and we used it with the guards.

"We are looking for an inn in the town."

The largest one laughed and said something which I didn't quite catch but from his actions led me to believe he was saying they would be expensive. We both nodded our agreement and shrugged. He seemed satisfied and waved us through. I hoped that it would be as easy to get out of the town. We were now in the Papal States. I know that we had been told that their soldiers were all based in Rome but that was not very reassuring. There were a number of inns in the town and we headed to the nearest one. They had rooms although I suspect they raised their prices when they saw the quality of our horses. I wondered where the other four were. Charles and Tiny answered that when they arrived half an hour after us. We pretended not to know each other. I took the opportunity of checking on the horses. Tiny followed me and we were able to talk in the stables.

"Michael and Francois are in the inn next door. We tried to get in there but it is full. There is some sort of diplomatic group and they are heading for Rome."

"At least we got in through the gates."

"True. Sergeant I was really scared."

"I think we all are Tiny. This isn't something we do every day. You wouldn't be afraid if you were in a battle but this is different. You are doing well. Just keep the story in your head."

He nodded and then added brightly, "This is the first inn I have ever stayed in! I am excited."

I laughed. "You will cope."

We paid for breakfast in the inn and left early. The other two were there as well saddling their horses. As there were stable boys nearby, we just nodded to each other as though we were all travellers. We left and headed towards the southern gate. Michael was there ostensibly checking his horse's hoof. He said as we passed, "The party heading for Rome is leaving this morning and they are using the southern gate."

Jean stroked his horse's mane. "Good. We will leave with them and use them as cover. Stay close but not together." Michael gave him a puzzled look and then he worked it out. We halted at a stall near to the gate to buy some sausage. I heard the hooves clattering along the cobblestones behind us as the diplomats rode towards the city gates. We mounted and after they had passed us, we trotted behind. It would look, to those at the gate as though we were the tardy ones in their party. The guards bowed as the diplomats rode through. As we passed them, we nodded and they gave a half bow as though uncertain if we deserved the honour. Once we had left sight of the town we headed as quickly as we could for the road to Ravenna.

"We were lucky there but I think that we will avoid Ravenna and sleep a little rough." I gave him a curious look. He explained, "Ravenna was the capital of the Roman Empire for a while and there is a history of intrigue and espionage. I think that we will not court disaster so early in our journey."

It was a hardship to sleep rough and we shivered through a frosty night under our blankets which seemed to be thinner than we had remembered. As we ate a cold breakfast Jean said, "Hopefully we will not have to suffer like that again. We will stay in stables at the very least."

San Marino was not one of the Papal States. Jean explained that to me as we rode south. "It is an independent country but it is just one city. It has been here for hundreds of years on top of its hill. We will be safe there. It is not ruled by a king but a council of regents."

We rode together. Out story would not matter here. This country was one of the few not involved in the conflict raging in the rest of the continent. Once through the gates, we headed for an inn. All of us were desperate for a warm room, hot food and some decent wine. The inn had all of that and more. We were totally relaxed as we finished off our third bottle of wine. I thought that Pierre would have been more than satisfied with its quality. The happy look on his inebriated face seemed to confirm this.

Suddenly the door of the inn burst open and ten armed men stood there with muskets aimed at us. "You are all under arrest as spies of the French Government."

We had no arms with us and we had to submit. They grabbed us and bound our hands behind us. We would end our days on the gibbet in San Marino. We were escorted to the town prison. The people we passed in the street viewed us curiously and then went about their business. We were not from the city and our fate did not matter to them. There were few prisoners; we found out later that there had been an amnesty for Christmas and those with lesser offences had been sent home. We had straw for a bed and there was a tub to be used as a toilet. Francois smiled. "Well, at least it is dry and warm. And we ate first. It isn't all bad!"

For some reason that made us all laugh, even the dour Jean. "I did not expect this. San Marino is a small city and does not bother overmuch with outsiders."

Tiny asked, "I've never heard of the place, sir."

"It has been a separate country since Roman times. It has a good position in the land and has high walls. It means that it is difficult for an invader to capture the city. There were many such city-states. Mantua where the regiment is at present, was one, as was Ferrara. They were all gobbled up one by one."

We were silent for a while. "Then what do they want with us? I would have thought they would have wished us to be gone and they would be left alone once more. I mean if the general wanted this town he could easily capture it. It isn't as though it has the Austrian army behind it."

"I know Robbie and that has me worried. This is deliberate. What is behind it? I know it is pointless but check the walls and windows in case we can escape."

It was a fruitless task but one which we had to perform. There was one door in and it was a solid one. It was guarded by two men. The window was so small that I doubted I could have got my leg through it. The bars would have prevented even that.

111

The floors and walls appeared solid too. The prison was in the main castle and was ancient. I suppose that if it had survived this long then it would have been well built.

We all slept uneasily that night. It was not the discomfort, we were used to that, it was the uncertainty of our position. We were many miles from friends and we had been disarmed. We could end up rotting our lives away in San Marino prison. The alternative appeared to be the noose. It was the smell from the tub which awoke me. Its acidic and pungent smell almost made me gag.

The others were awake. "Michael, ask the other prisoners how long we have to put up with that smell."

The three prisoners we shared our cell with were all chained to the walls by the means of a long chain attached to a large ring. We were free to wander. He came back. "He says that one of us will be asked to take it out to empty it when they bring our food and water."

Jean brightened at that. "Then that might be our chance to escape. Be ready to rush them when they tell one of us to remove it from this cell. The rest take the guards and flee. We'll take our chances outside."

It sounded suicidal to me but, like the others, I nodded. I did not want to end my days in a prison cell smelling of other men's waste. We all stood and stretched. We would need to be quick when our chance came. Jean apart, we were all fit young men and I did not think that the guards would pose too much of a problem. Jean might be older but he had kept himself fit and he would not slow us down. We were soldiers who were used to fighting. They were guards in a prison.

We heard the murmur of voices which told us they were coming. We all stood and Jean nodded to us. I clenched my fists. They were my only weapons and I would have to use them to escape from this cell. The door opened and we readied ourselves. The first thing we saw was the seven bayonets forming a circle of steel. One by one, seven guards entered and each of us had a bayonet pressed against our middle. The eighth, a moustachioed veteran, watched us. He barked something in Italian and Michael said, "We are to go with them. If we try to escape then we will be shot!"

I was the first one to be prodded out and I was met by another two guards. They were taking no chances. One of the guards led us down a spiral stair which kept going until we reached a heavy door. Another guard opened the door and the bright December light blinded me as we stepped into the courtyard. As soon as my eyes became accustomed to the light I looked around for a means of escape. My heart fell when I saw that the only way in or out was through the one door. There were just blank walls. We were not to be hanged we were to be shot. The wall looked to have been used before for it was peppered with bullet holes. This looked like a perfect place to line us up. I estimated that there were at least ten guards with muskets. We would be shot. As the rest were brought out, we were lined up against the wall. The guards stood in a line close to the door. I glanced up at Jean and motioned with my head. Perhaps if we rushed them, we might reach them before they hit us. I knew how hard it was to hit a moving target with an army musket. Jean shook his head.

Suddenly the firing squad snapped to attention and a well-dressed man with the look of authority stepped into the courtyard. He spoke to the guards and they left, closing and bolting the door behind them. The man stood there adjusting the lace cuff of his richly decorated coat. He did not appear to even notice us. I wondered why he was just waiting and then he looked up to the covered walkway halfway along the wall. The guards who had left us suddenly appeared and they aimed their muskets at us. Satisfied that he was now protected the grey-haired man strode across to us. He had a Spanish beard and moustache and was slim. The thing you noticed about him was his stare. He had piercing eyes which reminded me of a hunting hawk and he scrutinised you as though preparing to devour you.

Ha halted before us and appraised us all. He addressed Jean in French. "I am Antonio Onofri and I am one of the Regents of San Marino. You are six spies sent by General Napoleon Bonaparte.

You are all French soldiers. We have found your uniforms and weapons." He saw Jean about to speak and held up his hand. "Do not speak for the words will be lies. I know what I speak is true. You may not be here to spy upon my small country but you will report back to your general and I know that he has ambitions beyond leading an army."

I knew that to be true but I wondered how he knew this. San Marino was detached from the world and yet he appeared to know what went on beyond its borders.

He had been addressing Jean who now spread his arms. "True we are soldiers of France but we are passing through your city. Surely that is no crime? Had we worn our uniforms it might have been thought an act of war."

The Regent smiled and nodded, "So the general is wise in his choice of spies. You have intelligence and can reason. Good. I know that you are not spying on my land yet but I wish to forestall an invasion. My city enjoys peace and prosperity and I would wish that to continue." He pointed to the guards on the covered walkway. "I am here out of earshot and speaking in French because I wish to offer you a proposal."

Suddenly things did not look quite so bleak. There was a chance that we might survive. Jean's face remained impassive. "What sort of proposal?"

"When you return to your general tell him that I am a friend of France and the Revolution. We have no king here nor do we need one. In return for our sovereignty, he will have the friendship and cooperation of San Marino."

Jean nodded, "And that sounds reasonable but I cannot see what you will gain by letting us go." I looked in horror at Jean. Why was he spurning the opportunity of freedom?

"You are a wise choice of leader. I will be frank with you, I could have sent an emissary to the general but that would have risked capture. He might have been ignored by your general. This way your General Bonaparte owes me a favour." He shrugged, "He may not be an honourable man, I do not know, but this is a risk. Besides I suspect you will be eloquent on my

114

behalf."

"And why do you think that?"

"Because you know that the alternative would be to rot in our prison until you were old and grey."

"Or until our army rescued us."

The Regent's eyes narrowed and his face hard. "Oh no, my brave cavalryman; you would be the first to die once anyone fired on our city."

"And what if we leave and then tell our general nothing of your offer."

"How refreshing to meet an honest and truthful man. You have answered your own question. You will tell him of the offer because you are grateful for your life and those of these fine young men."

Jean smiled for the first time, "You are right." He held out his hand. "You have my word that we will be eloquent on your behalf. I just wanted to make sure that there was no trick to this message."

"Quite so and I understand." He waved a hand the muskets above us disappeared. "Now we will feed you and then you will be on your way. I will not ask where you are going and then I can answer my neighbours honestly when I express surprise at the six spies in their lands."

We were well fed and our clothes and weapons returned. I was pleased that they had looked after our horses. The Regent took us to the gate. His servants brought us bread and cheese for the journey and a jug of wine. He spoke quietly to Jean. "I suspect you are heading south. I would avoid the larger towns if I were you. There are garrisons in Ancona and Pescara." That dashed any hopes I might have had for a comfortable journey for they were to have been two of our halts on the way south. "However, it is Christmas and there will be more hospitality in the smaller towns. I assume you have money and that will buy silence." He patted Jean's horse on the rump, "Farewell it has been an interesting introduction to the soldiers of France."

"And thank you, Regent, although a conversation last night

might have prevented an uncomfortable evening."

He spread his arms, "Ah we had to search your belongings carefully and I wanted you in the correct frame of mind. Oh, one more thing; the illusion of travellers in small groups does not really work. You look and act like soldiers. We knew to watch out for you when the rider from Ferrara told us of six French soldiers. You might as well stay together for you fool no-one."

We headed south. Jean laughed when we were a mile or so from the town. "Well, I don't think that we have a future as spies do, we?"

"We still go on then sir? Isn't there a risk that he might have been lying to us?"

"He could have been but I can't think why and what he would gain. No, we will take his advice and carry on."

The advice turned out to be good. We were welcomed in the two small towns in which we took shelter. It was not an act of kindness but business. They happily took our money. They did not mind that we were French. They had no love for the Austrians and the war seemed a long way away. Their King Ferdinand was not a popular man anyway. The view of those in the country was that so long as they were left alone, they were happy. And so, on the seventh day after leaving the general, we reached our destination and we looked down on the city of Naples with the brooding Vesuvius close by. As we looked down, we saw the flags flying from the jack staffs of the warships. There was a British Flotilla in the harbour. I suddenly realised that Michel's part was almost over and, now, it would be my turn to be the spy.

CHAPTER 10

We did not enter the town as we still had Onofri's warnings ringing in our ears. Jean pointed to Vesuvius. "We will skirt the volcano and find somewhere where we can observe the harbour from a safer vantage point."

A mile or so from the city we found Portici which was a small port with enough houses and places to eat to provide accommodation and cover. There was a fine palace in the town but as there were no flags flying, we assumed that it was unoccupied. There were two overweight guards at the gate but we assumed that they were largely caretakers.

"Michael ride down to the port and find out if there are any small boats for hire. We will try to get some accommodation."

We now had enough Italian to be able to ask the basic questions. There was only one inn which had any spare rooms for travellers but it was quite a good hotel. We discovered later on that the servants of visitors to the palace often stayed there if the palace was full. The rooms were pleasant and had the most fantastic views across the bay of Naples to the island of Capri. The coastline looked rugged but beautiful. We left the inn and waited outside for Michael to return. After he had stabled his horse, we walked to a small hill which afforded us a good view of Portici and Naples and we could make our decisions away from any prying ears.

"There are boats in the harbour. They seemed quite happy to talk about the ships. They are part of an Admiral Nelson's squadron. They regularly use this as a base and then sail to attack our coastal defences. The arrangement seemed to suit both Naples and Britain but the rumours we heard are true. Ferdinand is not a popular king. One of the reasons the British are here is that they support him."

"That is good information Michael and I think our general will like that."

Tiny asked, "Does that mean our job here is done and we can go home?"

"Sorry Tiny, we need more information about the ships and their numbers. Robbie here will need to go into the town and talk to the sailors."

I had been puzzled by Jean's orders to Michael. "Sir, why do we need a boat? Can't we ride into Naples?"

"We could but the Regent was quite right, that would mark us as soldiers and we are at war with Britain. If we arrive by boat then we will arouse less interest. We just need to find a boat owner who can be discreet. We might as well try this now. Charles you, Francois and Tiny remain here. The three of us will go to Naples. If we are not back by tomorrow morning then return to the general with the information we already have. The San Marino intelligence is too valuable to lose with us."

That was a sobering order. Jean was preparing for the worst. Although there appeared to be few men working Michael had identified a boatman already. He was an old man and he was sewing his nets as we approached. The boat looked big enough for all six of us. Michael did the talking. "Are you busy at the moment?"

Without looking up he said, "I am mending my nets."

Michael chuckled, "Is that why you are not fishing?"

He looked up for the first time. "My crew are still recovering from the Christmas celebrations. They have no head for fine wine."

"We would like to hire your boat."

He put down his net. "Why?"

"We wish to visit Naples."

He pointed at the spurs on Michael's boots. "Then ride or do your horses need mending?"

"We would enjoy a sail across the bay. We have heard of its beauty."

"And why would three Frenchmen wish to see Naples?" I wondered how he knew that we were Frenchmen but as Jean let it pass so did I.

"We are travelling through Italy, that is all." Michael had grown into his role and could make up a story as quickly as anyone.

The old man nodded. "One gold piece and you will help me to fish." We looked at Jean. The old man smiled and I noticed he had no front teeth; it gave him a bizarre look. "What does the leader say to that?"

Jean understood enough Italian to grasp that and he nodded. He smiled, took out a coin and gave it to the old man. "Thank you."

"I am Carlo. Take off your spurs they will damage my boat and you do not wish to arouse suspicion when we step ashore eh?" He was wise and had seen the problems we might encounter already. I wondered why we had not thought to take off the spurs; it gave us away as cavalrymen. Our hair and moustaches were not as noticeable here in Naples but the spurs were. I suppose we were so used to them that they had become invisible.

The nets he had been mending were not his only ones and he had another set on board. We clambered into the boat and within a short time were skimming across the bay. We had to learn to duck. Michael was a little slow and the sail cracked him on the head. The old man chuckled. "You will learn. All young men have to learn things the hard way."

We sailed a mile or so offshore and he lowered the sail. He pointed to me and Michael and gave us the net. He said something in Italian and Michael said, "When he tells us, we drop the net over the side but keep hold of one end." Carlo said something else and Michael laughed, "He said if we lose his best net it will cost us five gold pieces." We drifted for a few minutes while

Carlo peered into the blue waters. Suddenly he said something and Michael said, "Over the side with it." As we did that Carlo tapped Jean on the head and handed him a rope, he mimed pulling. As Jean hoisted the sail we slowly moved inshore. He spoke again to Michael and our translator said, "Right Robbie, haul it in!"

I am a strong man but my back nearly broke as we pulled the silvery mass of fish on board. They were writhing and wriggling as we dropped them to the bottom of the boat. There was a huge variety and I was amazed for we had not been there long.

Carlo looked pleased and he smiled his gap-toothed smile. He turned the tiller and headed for the shore. He gave a wink to Jean as we sailed close to the British ships. The sailors on board peered down at us as we sailed by. Carlo waved and they waved back. I saw the names of the three ships. There was the Minerve which had guns on two decks and two smaller ships, the Juno and the Spitfire.

Jean smiled at Carlo and said, "Michel, ask him why he is so happy."

After an interchange, Michael said, "There are no other boats out today. When we land this fish, he will make much money. He said that it is a good day and we both have what we want."

There was a jetty devoid of ships and Carlo headed straight for it. We bumped to the side and he barked an order. Michael leapt over and tied up the small boat. He said something else and Michael nodded. "Carlo wants us to put the fish on that table there." I could see some stone tables nearby. Obviously, this was the fish market. The three of us gathered the fish and piled them up haphazardly on the table. When Carlo had finished with his boat, he tut-tutted us and began to arrange the fish into type and size. We quickly worked out what he wanted and we complied. When it was arranged people began to wander down. Carlo whispered into Michel's ear. The old Italian then began to haggle for the fish.

"He said he will wait here until we have finished." He pointed to the quayside and a busy looking inn. "He said the British like to use that inn."

Jean shook his head and said, "So much for our disguise." He leaned in. "Michael, talk to me in Italian in the inn. I will nod and smile. Robbie, you listen to the English. Pretend you are dumb."

Michael laughed, "That should not be hard, sergeant!"

I noticed that, as we neared the inn, people began to look at us. For a moment I worried and then I realised why we smelled of fish. Carlo had given us the perfect cover. Michael entered first and he headed for the English officers gathered at the table near the bar. He ordered the cheapest jug of wine he could and then began to talk in Italian. I leaned at the bar and smiled but all the time I was listening. It was early afternoon and we had plenty of time. So long as Michael could talk and Jean give an occasional comment, we were safe. When the English officers had the food brought to their table, I knew that they were there for some time.

It took me some time to attune to their accents. They were far from Scottish but, as they discussed the food and the wine, I discovered that I understood more and more. When they went on to the grappa and cigars their tongues became looser.

"I think that it is a damn shame. Admiral Nelson has done a fine job here. Why do we have to leave?"

"Politics, dear boy. With no Genoan bases and the loss of Corsica we have nowhere left this side of Gibraltar to supply our ships."

"I like this billet. Weather is pleasant. The food and wine damned cheap and the frogs are useless sailors. If we end up in the Atlantic again it will be horrendous."

"Don't worry; Nelson will be back here soon enough." The officer leaned in and tapped his nose. "A little bird tells me that he and Lady Hamilton are more than fond of each other."

"I say, Rodney, that is going a bit far!"

"Just saying what is common gossip."

Their conversation drifted into a discussion about the beauty of Lady Hamilton and then they paid their bill and left. The inn began to empty and Jean nodded towards the door. When we reached the quayside, Carlo was looking happy. There were just a few fish left and, as we approached, he deposited them in a bucket of salt water in the bottom of his boat. He happily jingled a pouch of coins. He said, in awful French, "A good day."

We headed back across the bay. The sun was setting and the bay looked golden in the dying sun. I envied the Neapolitans. They had a beautiful country, a magnificent climate and peace. As we pulled in Carlo said something to Michael. "He has invited us to eat with him. He says we brought him luck."

Jean shrugged, "We might as well. It will make us look less conspicuous."

Carlo knew his fish and the fish stew he made for us was magnificent. He brought out some powerful wine and we enjoyed a good meal. It was probably the best meal we had had on our journey. He pointed to me and Michael and said something. "He said any time we tire of soldiering we can work for him. We are stronger than the boys who work for him."

I took that as a compliment. I liked Carlo. He was a hardworking man and he was honest. He gave his word and kept it. A man can do no more.

When we reached the inn, our three comrades were looking worried. "I was praying you would come. I did not relish returning to the colonel and telling him that you three were dead!"

"Do not worry, Charles. We leave before dawn. We return to the regiment. Our days of spying are over. We have the news I think our general wants. The British are leaving the Mediterranean."

We left before dawn the next day and, this time headed up the west coast. Jean explained, "The Regent told us that we had drawn attention to ourselves and this way we are travelling in a new country."

I was not too sure, "We will have to pass by Rome and we were warned of the dangers."

"True but we can keep to the coast. We will head through Florence and then Bologna. It will save a day."

Jean made a good decision. The weather was fine and the journey was not difficult. When we neared Ostia and Rome, we were nervous but, once we neared Pisa we relaxed. Our Italian was now much better. I had begun to speak Italian to Michael and I felt more confident. I was by no means fluent but I could hold a conversation.

Tuscany would be the difficult section of the journey as they were quite close to the recent gains made by our army. Jean told us, as we crossed the border, that we should speak only Italian. Even bad Italian was better than French for that would mark us as the enemy. When we climbed the hills beyond Florence, we relaxed a little more. We were on the final leg. It was just fifty miles to Bologna and less than that to Mantua. Our only enemy now was the range of mountains and the snow. We hit our first problem when one of the pack horses went lame. They had all done remarkably well up until then. There were few settlements in the high mountains and we were forced to shoot the animal. It would have been cruel to leave it to the wolves. We camped close to a rock overhang which afforded us some shelter from the biting wind. The snow had not been deep but the wind had blown flurries of it into our faces all the way and we were all bitterly cold.

The fire was soon blazing and we cooked up a stew using some of the meat from the dead horse. Although we all loved horses none of us was squeamish about eating them. We had to survive. The food and a swig of grappa made us all sleepy. I knew that I would be on watch in a couple of hours and I snuggled down into my blanket with my back to the fire.

"Sergeant," Tiny whispered in my ear. I could hear the alarm, even in the whisper.

"What is it?"

"I think I heard something but I'm not sure."

"Go and wake the others but do it quietly."

I grabbed my two pistols and quickly put in a fresh charge. I strapped on my sword and then listened. If there are enemies around it is normally the absence of sound which alerts you.

There was total silence. The animals were still which meant only one thing, there was someone out there. I had not turned to face the fire as I did not want my night vision to be ruined. Jean joined me. "Do you hear anything?"

"No, and I should be hearing the noises of the forest. There is someone out there."

"You watch this side." He hissed. "Tiny, get yourself next to the sergeant."

As Tiny joined me, I motioned for him to lie down behind his saddle which was next to mine. "Make sure your pistols are loaded and watch for movement in the forest."

To anyone in the forest, it would look as though we were all sleeping with our feet pointed towards the fire. I had a gun in each hand and I kept flicking my eyes from side to side. Then I saw the movement. It was only a slight judder of a branch but it should not have moved; it was four feet up the tree. I aimed my pistol to the left of the tree and, when I saw a shadow move, I fired. I saw the bandit in the flash from my gun and then I heard the scream as he fell. Suddenly there were men all around us and guns firing. I just had time to fire my left-hand pistol at the man who raised an ancient two-handed sword above his head. He was less than four feet from me. It was so close his face disappeared.

"Tiny! On your feet!" I grabbed my sword and looked for another enemy. Three men lurched toward me. In an instant, I saw that one had a halberd and the other two swords. The longer halberd was the more dangerous weapon. As the man lunged at me, I rolled and stabbed at his leg. I felt the blade enter his leg above the knee and saw the bright arterial blood splash all over the snow. As he fell the two other bandits came at me at the same time. I parried one blade and took the blow from the second sword on the pistol I still held. They did not have good swords. I saw one was already slightly bent. I kicked the first opponent in the knee and as he winced stabbed him in the throat. I threw the pistol into the face of the other bandit and then charged him as he recoiled. He fell over the dying halberdier and

I gutted him like a fish.

There were no other bandits before me and I whirled around. Tiny was trying to fend off two men. One had an axe. Tiny fell backwards and the giant with the axe swung it at his head. I was too far away to stop it and so I threw the sword. The giant's side was impaled by the blade. I continued running as I saw that the sword had merely slowed him down and the axe was inexorably sliding towards the unprotected head of the young trooper. My shoulder hit the man with the axe and he lurched to the ground. The force of my body drove the sword through him and pinned him to the ground. I pulled out the sword and swung it backhand to sever the neck of the man who was trying to stab Tiny. I was panting with the exertion and I stared around looking for another enemy. There were none. Tiny clutched his left arm. I saw that the last blow of the dying bandit had cut his arm. I took the dead man's shirt and ripped a piece from it. I bound the arm above the wound. "I'll be back."

I looked around. Jean was unscathed. He raised his sword in salute. "Nice sword-play Robbie, although I don't remember teaching you the throw."

I grinned, "Improvisation. You taught me that!"

The other three were wounded but only slightly. Michael had a bleeding head whilst the other two had suffered cuts to their arms. None were serious. All of the bandits were dead.

"Francois, check and make sure they are all dead. Robbie. Make sure they have gone. Here," he threw me a pistol. "This one is still loaded."

I held the pistol in my left hand and the sword in my right. I went into the woods. Fifty yards in I found one bandit dying. Someone had sliced their sword across his middle. He must have staggered this far and then fallen. He was barely conscious when I reached him. I stopped and listened. I could hear nothing else. I turned to my right and did a complete circuit until I came upon the dead bandit again. I had found no-one else.

I searched the bandit and found a few coins and a wicked looking stiletto which I slid into my boot top. By the time I reached the camp dawn was breaking and the wounds of my comrades had been dealt with. "One dead bandit and I could see no signs of any other."

Jean nodded, "They will live but we were lucky. Well done Tiny but next time you are on sentry duty wake someone the moment you hear anything."

"Sorry sir, yes sir."

I patted him on the back. "You did well and you have a wound to tell the ladies about."

We packed up the horses and left by dawn. We were not sure if there were friends of the bandits around but we were taking no chances. As we rode along Jean said, "It was when we killed the lame horse that they knew of our presence. We should have cut its throat."

I shook my head. "I am not sure I could do that."

"We love our horses Robbie but they are like a sword or a gun. They are a weapon. If your sword breaks you replace it."

He was right but I was not sure I could ever cut Killer's throat. He was as much a friend as Pierre and Jean. We avoided Bologna, even though we could have done with acquiring a new horse and, once we reached the flatlands we changed into our uniforms. We stopped at the first farmhouse we found and gave them our civilian clothes. They were of good quality and they were delighted.

As we left Michael was laughing. "What is it?"

"They said they had heard that the French were devils but they think we are saints."

Jean shook his head, "Well we are no devils but I think calling us saints is pushing it a little."

We reached the army the day after. Mantua was still under siege but things were going well.

CHAPTER 11

I accompanied Jean when we reported to the general. Bessières actually showed deference as we waited to be admitted. "I have to confess that I thought the task would be beyond you. Despite any differences, we may have had before I admire your tenacity and the fact that you support the general as much as I do."

I didn't like to say that we would have refused the mission had we been given the choice. Instead, we both gave a modest smile and a slight bow of acknowledgement.

Bonaparte was eager to hear our information. We told him of the Regent first and he slapped his hand on to his desk. "If you had returned with that news only, I would have given you a promotion! Well done!"

The news of the British and their departure from the Mediterranean was even more welcome. "Our Navy is not the best and I am just delighted that our armies have driven this Nelson to Gibraltar!" He stood and shook our hands vigorously. "Well done! Well done!" He looked at me first. "Have you reconsidered Scotsman? Would you not like to join my Guides? You too, Captain, can join them at any time."

We looked at each other. Jean said, "I think I can speak for both of us when I say that we are flattered beyond belief but too many of our friends are in the 17th. We may take you up on the offer in the future."

"Normally one would say that the offer may not be there in the future but in your cases, I will just say that the offer is a permanent one." He gestured to his secretary. "Now then, promotions, as I promised. Captain, you are to be major, sergeant, sous-lieutenant and your three men sergeants." He pointed to the scribe. "Give him their names. And now I must leave you for tonight we make the Austrians think that we will assault Mantua. I take your return as a sign of good fortune."

He left like the whirlwind he was. We gave the names to the scribe and we left. "He certainly is impulsive sir."

"He is that. Let us go and see the colonel and give our comrades the news of their promotions."

Everyone was delighted and Tiny speechless. Pierre, of course, had a comment on the whole situation. "I cannot believe that I have to call you sir! What is the world coming to?" He was even more put out when we told him of the food, the wine and the climate of Naples. "That is it! I desert tomorrow and join the Neapolitans!"

After the excitement of a chase across Italy, not to mention a spell in prison, life on the Italian front was slightly dull. Now that I was promoted to sous-lieutenant Pierre became my sergeant and the four officers in the regiment each led thirty men. I frequently gave Pierre half to enable us to cover more territory when we were scouting. Tiny and Charles were still in my section although Francois had gone to Jean. The poor state of equipment in the French army was brought home to us when we received orders to begin to raid the Austrian supply depots.

Albert was cynical enough to understand why. "If we were trying to weaken the enemy, we would destroy them but we are ordered to bring them back." He pointed at the camps. "Many of the soldiers who join us have no shoes and no uniform. The Austrian white can be dyed quite easily." He shrugged. "We do our duty!"

The problem with raiding the depots was that they were well behind the Austrian lines. The Tyrol is a mountainous area with narrow passes which are easy to defend. Jean came up with a solution. "I will take my section and travel at night. That way we can raid first thing in the morning before they are awake.

It means a night without sleep but if that means we lose fewer men then it is a good thing."

I was tasked with a patrol towards Verona. It was a beautiful town and the mountains rose majestically behind it. The problem was that it made getting close and remaining unseen difficult. We saw no signs of the Austrians as we left our siege lines. Two of the troopers had proved adept at scouting ahead. Paul and Alain were younger than I was but both were country boys who loved horses. It was they who found the trackway which led around the town. It looked ancient. The bushes and hedges formed an arch. I wondered why it was no longer used but, as it twisted and turned, I could see that wagons would find it slow and difficult to negotiate. Even we found problems for we had to duck beneath the branches. It passed close by the bridge near to the Castelvecchio, one of the old forts. Verona was part of the Venetian Republic at the time and so we did not want to be the instigators of another war. Once we were beyond the city walls the land began to rise. Paul and Alain came galloping back with the excitement plain to see.

"Sir, there is an Austrian column. It is on the main road to Breschia."

Breschia lay to the west and I knew there was a garrison there. "How many wagons are there?"

"Five wagons and twenty horsemen guarding it."

"Good. I take it there is a guard on each wagon?"

Paul became less certain, "I think so. I just assumed there would be a driver."

"Were there any men or guards inside the wagons?"

They both looked crestfallen. Alain shook his head. "We didn't check."

"It is not a problem. We will go and have a look anyway." I turned to Pierre. "Makes sure their muskets are all loaded."

"Are you going to take them on? It sounds like we are evenly matched."

I laughed, "I cannot believe it. Sergeant Boucher doubts his beloved chasseurs. I thought there was nothing they could not do."

Pierre became embarrassed. "No, it is just we have a lot of young troopers..."

"And the officer who leads them is still wet behind the ears. I know."

"I didn't mean that sir."

"I will try to come up with a plan while we travel. If I do not think we can take them then we will just slow them down."

While he checked the men, I wondered how we would manage to do it. I put myself in the position of the commander. I would keep my horsemen close to the wagons. I might have a scout or two out but with only twenty men that would be difficult. I would be looking for trouble from the south as there is where we, the French, were.

"All ready sir."

"Head north. I want to approach the road from that direction. Paul and Alain, you keep contact with the wagons. If they deviate from their route then tell me. We will always be to the north of the road."

Once we left the cover of the hedgerow, we were exposed but we travelled much faster. Charles rode next to me. "Sir, as I recall the road to Breschia runs close to Lake Garda up ahead and the hills are close to the south. The road narrows and it might be a good spot to ambush."

"How far ahead is it?"

He stood in his stirrups and peered to the north. "I would say about five miles."

"Then we will get ahead of them."

We rode hard to reach the lake but it was a pleasure to do so. All of us loved riding and, jumping the low walls and streams was as exciting as riding ever got. When we reached the lake, we headed south. There was a bridge carrying the road over the river which fed the lake. "Pierre, take ten men and hide on the other side of the bridge. When the first wagon reaches your end of the bridge, take out the riders and the two men on the wagon. I want them held up."

"What will you do? You will only have seventeen troopers and they will outnumber you."

"I am counting on the fact that their attention will be on you. I will keep Charles and Tiny with me."

Pierre chose his men and they quickly concealed themselves. I led my men up the slope of the small hill. We were halfway up when Paul and Alain broke cover and raced across the road to join us. "They are half a mile down the road sir."

I had cut it too finely. If it were not for the slope of the hill we would have been seen already. "Move yourselves and get over the crest as quickly as you can."

I breathed a sigh of relief as they formed a line behind me. I could hear the creaks and groans of the laden wagons as they rumbled along the cobbled Roman Road. I could just see the eastern end of the bridge. Two white-jacketed horsemen stepped onto the stone bridge followed by the first of the wagons. "Charles, I want you and ten of the men to use your muskets. Make sure you halt before you fire. I want you to aim for the cavalry. Hit the horses or men it doesn't matter which. When you have fired then join us. Corporal, you and I will take the other five and see if we can frighten them with our swords. Forward!"

We headed across the side of the hill. We would be hidden from sight for a while. The first wagon was halfway across and we saw that three others were on the bridge. The cavalry had had to wait to allow the wagons to cross as the bridge was too narrow to accommodate a wagon and two riders. It was all a matter of timing. We would have the speed from the slope on our side when we struck and Charles and his men could fire over our heads. Suddenly ten musketoons sounded at once and I saw the two lead riders pitch from their horses into the river. The driver of the first wagon also fell to his death. "Charge!"

The attention of the cavalry was on the far side of the bridge and their commander was desperately trying to get his men across. He had no idea we were coming. Then I heard a shout, there were men in the back of the wagons. Pierre was correct, we would be outnumbered. I could hear him and his men firing as Charles shouted, "Fire!" Not all of the balls struck home but enough did to disrupt the line.

I aimed Killer at the officer who was trying to organise his survivors. He took his eye from me and the distraction of Killer's flared nostrils allowed me to stab him in the throat. I gave a flick of the wrist and his body fell. One of the men in the wagon raised his musket to fire and I closed with him. I moved my head slightly and I felt the flash of the muzzle along my cheek. My sword punctured his chest and he fell dead. I turned and saw an unprotected back. I jabbed my sword into the sergeant's back, not enough to penetrate but to tell him I was there, "Sergeant, surrender or die!" He hesitated and I pushed forwards so that the sword broke the skin.

He threw down his sword and shouted, "Quarter!"

"Corporal, check our wounded!" Charles ran off to give aid. "Sergeant Barriere, Secure the prisoners!"

Pierre raced up with his men. He looked worried. "That was close."

I was puzzled, "What was close?"

He rubbed his own cheek and pointed at me. "That was."

I rubbed my cheek and it came away black. That was how close I had come to death. Another inch and half of my face would have been blown away. "I survived. Check the wagons and see what we have."

Charles came back, "Five wounded, one, Trooper Ney is quite badly injured." He shook his head.

"Put him in one of the wagons and one of the lesser wounded to look after him."

Tiny rode up grinning. "Ten prisoners, five more wounded and the rest dead."

"Put five of them as drivers and tie the rest up. Sergeant, what do we have?"

"Three wagons of muskets and two of the ball. A good haul."

"The trick will be to get it back to Mantua." I took out my map. "There should be a road heading south, through Goito. By my reckoning, we are just twelve miles from Mantua."

Pierre peered over my shoulder at the map. "Yes sir but will there be a garrison at Goito?"

That was the key question. "Take Charles and four men and scout it out."

"That will leave you short-handed."

"The officer is dead and the sergeant lacked conviction. I will leave Tiny in charge of them. You know what he is like when you give him an order. He is like a dog with a bone. He won't let go."

The Austrian cavalrymen were subdued as they rode in the wagons. A cavalryman is only happy when he is on a horse; anything else isn't good enough. Tiny had the sergeant on a horse but tethered to his own. The trip to Naples had helped to mature Tiny. His strength was phenomenal and his attitude exemplary. I did not worry about him. The wagons would slow us down but we could still make the lines in two hours or so, well before dark. I rode to the wagon with the wounded inside. The trooper with Ney shook his head, "I don't think Patrice will make it sir."

"Do your best for him Trooper Lannes. If it is his time then it is better to go with comrades around you." I looked at his bandaged head. "And you?"

"Just a knock with a sword sir but I did for him."

"Well done. Is Trooper Ney conscious?"

"No, sir. The sergeant gave him half a bottle of brandy and he went out like a light." He opened Ney's tunic; I could see where the sabre had ripped him open like a ripe melon. He would not survive.

I heard a voice from the front. "Lieutenant Macgregor." I always smiled when I was addressed as such. When my mother pronounced our name, it had a rolling sound in the middle. The French missed it out altogether and made it softer. I was used to the sound but it still made me smile.

"Yes?"

"It's the sergeant and the patrol."

Pierre reined in. "There are half a dozen or so soldiers in the town but no garrison and no checkpoint. They look to be engineers with an escort."

"What do you think they are up to?"

"I would guess they are sighting a redoubt for when we come through here. They are digging on the far side of the town close to the bridge."

I suddenly had an idea. "Then we ride through as though we own it. Corporal, bring the sergeant here."

Tiny tugged the sulky sergeant to the front of the column. "When we ride through the town, you two ride in front. I will be behind." I looked at the sergeant and said, in Italian, which I hoped he would understand, "One false move from you and I will blow your back in two." I showed him my horse pistol. "Understand?"

His eyes widened in fear and he nodded.

"Sergeant, you take your men to the rear. You can be the rearguard and watch to see that our prisoners don't make a break for it."

The town itself was quite a pleasant little place. It nestled next to a river in a beautiful valley. As we descended into the town, I could see the bridge which could be defended to prevent our army advancing. Had they had men on this side of the bridge then we would have had trouble. As it was our leisurely approach and the white Austrian uniform allayed their fears. I had six of my men load their muskets and ride behind me with the guns across their saddlecloths. They could be levelled in an instant.

Tiny played his part brilliantly. He shouted, "Buongiorno!" cheerily to all the townspeople he saw. They must have thought his green uniform was that of a Neapolitan. It was a superb performance.

As we approached the engineer and his workers they halted in their work and smiled at us. They asked the sergeant something and I pulled out my pistol and levelled it at them. My six troopers had their muskets levelled in an instant. My German was not good but "Hände Hoch!" seemed to do the trick and they looked bemused as they raised their hands. We bundled them into the wagons and I took the plans the engineer had been clutching. They would provide good intelligence.

We knew we were close to the siege works when we heard the crash of the general's cannon. He was an artilleryman and, although he did not think he could break the siege through assault, he enjoyed the challenge of destroying its walls by gunfire.

Captain Bessières had now been promoted and was working as an assistant to the general. He seemed better suited to that role. He was delighted with both the wagons and the prisoners. When I gave him the plans, he positively gushed. "This is just what the general needed. You have a bright future in this army Scotsman. You and I will go places with this mercurial general."

I didn't like to upset him by saying I was happy where I was and so I just smiled and went back to the rest of the squadron. When I reached the camp, I saw the sad faces and knew that Ney had died. This was the first of the men to die under me; it would not be the last but it did leave a scar. I wondered if I could have done anything to change events. When I told Jean of my doubts, he shook his head. "Trooper Ney died because the man he was fighting was a better swordsman. The officer you killed died because you were the better swordsman. It is life. The men know that you did everything to stop them from dying needlessly. We are good officers. Believe me, there are much worse as I found out when I served."

"You mean like my father?"

"He was not as bad as some."

"Then why did you leave the regiment to follow him."

"He saved my life. I would have died before you were born and so I followed him. Now I see that Fate determined this and I was meant to meet your mother and to help you."

"You loved my mother, didn't you?"

"She was an easy woman to love but it was pure love. She was honourable and even though your father did not marry her because you were their child, she was loyal to him. I wish she had not been; she might still be alive."

"What do you mean?"

"If she had run off with me as I asked and taken you with us then she would not have suffered as she did."

"But I don't understand. What could have been done to save her?"

He became silent and then he put his hand on my shoulder. "I never told you but there was a letter for me from Madame Lefondre. She confirmed that Mama Tusson poisoned your mother. She was jealous."

I suddenly went cold. I felt my whole body become rigid. I became numb. Poisoned! "Why did you not tell me when you found out?"

"The wounds of your mother's death and the execution of your father were still raw. I thought you needed time. Besides, you could do nothing about it. But now I see that you are a man and you can handle such things."

"I will kill the black witch!"

He nodded. "I understand but she is quite powerful now. She has influence around Breteuil and has become the new count in all but name. If you kill her then you will become a hunted man and you will face the guillotine."

"It matters not. I will kill her."

He nodded, "Then I am honour bound to help you for the woman I loved."

We both knew that this would not happen soon but it was a promise we both made to each other. We did not speak of it again for we did not need to. It was an unspoken bond joining us together.

The news that we brought turned out to be momentous. Jean and his patrol had captured Austrians too and the combined intelligence from the papers told the general that the Austrians were massing huge columns to the north of Verona and Breschia. He mobilised everyone. We were, once again, attached as scouts, to General Massena.

We were assigned the left flank. There was a mighty gorge

there and General Massena had placed some of his weaker battalions there to protect his flank. General Bonaparte had his main attack planned for north of Rivoli. I could see that we were just a small part of the larger battle. General Massena called the colonel over.

"You only have a couple of squadrons and I cannot use you in my attack. Take your men on a sweep to my left and keep watch for the enemy."

As an instruction, it was a little vague and more than a little insulting but Albert took it in good part. We rode well to the west to enable us to climb above the gorge. We twisted and turned around the hill called Monte Moscat. Claude and his section were at the front. The terrain meant that we could only ride in a column of twos and it was difficult to manoeuvre through the trees around the base of the hill. Suddenly, as we emerged from the trees, I saw a huge column of dragoons below us and to our right. I shouted to the colonel, "Austrians colonel!" He turned as I pointed. The ground was rock strewn and totally unsuitable for cavalry. Albert Aristide had been a cavalryman all of his life and he did not panic.

He turned to a trooper and sent him back the way we had come to warn General Massena of the danger. "Squadron dismount. Muskets!"

The range was too great to be effective and we could only hope that we would distract them. As one man in four held the horses I led my section down the slope towards the dragoons. There were at least two regiments of horse and two of infantry. This was a major attack.

"Get as close as you can otherwise, we will be wasting ammunition." It is not easy racing down a slope with cavalry boots and spurs. I saw at least three troopers take a tumble. The head of the column was almost level with us. The range was a hundred yards and that was probably too great for our musketoons but we had to do something. "Halt!" They all raised their weapons. "Fire!"

My twenty-four men fired as quickly as we could. Normally

we only fired one volley and then engaged with swords but here we would have to be light infantry until the general could organise the defence. As I glanced down the valley towards Rivoli I saw that General Massena was organising cannons and infantry but we had to buy them more time. I fired so quickly that the barrel became hot. And then we were taking casualties as a company of light infantry detached itself from the column and began to make their way up the slope. These were real light infantry and not playing at it as we were. My young troopers began to die. I was grateful when I heard the boom of the cannon which told me that Massena had his defence prepared. The colonel sounded retreat and we began to fall back. I slung my musket and drew my sword. We ran back up the hill. A young Austrian ensign, who seemed keen for glory, raced eagerly after me. I heard his shout as he closed with me and turned, just in time to parry his sword. I had the advantage of the slope but, as I heard the musket balls fly around me, I knew that I did not have much time. The ensign was good but he had been taught to fence properly. As I parried one stroke I stepped in and head-butted his nose. I heard it break and he dropped his guard. As I ended his young life, I admired his bravery but not his reckless disregard for his life.

I was one of the last up to the slope and a volley from the quadroon sent the light infantry packing. "Mount! Captain Alain has found a way down from the slope. Follow me!"

We all galloped after the colonel. It seemed odd to be riding away from our own men but I could see why he was doing it. We would be able to fall upon the rear of the column. It was the role Chasseur à cheval regiments were made for. We halted above the Tasso River. We formed two lines and drew our swords. Claude had brought us out slightly behind the advancing Austrians.

"Trot!"

I had to hold Killer back for he was always eager to close with the enemy. My sword rested on my right shoulder. I glanced down the line. "Trooper Lannes, hold the line!" The trooper in question tugged back on his reins.

"Gallop!"

As Killer opened his legs the motion became easier; I hated the trot. The gallop was much easier for both man and horse.

We were a hundred yards away when the colonel shouted, "Charge!" The bugle sounded and we all thrust our swords forwards as we gave our horses their heads. There was no way we could all stay together but it would not matter. The infantry had been taken completely by surprise. There may have been little more than a hundred attacking but the Austrians just saw a wall of horseflesh. One or two tried to fire their muskets but there was no coordination. A couple of sergeants tried to get their men to form a wall of bayonets but it was too late.

I slashed down with my sword and cracked open first the shako and then the face of the musketeer. Killer trampled a second. I stabbed at the back of a fleeing soldier and felt the point penetrate jacket and then flesh. I saw a sergeant with a bayonet. I flicked the end of the musket away and leaned Killer into him so that he fell beneath the feet of Tiny's horse following close behind. There were so many targets it was almost hard to choose. The river was looming up and the ones at the front were throwing themselves into it despite the fact that Massena's light infantrymen were shooting them as they floundered in the water.

When the recall sounded it was almost a disappointment. I saw two of my young troopers still going forwards. "Fall back!" My bellow carried to them and they reined in and joined me and the rest as we made our way back to the ridge, we had left a few minutes earlier. Our horses walked across a carpet of corpses. I noticed that although we had lost few men there were dead troopers lying amongst the white uniforms of the enemy.

When we made the ridge the colonel said, "Well done! Rest your horses we may be needed again soon." He pointed to where the cannons of Massena were carving holes in the Austrian ranks. The dragoons would not be able to suffer that kind of bombardment for long. We would have to attack them as they retreated. I could see that all of my friends had survived. That was always the first thing we all did. The ones who had fallen were comrades but they were not friends.

We heard the wail of the Austrian bugles and knew what it meant; they were falling back. As Massena's men moved forwards many Austrians surrendered. The dragoons did not come back towards us but headed up the slope where their own men were standing in serried ranks waiting to attack.

"Forwards!" We cantered down the hill after the dragoons. Our horses had had a rest and we were soon gaining on them. The dragoons had metal helmets but no breastplates. Their bare backs were easily pierced by our blades. As the men fell from the horses the dragoons' mounts galloped even harder and there were no riders to guide them. As we thundered up the slope to the heights leading to Monte Baldo, the runaway mounts trampled through the waiting musketeers. Nor did the dragoons make allowances for their own countrymen and soon there were huge gaps in the Austrian lines. I glanced behind and saw that Joubert had launched our own dragoons and they were galloping after us on fresh mounts. As we reached the infantry we slowed down. Our horses were tired and we had crested the rise but there were many men for us to kill.

Musketeers can stand against cavalry when in square and with a three-deep bayonet-tipped defence. These had neither and they were slaughtered. My arm grew tired from chopping and slashing. I felt more like a butcher than a cavalryman. I drew one of my pistols and fired left handed at the officer who loomed up at me from my left. Killer had stopped and I must have looked a tempting target. The Austrian's face disappeared as my pistol took him at point blank range.

When the colonel sounded recall I was grateful. I had had enough of slaughter, and that is what this was. The Musketeers were surrendering in their thousands. I sheathed my sword and took out my fresh pistol. I gestured for them to raise their hands. My mouth was so dry that I could not even say hands up in any language! Our own dragoons thundered past. They had not been riding all day up and down slopes. It was a day for cavalry. As we gathered the prisoners together wondering how we would guard so many we heard the thunder of hooves as Napoleon Bonaparte and his Guides galloped up.

"Well done my chasseurs, once again you perform like a brigade and not a squadron. I wish that I had another regiment like yours."

The colonel nodded, "Have we won general?"

Napoleon laughed, "Of course! It was a close-run thing for they attacked down the two gorges but your message bought us enough time and General Massena broke their backs as you broke their hearts." He pointed down the slope. "The infantry will take care of these prisoners. Well done Colonel."

Bessières came over to speak with the colonel and shake his hand and the victorious general and his escorts continued their tour of the battlefield.

I looked around and saw that Pierre, Tiny and Charles had survived. Claude waved from the opposite side of the prisoners as did Michael and Francois. Finally, I heard Jean behind me. "You will have to learn when to leave the battlefield; I thought that young Austrian had you."

"He could fence Jean, he could not fight. We both know there is a difference. When I joined, I could fence but, thank god, I have had the time to learn how to fight. The young Austrian didn't. I think we need to teach our young troopers how to fight."

"That is a good idea and the colonel has just discovered that we are to receive more recruits just as soon as Mantua falls."

"It has been months. Will it ever fall?"

"I think that it will now. This was the last throw of the dice. There are no more Austrians left to relieve the siege and they must be starving by now. It will end soon."

Jean proved to be remarkably accurate in his predictions. Two weeks after we had cleared the heights above Rivoli it surrendered and, more importantly, a peace treaty was signed. This part of the war was over.

CHAPTER 12

If I thought that the end of the siege meant a quiet time then I was wrong. Firstly, we received a hundred new troopers and even before we had time to half train them, we were sent north to the mountains of the Tyrol. The 17th Chasseurs were needed as scouts once again. Just as when we had left for the south, we had to try to train them as we headed north towards Rivoli and the passes into the Alps. I had to use Tiny and Charles to keep on to the men about their riding. It was the road to Paris all over again. They were slouched over their saddles and waddling from side to side. This time, however, I had more experience and no-one got away with slack discipline.

Fortunately, the first part of the journey was through the plains north of Turin and Milan and the Austrians had fled back to their mountain homeland. The Italians were not sure if we were liberators or oppressors. The Ligurian Republic had shown us in a good light and we were generally welcomed by the locals, albeit warily. The troop was knocked into shape as we headed north. Pierre was as relentless as I was and he was determined that when we got into our next fight the men would be ready. The tradition of sergeant major carried on strongly with the new occupant of that office.

We were close to Legnano when we had our first desertion. Gregor Lapin was a huge unpleasant lump of a man and he belied his name of rabbit. He was slovenly and lazy. Both those characteristics could have been accepted but he was a thief and a bully. Since the revolution we were no longer allowed to flog a man but when Jean-Noel found him stealing something had to be done.

Pierre came to me, "Sir, there is a way around this. We will hold a trial and, if he is found guilty, and he will be, then the men he stole from will deal out the punishment."

"I am not sure Pierre. Isn't there another way?"

"This way is as old as time. I have heard the Roman legions used a similar punishment. It will show anyone else that bullying and stealing will not be tolerated and it will give hope to others that there is discipline." He paused. "The colonel will approve, just ask him."

I went to the colonel and told him what had happened and what we thought we ought to do. He nodded. "It is hard when you have a thief. The men hate that more than anything. When you go to war you must trust those you fight with. If there is a thief then they cannot trust them. It is not pleasant but it must be done. Pierre is quite right."

I was pleased that I had asked him. After the trial, Pierre came to see me. "He is a bad 'un sir. He has been taking money from some of the young recruits as well as thieving. I hope they break something. We can do without him in the troop."

"I don't want him hurt so badly that he cannot ride."

Pierre grinned. "Don't worry sir; he made the mistake of stealing from Tiny. He is in charge of the punishment party."

I saw the thief as he made his way back to his tent. He was able to walk but his face showed the pain as he winced through the camp to his tent. I thought that we had dealt with it until the next day when Pierre found me. "Sir, it's the thief, Lapin. He has legged it."

"Damn. See if you can find his trail and I will see the colonel."

Albert was not surprised. "He is a bad soldier. We are well shot of him but you must catch him, lieutenant. Bring him back and we can shoot him as a deserter. It will discourage others from copying him. You have two days to catch him. Jean will look after your troop until you return. Take Pierre. He is like a bloodhound."

Pierre was not surprised by the colonel's decision. "If you have one desertion, it spreads. Besides this will be a good lesson for all the young lads." He pointed south. "He headed towards Mantua. He will be trying to hide out in the confusion. The trouble is he is dozy sir. He is so big and he is wearing a chasseur's uniform. He will stand out like a huge ugly sore thumb!"

We took nothing but what we needed. I left my musket; it would only get in the way. I took money from the quartermaster in case we needed accommodation. I hoped to catch him before the day was out.

We quickly picked up his trail. As Pierre had said a big ugly chasseur was easy to find. People along the route all told us of the giant in the green uniform who recklessly galloped through their towns. He was heading for Mantua. We both had better horses and I knew that we would be catching him. Once we reached Mantua we reported to the Gendarmerie. I did not want to be arrested for desertion myself.

"We are looking for a trooper who has deserted."

"A big ugly fellow wearing your uniform?"

"Yes. Have you seen him?"

"He rode in an hour ago. I was busy with some wagons or else I would have spoken with him."

"Where would he go to hide in this town?" I could see the damage our artillery had done and it looked as though half the city had been destroyed.

"The eastern quarter has the most unsavoury bars and that is where the local villains hang out. When we have time, we will clear out that nest of vermin but it is early days. I would leave your horses here. There is a stable and we will watch them for you. Do you need any help?"

Pierre grinned, "Not us!"

He inclined his head, "Watch out for yourselves. It is filled with criminals and deserters. We should burn the place to the ground."

I was not so sure I agreed with Pierre. Perhaps we could do

with the Gendarmerie. After we had stabled our horses, we loaded our pistols and stuck them in our belts. We headed for the eastern half of the city and we could see that it was the least damaged portion but the one which felt more dangerous the burnt-out parts. There were eyes all over us. It was Pierre who recognised the saddle. It was for sale on a market stall selling a variety of disparate items. "I recognise the saddle, sir. He will be somewhere near here." We knew that he had taken his weapons and we had to be prepared for violence.

We did not enter the nearest tavern but the second one we found. The first was largely empty and Lapin would hide in a crowd. The second was packed. When we entered the smoky room fell silent. An Italian deliberately spat on the floor in front of us. He looked belligerently at us. Pierre smiled and then in one movement picked the man up by the shirt and head-butted him. I heard the nose break and he collapsed in a heap in front of us. Pierre leaned down to wipe the spit from the floor with the man's woollen hat. "I can't abide a dirty floor." He smiled and we walked to the bar. Everyone moved away.

There was a surly looking man at the bar. Pierre walked up to him and asked, "We are looking for a trooper. He is dressed like us. Have you seen him?"

They feigned ignorance spread their hands and smiled at him. Pierre tried again; he pointed to his coat and said, "Soldiers like us." He pointed to me. This time the barman shook his head. Pierre looked at me and spread his arms. "Not in here sir. Shall we have a drink?"

"We might as well."

Pierre said, "Two glasses of wine."

As soon as the man served us, we knew they spoke French but we smiled at them. What they did not know was that I spoke a little Italian. The barman turned to the woman next to him. "When they have gone, bring the big man downstairs. We will get more money from him than he paid."

I winked at Pierre. "I am just annoyed that he took the pay-master's chest. With that kind of money, he could hide anywhere."

"Yeah, he was always a sly one. There must be a thousand gold pieces. I bet he is staying at an expensive hotel. He could afford it."

I saw the reaction on the faces of the two behind the bar. They were already spending the money. We slowly finished our wine and then paid. I could see they were desperate to get rid of us and then they would search Lapin for the chest he didn't have. We said goodbye to the barman and then I said to Pierre, "Let's see if he headed for Venice. It's where I would go to get a ship."

Once outside we walked purposefully away. As soon as we reached the corner and turned, we stopped. "You take the back door and I will take the front."

Pierre grinned and rubbed his hands. "Right you are sir."

I walked slowly back to give Pierre time to reach the back of the inn. They had neglected to put a watch on the door and I stood outside. Lapin was being beaten up. "Where is the chest of money you fat pig. We know you have it."

I could hear the trooper crying through broken teeth, "They were lying. I only have the money from my saddle and my horse. Honestly!"

I smiled, that was a lie in itself as he had stolen from his comrades just before he deserted. He had to have hidden that money somewhere. I took one of my pistols out and made sure it was primed. I stepped through the door. One of the men on my right lurched towards me with a blade in his hand. I struck him with the barrel of my pistol and he collapsed to the ground. They all looked around. I pointed my pistol at the barman.

"Now when we were just in you said that this man was not here and yet he has miraculously appeared. How is that?"

The barman looked to my left and said, in Italian, "Giuseppe, kill him!"

I turned and fired in one move and then drew out my second pistol. This time, when I spoke, I spoke in Italian. "Now you are really starting to annoy me." I walked towards him and placed my gun in the centre of his forehead.

The barman just said, "You have one gun and you are alone. There are many men behind you. Give up now!"

I smiled as I saw Pierre appear with a shotgun in his hand. It was the one with a short barrel used by the locals when finishing a feud. "And that is a shame because I only have one man behind you but he has got a shotgun."

The sound of the two hammers being cocked seemed unnaturally loud. Pierre shouted, in French, "Drop your weapons! Now!"

I didn't turn but I heard an assortment of objects being dropped to the ground. "Now, you lousy, little, lying Italian. I should kill you for not telling the truth and threatening me." I smiled, "But I won't." I saw the tension leave his face. "I'll just give you a headache." I smashed the barrel of the other pistol on his skull and split his head open. I then put the barrel to the head of the woman who I assumed was his wife. "Now I want the money this man paid you because we have to buy back his equipment. If you think I wouldn't shoot a woman, believe me, I would."

I saw resignation on her face and she grabbed a handful of coins and thrust them into my hand. I pointed the pistol at Lapin. "You, get on your feet. You are coming with me. Can you watch them until we get out sergeant?"

"It will be my pleasure, sir."

Lapin looked as though he might argue so I pressed the barrel into his huge nose. "I personally do not mind shooting you here. Understand that!" He stood and we backed out of the door. As we reached the door I heard, "Well you get things done. I will say that."

I glanced over my shoulder and saw the Gendarmerie officer and four men we had met from the gate. "There is one dead Italian in there."

"He probably deserved it. We will escort you to the gate. Where is that resourceful sergeant of yours?"

Just then Pierre appeared with the trooper's horse. "It looks like they planned to steal the horse from the trooper as well sir. Shall we call and get the saddle?"

We headed out of Mantua with a very sore and sullen Lapin. We had taken the precaution of binding his hands and leading his horse. Having gone to so much trouble to capture him I didn't want to risk losing him. We were exhausted by the time we reached the camp and it was well after dark. Albert came to greet us, "I knew you would get your man, I just didn't think it would be this quickly." He shouted for his orderly. "Have this man chained and guarded. We will try him tomorrow."

The trial was a foregone conclusion. He had not got a leg to stand on. I think the two beatings had taken any spark of resistance he had left in him. When the colonel announced the punishment, death by firing squad, his shoulders slumped in resignation. The firing squad was chosen by ballot but most of the squadron would have been a member without a second thought. Lapin had not been a popular man. The effect was that Lapin was the only man who ever deserted from the 17th Chasseurs and that was a claim which not too many regiments could make. We left for the Tyrol with a regiment determined and of one mind.

The closer we came to the mountains the worse the roads became. We also saw more signs of the enemy. They were destroying anything we could use as they left each town. Bonaparte's armies famously travelled light and relied on local supplies. That had gone awry at Montenotte and the general had scoured the lands to the south to ensure that his army ate well. The scorched earth would not hurt us.

The land itself, and the terrain through which we had to travel was another matter. The roads twisted and turned around blind outcrops of rock. Trees suddenly obscured the roads to the side and the rivers were only passable by their heavily guarded bridges. General Bonaparte quickly assessed the situation. He brigaded light infantry with the cavalry so that when we found the defended bridges and rocky outcrops the sprightly light infantry would scramble, duck and dive to winkle out the enemy. They did not have it all their own way for the Jaegers we encountered were masters of the mountains. The solution the general found to that problem was to give us a four-pounder horse gun which would blast the defenders with grapeshot. It was slow work and it cost us many men but we managed to reach the land of old Austria.

We had to use all three arms as well as calling upon a brigade of infantry when we reached Trento. The mountains reared up on one side of the valley in unscalable peaks. The river twisted its way along the valley and nestled on the opposite bank from the town was a small hill topped by a fort. Its guns covered the town, the bridge and, more importantly, the road north. We had to eliminate the fort's threat. Colonel Aristide was the senior colonel. Colonel Dayan of the light infantry had only been a colonel since Lodi and was only twenty-two. The lieutenant with the horse artillery was a mere eighteen years old. We placed pickets in the town close to the bridge and Albert held a meeting with the officers of the three units.

"I think that we need infantry for this job. Jean, send a rider back to the general and request a battalion of line infantry."

Colonel Dayan bridled a little. "My men can take the fort!"

Albert smiled graciously, "Of that, I have no doubt but they would lose many men would they not and your light infantry are too valuable to throw away without good reason."

The light infantry captain, Captain Senonche was a bright man. "And is the colonel saying that the line infantrymen are?"

"No Captain Senonche, I am just saying that if they die then less training would have been wasted and we have many more of them." He held up his hands, "I am not saying we sit and do nothing. We will attempt to take the fort but not by assault. Not yet anyway."

I was sent to the northern approach road to the town. My job seemed the least glamorous of any of the troop. I was to stop anyone entering the town. It was not a siege but we needed to prevent the Austrians reinforcing the garrison. Jean explained it to me. "General Bonaparte is a clever man and he has columns and brigades like ours throughout the Tyrol. We are probing for weaknesses so that we can bring them to battle. We have found a strength which is why the colonel has decided to send for line troops. Your job is important."

I understood but it seemed a little mundane after the exciting missions we had been on lately. Even hunting a deserter had enlivened my life. Pierre was quite happy to be a watcher. "This will suit me for a while, sir. It will give the horses a chance to recover and some of the other troops can be at the sharp end for a change."

The rest of the troops were joining with the light infantry and the horse artillery. They would be probing for weaknesses in the Austrian defence. As we headed north, we heard the pop of muskets and the crack of the cannon. So far, the Austrians had not replied but it was obvious to us all that the bridge could be a killing zone. We had left before dawn to avoid being a target for them. The castle had round walls and could fire either north or south of the town if they chose.

We rode north towards San Michel Alla'adige. This was a small town eight miles up the road. Pierre was delighted as he was sure that there would be an inn. An inn meant he would have his two staples, food and wine. I placed Tiny and four troopers at the northern end of the town while we occupied the small square. The villagers were wary of us. It was what I had expected. We were polite and paid for what we needed. I began to teach Pierre some Italian as it broke down many fences and barriers. After one such lesson, I said, "Rotate the guards at the northern end of the town every three hours. I want to give as many of the new recruits the experience of sentry duty."

I examined the town. It was like many of the towns we had passed; it was a string of houses along the main road with a square in the middle. There was a complete lack of military presence and I put that down to the fort at Trento controlling the valley. We could not find accommodation and so we camped at the southern end of the town where the houses stopped. It made our presence less obvious. I knew that the locals would like to enjoy their square at night time.

Pierre managed to slope off to the inn for a drink each time he relieved the guards at the northern outpost. I did not mind as I knew he would not abuse the privilege. Just before eleven he galloped in and entered my tent. "I think someone slipped out of the town sir."

"How do you know?"

"I was in the tavern having a drink. Just as I was finishing it a young lad, about eighteen years old left. He mounted a horse and headed north. I didn't think anything of it as I was going that way. Halfway down the street I noticed that I couldn't see him. I thought he must live just outside the town. When I reached the lads, they said they had heard a horse to the east. I went back down the road and found the place I lost him. There is a track there. It heads towards a tiny hamlet called Barco and then it rejoins the main road further north. There was no sign of his horse and I think he has gone for help. Sorry, sir."

"No, it is my fault. I should have explored the whole town and not just the main road. It is shutting the stable door after the horse has bolted but stick Charles and a couple of lads at Barco. It will take someone a couple of hours to get to the nearest garrison. Hopefully, we can hold them up for a while. Wake the troopers before dawn and have them stand to at the northern outpost."

After Pierre had gone, I could not sleep and I took out the map. There was a fort at Bolzano about thirty or so miles up the valley. The road followed the river which actually touched the road at Tiny's post. By the time the garrison reacted it would be dawn so we had to do something to slow down any advance from the north. We had to build a barricade. We could not hope to stop an enemy but we could slow them down. I didn't want to alarm the colonel with false news. I would send a rider when I knew what we were facing.

I did not get much sleep and, leaving Pierre to wake the rest of the troop and bring them to join me, I headed for the northern post. It was Tiny who was on duty. He had set up the outpost and knew it better than any. "I think, sergeant, that we may have company today. We need to slow them down. Any ideas?"

He pointed to the lumber mill along the river. It used a water wheel from a leat to power it. "There is plenty of timber there. We could build a barricade. It would not take long to build."

"Good, get the boys started on that. What about the bridge?"

There was a wooden bridge across the river and it would enable the enemy to outflank us. "It is a bit rickety. It wouldn't take much to destroy it."

"You mean if too many men were on it then it might collapse?"

"Yeah. I walked across it and it shook. More than a handful and they will get wet."

"Good. You get your boys started on the barricade."

When Pierre reached me with the men, I had my plan formulated. "I want some of the timber from the lumber mill. Build a barricade here to cover the bridge. Put four troopers there. Pick the best six shots and place them in the rocks over there." I pointed to the rock strew slope above the road. "Make sure the ones you pick are quick. They will have to run back here as quickly as they can. Send another four men to Charles. He will have to hold the Barco road. What was the road like?"

He shook his head. "A track really sir; men and horses could only approach in twos or threes."

"So, he could be the cork in the bottle?"

"Exactly."

"Good, tell him what he has to do. I want a rider ready to ride to the colonel in case they do come. It may be that they don't bother in which case..."

"In which case, the men will have worked out for nothing." He grinned. "An idle trooper gets into trouble. This is for the best sir."

He was right, of course, the men moaned but they worked with a will and soon we had two barriers built. The one to the north was six feet high and the one near the bridge four feet. We wanted an attacker to be tempted to force the smaller barricade. We had a firing step on the larger barricade for that would be the position we would put all of our firepower. We ate at our posts. I contemplated sending a rider up the road to scout out the area but we had too few men as it was. We would have to wait, patiently.

The Austrians signalled their arrival with drums. They were marching down the road and we heard them a mile away. One of the men on the hillside saw the white uniforms and sent us a message. "Right sergeant, send the rider to the colonel and warn Charles that he is about to get company."

I hoped that the Austrians would see the barricade and charge it. That would enable my men on the hillside to attack their flank. Our weapons were not the best but by splitting the men behind the barricade in two we could keep up a constant volley. We all had our pistols on the firing step so that when they closed to within ten yards, we could blast them and hopefully send them packing. I was counting on the fact that they would not expect stiff opposition from horsemen.

They saw us from some way down the road and the battalion of infantry prepared to charge. The hillside and the river narrowed their options and they began to march resolutely down in a ten wide column. Pierre and I were with the main force while Tiny had taken charge of the bridge. He had the right attitude for such a task. I would order my ten men to fire and, while we reloaded then Pierre would fire his ten. With the men on the hillside adding to the onslaught we had a chance of denting their morale. With luck, they would have to send for cannon. The fact that none had appeared so far was a good sign.

"Remember men; wait until they are fifty yards away. They should be starting their charge about then." I peered over the top and saw a keen officer urging his men forward. I lifted my gun over the top and aimed at him. "Ready!" We had placed white stones at the fifty-yard mark and as soon as I saw that they had reached it I shouted, "Fire!" Almost as soon as we had fired, I said, "Reload!" Pierre's men then fired. I could hear the popping of muskets on the hillside but I could not see the effect for the smoke.

As I stood and aimed, I saw that the Austrians had fallen back and left bloodied white uniformed corpses littering the road.

My men from the hillside raced in. I counted them and saw that they had all survived. "Thought we ought to come back, sir. They sent some jaegers after us!"

"Well done. Join the sergeant on the bridge."

Then I heard the crack of muskets to the east. Charles was under attack. I peered over the top and a flurry of musket balls cracked into the barricade. "Keep your head down sir. There are gaps in the barricade."

"Thank you, Sergeant Major! It is like having my mother with me again." The men laughed and Pierre shrugged.

The Austrians must have realised that they could out range us and they peppered the barricade with musket balls. It was a waste of ammunition but I knew why they were doing it, they were trying to outflank us. I knew that Charles could not hold them for long at Barco but that route did not bring them close to us. The two troopers who guarded the horses in the square would ensure that we had a means of escape. It was the river where we were most in danger.

Trooper Simenon pointed. "Sir. They are on the other side of the river. I could see that they had sent four companies to cross the bubbling mountain river by the bridge. I hoped that Tiny's nerve would hold. I heard the muskets of my men as they targeted the officers and sergeants. The bridge was only wide enough for four or five men and with nine muskets firing at them it should slow them down.

I nodded to Pierre. "You take charge here; I am going to see the bridge."

I crouched and ran the hundred or so yards to the bridge. Tiny was grinning. "They keep trying it in ones and twos sir. So long as they do that we can easily take them out."

Even as I watched an officer and six men tried to sprint across the thirty-yard bridge. They must have thought that we had run out of ammunition or something. Tiny did not fire until they were halfway across then he yelled, "Fire!" I added my musket to the volley. Every man was hit. Four of them staggered back but three remained where they were.

Griff Hosker

"It looks like they have a senior officer there now, sir." I peered over the top and saw the officer on the white horse lean down and speak to an officer.

"Well, sergeant. I think they have had enough of you and intend to brush you aside. It looks like a column attack." We, the French, liked the column attack. Ten men wide and up to a thousand ranks, it was like a human battering ram. Even if the ones at the front were killed the others, coming on behind, kept on pushing. The Austrians were trying the same. "Remember men, when you have fired your musket give them both your pistols and then reload. I want a barricade of bodies across that bridge."

They roared a, "Yes sir!" I had told them exactly what we intended before the Austrians arrived and it had given them an insight into the action. Men fought better knowing the plans.

We heard the drummer beginning to strike up the beat and then their bugles sounded. With a shout, they raced across the bridge. Once they reached the middle Tiny shouted, "Fire!" They all unloaded their muskets and began firing their pistols. I reloaded my musket and saw an officer, bleeding but holding his sword aloft stagger towards me. I shot him in the head. Suddenly we heard a creaking and groaning. Then there was a crack like thunder and the ancient bridge collapsed beneath the weight of the living and the dead. The white-coated Austrians were swept downstream.

We had no time for self-congratulation. "Sergeant, take your men to the horses, Charles may need some help."

"Yes, sir and don't be too long yourself eh?"

"I won't. I'll be listening for the trumpet." Our bugler was with the horses, as soon as the enemy was sighted, he would sound recall and we would get to the horses as quickly as we could.

Back at the barricade, they were still peppering the timber. Pierre smiled in an evil way, "I take it they went for a swim, sir? We heard the bridge go."

"Yes, although they can still reinforce the castle on the far side of the river if they want to." Just then we heard the bugle. "Right boys, back to the horses and don't hang around!"

Cavalrymen look strange when they try to run in boots and spurs but we had no time for either laughing or watching. If they had sent two companies to outflank us, we would be seriously outnumbered. As we reached the horses, I saw that the Barco defenders had suffered wounds and losses.

"Sir there is a company and half there." He pointed to the east.

"Well done sergeant. Get your men to the colonel now and report that we are on our way."

Pierre pointed up the track. "They are just charging sir, no order."

I looked at my men. There were still twenty-five of us. "Column of eights. Let's see just how brave they are. Draw sabres!" There was a metallic hiss as twenty-five swords were drawn.

"Sound the charge!"

As the bugler sounded charge, I spurred Killer on. The Austrians were only thirty yards away and their look of exultation was replaced by one of horror. I do not think any had reloaded and there was no order. One or two attempted to present bayonets to us but the rest ran. As I kicked one musket and bayonet away, I slashed down at the musketeer. The next man had his back to me and I split the back of his head open. It was a rout. They might have outnumbered us but they had not stood and we were invincible. We chased them all the way to Barco. I shouted, "Sound the recall."

As we halted, I looked to see how many men we had lost. I could only see one riderless horse although there were a couple with bayonet wounds to the legs.

"Sir, that barricade will not hold them for long."

"Quite a right sergeant. Back to Trento."

The lane was littered with the dead and the dying. Pierre halted and picked up Trooper Roux's body and draped it over his horse. We would bury our own.

As we re-entered the main square, I could see that they had half demolished the timber of the barricade. We had plenty of time and we did not need to thrash our horses. They had served us well. We rode at a steady trot back to the brigade. As we neared the town I saw, to my great relief, the Tricolour flying from the fort. The colonel had succeeded and the Austrian column racing down the western side of the river would get a real shock when their own cannons stuck them.

CHAPTER 13

The next couple of weeks saw us gradually close with the heart of the Tyrol. It was hard going but we rolled northwards like a huge machine. The Austrians could not hold us anywhere. The Austrian defence was like a sieve and we flowed through it undeterred. In April the Austrians were forced to sue for peace. We had won. It would now be down to the politicians to make the best peace they could with the smallest loss of territory. We had bought the land with the blood of our soldiers. Those untrained and ill-disciplined recruits had now become trained soldiers who could hold their own against anyone.

Our hard-worked regiment had taken many losses and we were sent back to Verona to re-supply and to receive recruits. With the losses amongst the sergeants and officers, it meant that I was promoted to full lieutenant and Pierre became a sous-lieutenant. Tiny became Sergeant Major while Michael was made the First Sergeant. The boys who had joined three years earlier were now men. I still could not get used to the new years dictated by the Directory nor the new months and so for me it was still April in 1797 when we reached our new barracks at Verona. It had been taken from the Venetians by the Austrians and we took advantage of their departure. We would sleep well.

And then Jean and I were suddenly summoned to Bonaparte's headquarters again. We were needed for yet another special mission. We knew this from Bessières' subtle tap of the nose when he asked us to have a secret meeting in Mantua with the busy little general. As we headed south, I asked the major what he thought was in the offing. Jean was always calm and thoughtful. I think that was one of the reasons mother must have liked him. The count had been a loud and ebullient man. Jean was nothing like him.

"Albert is not here and that means it is unlikely to be military."

I was not expecting that answer. "Then why us? We are soldiers."

"I think he believes we can get things done. I heard from Bessières that he was impressed with our Naples escapade. You can speak a couple of languages as can I. You showed how resourceful you were when you recaptured the deserter."

That took my breath away. "That! How did he find out about it?"

"The Gendarmerie officers have recounted the tale since we left for the Tyrol. You looked so young and yet you cowed the criminals of Mantua. It impressed the general I think." He shrugged, "I am guessing though. Perhaps he sees you as a resourceful young man who gets things done."

"Oh." We rode in silence for a while. "And you sir, do you think I am resourceful?"

"I know that you are. He turned to look at me. "You are not looking for compliments are you Robbie? I did not think you needed them. The men also admire you but they would not like to hear you asking to be told that. It is not our way is it?"

"No, and I am not, it is just I don't know if I always do the right thing."

"You have had enough promotions to know that you have. I do not think our lives will be in danger. I just think the general wants us to go somewhere his Guides cannot. Bessières is a fine officer but he is best suited to lists and looking good. We may not look good, Robbie, but we get the job done. No matter how dirty it is."

Bessières took us to a small back room in the Palazzo Te, a superb palace which had previously been occupied by kings and princes. Bonaparte had chosen a plain room for his meeting. This time Bessières stayed with us. "Make sure the guard is at the door. I do not want other ears to hear this."

Bessières went to the door and spoke a few words to the Guide there. "We will not be disturbed, general."

Once again there was a map in the middle of the table. Napoleon waved us to two wooden seats. They looked uncomfortable and I hoped this would not be a long meeting. "Here is the Venetian Republic. They have been very clever over the years at playing one enemy against another. They no longer fight wars but they do come out victorious, gaining land they have not fought for. I intend to gain as much of the Republic as I can for France." He shrugged. "I would prefer not to lose any more men as I have important plans for next year." He waved his hand as though a fly had entered the room. "That is not important now. Since you visited Naples I have been in contact with the Regent of San Marino. I wrote to him and he visited me here not long ago. He has agreed to be my emissary."

I could not see where this was going. Why did he need us? The questions must have shown on my face. "Be patient, young Scotsman, your role will be made clear soon enough. If I am to take Venice without a fight then I need some leverage. I need a threat to enable me to grab it. That threat, of course, is Austria. I wish you to escort the Regent to Vienna and negotiate with the Austrians."

Jean and I looked at each other in amazement. Jean found his voice first. "Why us?"

Bonaparte shook his head impatiently, "You are soldiers of France and you should not ask 'why me' but say 'thank you, general, for choosing me'."

"I am sorry general I phrased it badly perhaps. Why choose us rather than some other soldiers who might be better suited?"

He appeared a little mollified by that and smiled, "You know the Regent and he likes you. You can speak a little Italian and you have shown me that you can handle yourselves in difficult situations. I trust the Regent implicitly and I need to trust the

men who accompany him." He banged the table in a business-
like way. "Now you will be travelling as citizens of San Marino.
Bessières has your papers. You will need to act as bodyguards as
well for the Regent. There will be some who try to stop these
negotiations taking place. You will probably want your own
weapons. You will be given civilian clothes and horses which
are less military."

"Anything I have missed out?"

"I think, general, that a couple more men might be useful."

He looked puzzled. "More men? Why?"

"If we are to be his bodyguards too, then that will require more
than two men. We do need to sleep, sir."

He smiled, "I don't but you are right, you will need some relief.
Have you someone in mind?"

"Two of the men who went with us to Naples sir; one speaks
Italian and the other is handy with his fists. Both are skills we
will need."

"Very well, Bessières, make the arrangements. As with the
other trip you will be provided with funds." He leaned forwards. "This may not be like a battle, gentlemen but it could
win more for France than any battle you have fought." He stood,
which indicated that the meeting was over. "You will do all in
your power to ensure that this mission is a success. Be ruthless, I
am counting on you."

Bessières led us from the room and took us to an antechamber.
"He has great confidence in you, you know that?"

I shook my head, "Well he has more confidence that I think I
have."

He patted me on the back and opened a chest. "Here are your
clothes and your papers." He handed a leather pouch to Jean.
"Here is the money you will need." To me, he gave a letter. "Give
this letter to your colonel. It tells him that you and anyone else
you need are to be detached for an undisclosed period. Do not
tell him what you are about. Return here tomorrow with your
two men. The Regent will be here and you will leave immediately he arrives. You can leave the chest here and the papers it

will be safer. You will use this room tomorrow to change. There is a wardrobe there for you to leave your uniforms."

I was still stunned as we rode into the camp. "You had better ask Tiny and Michael if they will come with us and I will go and see the colonel. I think he will not be pleased. He has troopers to train and we will not be here."

"No, but he has Claude and Pierre, and they are both better than me."

"Do not underestimate yourself."

When I reached the mess, I waved Tiny and Michael over. Pierre said, "I have a good bottle of wine. Care to join us?"

"Sorry Pierre, I need to see these two urgently." He looked a little put out but he smiled graciously and bowed. Once outside, they both looked at me with a worried expression. "Listen, I do not have much time. General Bonaparte has asked Jean and me to do another job for him and we would like you to come with us." They both smiled, "But I cannot tell you what it is until we are on the road. Sorry."

Michael nodded, "We trust both of you sir and besides it will be more exciting than training a bunch of clodhoppers how to ride and fire a musket."

"Good then meet us at the horse lines with your gear but tell no one what we are about."

"Not even Pierre?"

"No even Pierre."

As we rode away from the camp, I saw the puzzled look on a slightly drunk Pierre. He and I were good friends and I had deliberately shut him out. It made me feel uncomfortable and I brooded about. When we were clear of our lines Jean said, "Stop feeling sorry for yourself and we can tell our two comrades what this adventure is all about."

It was probably the best thing he could have said to me as I had to concentrate and remember all that we had been told. They were both excited and happy about travel into the heart of the enemy's lair. As Tiny said, "So far there is nothing about the Austrians that worries me. Besides we won't be Frenchmen we will be Italians."

Michael laughed, "Then we had better work non-stop on your accent. Robbie is fine and Jean can get by but you Sergeant Major are dreadful."

We spent the journey back to Mantua speaking Italian to get into the language. I had not had time to check on our papers and our identities but we would have to learn just who we were supposed to be.

We stayed at an inn just outside Mantua so that we arrived bright and early. Bessières was impressed. "The Regent has not risen yet so this will allow us to make sure we have all the details correct."

Since he had left our regiment, I had learned that Bessières was a master of detail. We first changed into civilian clothes. Tiny and Michael were given good clothes but the clothes of servants. Jean and I were given the clothes of young Italian nobles. My name was to be Roberto; Jean's was left as Jean. Michael was left as Michael and Tiny given the name of Cesar, a name he thoroughly enjoyed. I wondered about leaving my money belt at the castle but thought better of it. Who knew when I might need it? Bessières had provided us with much better pistols than our own as well as powder and ammunition. Jean insisted on sharing the money as we might end up separated. While we waited for the Regent Tiny and Michael went down to check on the horses. As cavalrymen, we needed the best.

Bonaparte himself brought Antonio down to us. The Regent was gracious as ever, "Good to see you." Then he stopped. "They will have to go."

I wondered what he was staring at and then Bonaparte said, "Of course. Bessières fetch my barber." He walked up to me and tugged at my pigtails and queue. "These mark you as a cavalryman and a French one at that. My barber will deal with this. You had better have the others done too."

I was in shock. It had taken me so long to acquire them and I felt more like a cavalryman with them. Our hair was trimmed and styled. It may have pleased Napoleon but it annoyed me.

Tiny and Michael were less bothered by it and Jean not at all. "It is hair, Robbie. It will grow again."

He also trimmed our beards and moustache to make them look Italian. That I did not mind so much as the style was quite dashing. Once we were ready Bonaparte was eager for us to leave. "It should take you between ten days and two weeks to reach there. By then our negotiations with the Austrian Army should be at stalemate. He smiled, "In two weeks I will become more amenable to their offers eh Regent?"

Antonio did like Bonaparte and he laughed, "Yes general."

We left quietly through a small postern gate on the eastern side of the city. Tiny and Michael led two horses with spare clothes for the journey. I felt almost naked wearing civilian clothes. They were well-made clothes and they were comfortable but they did not give me the reassurance of my uniform. I found my hat hard to wear and I was sure it would fall off my head. We had been trotting along for a mile when Antonio turned to me. "Your hat will stay on, believe me. I know it is hard not to wear a uniform but you will become accustomed to it. And now that we are out of sight of prying eyes; you two," he pointed to me and Jean, "as my companions and bodyguards should be in front so that I am protected. When we are in public you will need to call me sir. The people we will be meeting know who I am and you should be invisible to both them and to me. That way you can use your eyes to watch for danger."

Jean asked, "So you may be in danger, sir?"

He nodded and added almost casually, "Oh most certainly. There is a faction which wishes the war pursued at all costs. They want the revolution crushed it is a dangerous idea. It is why Britain will never stop until France is defeated."

"But what difference can it make to them sir?" I was confused. "It is an island."

"It is the idea they fear. Britain is as France was before the Revolution. The rich landowners exploit the workers. If the workers realised that and rose up then their way of life would be ended. Well, you should know Robbie. Your people, the Scots

are subjugated. They would join in any revolution to over-
throw the English and the Irish are always rebelling. Remember the American colonies recently rebelled and overthrew the
shackles of British rule. That wound is still raw. No, the British,
and some of the Austrians believe that the French need defeat-
ing to destroy the ideal of freedom."

Jean and I went to the fore and we rode on. Over my shoulder, I
asked, "If you do not mind me asking sir? What is in this for you?
If it is necessary to have an escort then why risk it?"

"Robbie!"

"No, he asks a good question. Your General Bonaparte is a great
general. I have no doubt that he will conquer the whole of Italy
when he chooses."

It was Jean's turn to be incredulous. "Really?"

"He has yet to be defeated. At the battle you call Rivoli, he defeated three armies and he was outnumbered. When he decides
he wants it he can take the whole of the country. You have travelled through all four parts. My own is the smallest but none of
them could stand up to France. Your general knows this. If I aid
you then San Marino will still be free. He is a ruthless man and
he drives a hard bargain. I like that. It is a small price to pay; a
month's journey to secure my country's freedom."

Putting it like that made it easier to understand. Once I knew
the reasons, I travelled easier. It was a pleasant enough journey. The land was free from war and summer was almost upon
us. We could see the mountains to the north-west of us but we
travelled over the undulating country which did not tax the
horses too much. For the first part, we had no problems with the
language as we travelled through Italian lands. It helped Tiny to
develop an accent. By the time we reached those parts where
they did not speak Italian, he could pass for someone who had
lived on the Italian border.

We crossed into Austria from Venetian territory. I was not
aware of the actual point, there was no border crossing as I had
imagined it was just that the Regent said, "And now we are in the
Austrian Empire."

"What language do they speak here sir?"

"There are many, German and Austrian of course. There are some Slavs here and they speak their own language. When we get closer to Vienna some will speak Magyar which is incomprehensible to all but the Hungarians. Those who are educated will speak French or German. It will not seem strange if we speak French but remember we only speak Italian to each other. We only speak French if I do. Is that clear?"

That was the first sign that we might be in danger; Antonio was always calm and unruffled but there was an edge to his voice. I did not find a problem with Italian. Having grown up with two languages it was easy enough to drift into a third. When we reached Graz, we were approaching the last third of our journey. This was a huge place. Not quite as big as Paris but certainly the second biggest place I had ever seen. This would be the first time we would not be staying in an inn. The Regent was expected and the Governor greeted us. He spoke in Italian, "We have quarters for you and your companions on the first floor. Your servants have rooms close to the stables."

The Regent smiled, "Cesar take the horses to the stables. Roberto and Jean when we have found our rooms you can collect our luggage."

We had all been practising our bows so that it would look like second nature. Antonio gave a smile. The residence was the old Imperial Palace. Jean and I shared a small room connected by a door to that of the Regent. The Regent's room was superior to anything the count had had. While Antonio was entertained Jean and I were taken to the stables to get the luggage. As we took the two chests, we needed Jean said to the other two, "Keep your ears open and speak Italian all the time."

We were not invited to eat with the Regent and the Governor, instead, we were stationed close to the door with the Governor's two guards. The two men were ruddy-faced men with hands like hams. These were not gentlemen, they were thugs. None of us spoke we just watched the two men eat. The conversation appeared to be banal rather than diplomatic but they did venture on to the subject of Napoleon Bonaparte. I got the impression that the Governor knew nothing of the specifics of our mission and had no inkling that the Regent was negotiating for France.

"What do you think of this Bonaparte?"

The Regent dabbed his mouth with his napkin. "He seems competent enough."

"He certainly destroyed our armies." The Governor leaned in, "Between you and me I don't think the generals we sent were that good anyway."

"I wouldn't know. We do not have a large army in San Marino."

"Ah well we need one, we are the largest Empire you know."

"I thought the Russian Empire was quite big too."

The Governor reddened and they changed to less prickly subjects. "Well Governor, I have an early start tomorrow. Thank you for your hospitality."

"You are more than welcome. We get a few refined visitors these days." He seemed to notice us for the first time. "There is a table with food for your men in their room. We wouldn't want them starving eh?"

We were ravenous but we made sure that the Regent was settled before we ate. When we had stayed in taverns and inns, we had each taken a spell as sentry during the night. As we left the Regent's room he said, "I think we should be safe enough tonight. You can both get a good night's rest; after you have eaten, of course!"

The food was good and certainly better than the indifferent fare we had experienced thus far on the road. Before we turned in, we cleaned and loaded our pistols, as was our practice and sharpened our blades and my stiletto. I had yet to use it but I still sharpened it every day. There was something soothing and therapeutic about sharpening such a fine blade. After we had checked the corridor and the door, we both retired for the night. We did not sleep beneath the covers but merely took off our jackets and lay on top of the bed. We were both acutely aware that we were Antonio's only guards that night.

I think it was the fact that the bed was too comfortable which made me restless. I had never had a soft bed and my time in the army had made me more used to the ground. Whatever the reason, I rose in the middle of the night. I could hear Jean snuffling and Antonio snoring. We had left a candle burning as the room was completely dark; we wanted to be able to see the strange room clearly if we woke. I wandered over to the table and thought about eating another leg of pheasant. I found one and was nibbling it. I was not hungry but I thought eating might make me sleepy.

Suddenly I heard a noise. It was not a loud noise but it was an unnatural noise. It was not the creak of a bed or the rustle of a curtain. It was the sound of a handle turning. I grabbed my sword and shook Jean.

"I heard a noise!"

He needed no more and he was on his feet and so armed in a trice. Snuffing the candle out as we passed, we opened the door. Two men had entered the Regent's room and they looked to be armed. A third and the fourth were entering.

Jean yelled, "Assassins!" as he thrust forward with his sword. As his victim staggered when the blade entered him, I slashed down at the man who held the sword poised over the Regent. It slashed through the wrist and the sword fell. The other two drew their weapons to face us. They were fencers, that much was obvious, from their stances. As we circled each other on either side of the Regent's bed I saw that my opponent was young but he had a very flexible wrist. He would be dangerous. His blade was far thinner than mine with a rapier point. Mine was a blunt instrument by comparison.

He suddenly flicked his wrist in an attempt to disarm me. I had been taught that when I was eight. I countered with a thrust at his thigh. He had to beat my sword away. We danced around each other. This had to end. I feinted with my sword and reached down for my stiletto. I kept it hidden. He came in with his blade and I pushed mine so that they were both vertical and were close together. I smiled at him and slid the knife between his ribs. I turned to see how Jean had fared and his opponent lay dead.

"Are you hurt Regent?"

"No!"

"I wounded one. He must have…"

Just then there was the crack of first one musket and then another. When we reached the corridor, we saw the man I had wounded lying dead. The two guards from dinner held the smoking guns. The Regent stood behind us. "It is a pity we could not question him. We might have found out who hired him."

The Governor, guarded by another two guards entered the corridor. "My apologies Regent. I don't know how this happened."

The Regent shook his head, "Murderers will always find a way. Why did your men kill this one? We could have questioned him."

The Governor asked them a question and one answered. "They said he reached for a weapon."

"Ah!"

"I will have the bodies removed and you can continue your rest."

"Thank you although I fear sleep is over for me but thank you anyway."

After the bodies had been removed, I said. "That man could not have gone for a weapon I almost severed his wrist. They were lying."

"Of course, they were, Roberto, the Governor was in on it. Why else would he have had two of his own bodyguards guarding the corridor? They were to finish us off in case the murderers failed." He shook his head, "But for your vigilance… thank you. I owe you my life."

Jean said, "It was not me. It was Robbie heard the noise. Thank God for young ears."

We dressed and packed. Jean and I took the opportunity of clearing and finishing the food. Soldiers eat when they can for, they never know when there will be no rations to eat. The Governor could not apologise enough. He sent his servants to take the chests to the stables. "We have discovered that the four men were Italians." He looked sympathetically at the Regent. "You have enemies at home, obviously. I don't know how they got into the residence. I will hold an enquiry when you have departed and believe me, heads will roll!"

We said nothing to Tiny and Charles until we were well clear of the city. When we told them what had occurred, Charles nodded, "We were virtually held, prisoner. They had a guard at the door of the stables. He said that it was to prevent the Regent's horses being stolen but it was to keep us in. Every time it looked as though we might move, they provided whatever we needed. We were prisoners even though the cage was a velvet one."

The Regent nodded, "We now know what we merely suspected before. There are enemies all around us and we will have to be on our guard."

Jean looked ahead, "And I would say, starting now." He pointed at the forests which spread out before us. The road cut a lonely track through the middle. "That is perfect ambush country and they will not be sneaking around any more. Make sure your swords are at the ready. How are your sword skills, Regent?"

He smiled, "I am Italian. They will suffice."

"Make sure your pistols are primed too. They may use firearms."

Now that we had been in danger our senses were on the alert for threats of any kind. All four of us scanned the forest for signs of an enemy. The bird which suddenly flew up a hundred yards ahead was a palpable warning.

"Ready your pistols and when I say go, we ride like the wind."

Having seen the bird we knew that the danger would be from our right. That was their first mistake; our swords were on our right. It would have been far better to attack from our left. Their second was in scaring the bird. They should have been in position for hours. They had just arrived; no doubt the failure of the first attempt involved some improvisation. Improvised plans are more likely to fail.

Jean waited for a few moments and then shouted, "Go!"

The attack, when it came, was swift and furious. A dozen muskets appeared from the pine forest and fired at the position we had been in when Jean shouted his order.

He balls mainly missed but I heard a couple of pings off the chests on the pack horses at the rear. Jean shouted, "Stop!" We all reined in and stopped. "Fire!" I suspect the Regent had no idea what was going on but the four of us were looking were the smoke was coming from and we all fired at the smoke. Jean's orders were for the four of us and when he shouted, "Second weapon!" we knew what he meant. We aimed our pistols at the forest as the ten men rushed at us, assuming we had fired everything. I aimed at a small fellow who was trying to dodge and weave. When he was ten yards from me, I fired and his face disappeared. I holstered my gun and drew my sword. I charged the men coming at me. I saw three others hit and knew that the others would be doing as I did and charging. Our attackers did not expect that. I took the head from one murderer with a sideways slice of my sword. It was over ridiculously quickly. The four survivors fled into the forest.

I turned my horse and trotted back. The Regent was safe. One of the horses with the chests had been struck and was kicking violently. "Michael and Tiny ride into the forest, they must have had more horses bring back at least one. Robbie, deal with the horse."

I took it as a compliment that Jean knew I would be able to handle the dying horse. I took my knife and slit the ropes holding the chest. They fell to the ground. I put my left arm around the horse's neck and said, "Shssh, Shssh," I began to hum a tune and as she calmed, I slit her throat. I had learned the lesson of shooting a horse in a strange land. The brave beast just slid to the ground dead. Her fate had been sealed by the attack and the assassins who put three musket balls into her.

Tiny and Michael soon returned with two horses. "Another one of the killers died as he fled. They will remember this encounter."

As we packed the chests on to the horses the Regent began to clap his hands together. "I can see why the general picked you for this mission. You are soldiers of which France can be proud."

CHAPTER 14

We left the dead where they lay and headed towards Vienna. We had learned our lesson. When we reached the first inn I said to Jean, "My mother told me of the old kings of Scotland how they would have one of their bodyguards sleep behind the door. It is how they got their name, Chamberlains. I think that we should do that. We are all used to sleeping on the floor and it guarantees that no one surprises us."

The Regent was against it but the other three thought it was a good idea as we would no longer need each of us to lose two hours sleep a night. It made the next five days much easier. By the time we reached the fabulous city of Vienna, we had all had more rest and were prepared for whatever treachery our enemies could throw at us.

We were all warier when we were welcomed into the Imperial Palace. The last one we had stayed in had almost cost the Regent his life. The Austrians seemed regimented and had strict systems in place. Tiny and Charles were not in the stables but they were far removed from us in the servant's quarters. As before, Jean and I had a room adjacent to the Regent. We were not greeted by anyone important but a diplomat who grovelled obsequiously and explained that we would meet our negotiator the next day. I think the Regent was a little nonplussed by this rudeness. It was not the way things were done in a civilised country. It was not a quiet dinner that night but a full-blown banquet. The Emperor was not there but the room was filled with aristocrats and military uniforms. Jean and I watched from the side. It was, however, an illuminating experience.

We watched the politics of the dining table. It was quite obvious who was opposed to the peace with France, even though it was supposed to be a secret. They sat together and cast the most evil glances in the direction of the Regent and those who sat close to him. That number appeared to be a very small number and I wondered just how Bonaparte would achieve his ends. It seemed to me that there were few people who countenanced peace. The Regent did not appear to be bothered by all the apparent hostility. He smiled at all and was gracious even to those who were being rude to him.

When we were safely ensconced in our room Jean asked him about the dinner. "How did you suffer the insults?"

"It was simple. The Austrians have been beaten soundly by your Napoleon Bonaparte. They may have held the other generals but Bonaparte has beaten them. The days of the Austrian Empire are over and they cannot see it. That thought helped me. And, as I said to you, this is my country's freedom. Men have died to make their country free. What are a few insults?"

We kept the same arrangements as on the road. The first night I slept behind the door with a loaded pistol. It was a peaceful night.

The next day we were summoned to a room in the west wing of the palace. There was no-one in the room and it was laid for five people. Jean and I stood, as we always stood, by the wall and Antonio waited patiently.

The door opened and a military man stepped in. He had with him a young aide and no-one else. Count Philipp von Cobenzl had eyes that bored into you. He was a very clever man and far better educated than most of the generals we had seen the previous night. He wore a military uniform as did all the Austrians we met but he was not a belligerent man. He was a thinker. The Emperor thought highly of him which explained why the meeting was taking place. After they had introduced themselves, he sat down. He suddenly held up his hand. "Would not the two

French soldiers be better placed here at the table and then they can report back to their general more accurately what has taken place?"

I had no idea what to do or say. The Regent turned around, smiled and beckoned with his arm. "Come and join us."

Count Philipp von Cobenzl smiled and spread his arms. "I am not a devious man and I prefer transparency. My aide and I are fluent in French so we will use that language it will make life simpler."

The negotiations looked to have been started by letters for there was little disagreement. The Treaty of Leoben had already been signed by General Bonaparte and ended hostilities. From the discussion of the two men, there was much agreement already. We were witness to the final details and the lure that Bonaparte used to get his way.

"You have already given away or lost the Austrian Netherlands and Lombardy. The general does not wish your Empire to disappear. The Turks are still an enemy to us all; your Empire is a buffer against those religious fanatics. To make this treaty more palatable he proposes that you gain the Venetian provinces of Istria and Dalmatia."

The count looked both surprised and pleased at that. "That is generous. What will Venice have to say about that?"

"Nothing, as the general will convert the rest into the Venetian Republic."

"You mean like the Ligurian Republic, a French puppet?"

"I think that General Bonaparte sees it more as a state benevolently protected by the brave French Army."

"And I presume he can deliver this?"

"When I leave here, Count von Cobenzl I will be going with these gentlemen to Venice to inform them of their fate and to warn them of the dangers of opposing it." He paused, "Austria would be keen to gain the territories and to use force to acquire them?" Von Cobenzl nodded. This was the first we had heard of this additional journey but we both kept impassive faces.

The Austrian smiled his approval. "We will, of course, need

written assurances of the general's intentions. They will be kept secret but…"

"Quite." The Regent reached into his bag and took out three letters. He held them tantalizingly over the table.

"And we would need letters which approved the formal handing over of Lombardy and the Austrian Netherlands to the French Republic."

"Of course." Count von Cobenzl held out his hand and the aide handed him two letters. The two men exchanged the precious documents.

With that over, there was an air of calm around the table. Count von Cobenzl held his hands open, "I understand you experienced certain dangers along the road?"

"We had a little trouble in the Governor's Residence in Graz but my keen-eared young friend here helped us to snuff that out."

"And there was an attack in the forests north of Graz too?"

"Yes, ten or so fellows attacked us." He dismissed the action as though it was minor. "We dealt with it."

Count von Cobenzl's face creased into a frown. "I could give you an escort of horsemen if you wish."

"No, Count von Cobenzl, it is kind of you but that would merely draw more attention to me and my companions. The general is keen for all of this to remain secret. Besides we will not be passing through Graz. The road to Venice takes us in a different direction."

"Yes, I am afraid the Governor of Graz is of the hawk side of the fence and he is keen to pursue the war against the peasants of France."

Antonio leaned across the table, "And when did the Governor last fight in a war?"

The Austrian smiled, "I believed he served as an aide to a general for a while when he was quite young."

The Regent smiled and said to the aide, "If I were you, young man, I would get some experience of war sooner rather than later."

The aide blushed but I could see that he took no offence. The count asked, "If you do not mind me saying so, one of your companions looks even younger than my aide. When will he experience war?"

"This young man has been at war for three years and is now a lieutenant. He has met and defeated your men in the Netherlands and Italy."

Count von Cobenzl looked at me with steely eyes, "I apologise young man. You look too young to have done so much."

"I never went to military school sir but you learn more from the back of a horse in a battle than you will ever learn in a classroom."

The count looked at his aide, "There Joseph, there is a model for you."

"Yes, uncle and I would love to fight."

The Regent said, "Well good luck, but I hope you never have the misfortune to fight these men and their comrades. They have that rare combination, skill and more than their fair share of good luck!"

We left the palace and Vienna quietly. As we travelled through the beautiful city over the magnificent Danube, I regretted the fact that we had not had time to explore it. It certainly rivalled Paris and I could see the power that had been Austria. I was not so sure that it was equipped to deal with the new, faster warfare. I had not seen any evidence of either soldiers or generals who could stand up to the likes of Bonaparte and Massena.

As we rode south, I wondered about this visit to Venice. Nothing had been said before we left in April. Yet the Regent seemed to have planned it all along. I know that we were only soldiers and would not be consulted but it showed a lack of trust certainly. When we reached the outskirts of the city the Regent asked to be taken to the Doge's Palace. As they appeared to know who he was they acceded to his request. Tiny and Charles were sent to find accommodation. We did not expect to be given rooms in the palace, this was an unexpected visit.

We were taken to an antechamber where we cooled our heels

for a long four hours. Eventually, we were taken in and met by an official. He had a secretary to take notes. He looked rather bored with our visit already and we had only just arrived.

Antonio was, as we had learned, a master at diplomacy, he smiled. "I would have expected to see one of the Council of Ten. The news I bring is important."

The official gave a self-important smile. "San Marino is a valued ally but the Council have more pressing matters to deal with."

"Ah, I see. San Marino is too insignificant to be worthy of their attention. I quite understand. However, had you asked me my business and my purpose, I would have told you that I was here as an envoy of the French Government and General Napoleon Bonaparte in particular."

The man's whole demeanour changed. He raced from the room but spoke quietly to the guards whose attitude and stance changed to one of suspicion and caution. Within a short space of time, five powdered and bewigged men walked in. They took their seats. One of them pointed a heavily ringed finger at Antonio. "I am Carlo Abruzzi and I speak for the Doge and the council on this matter. Why does the Regent of San Marino side with the French aggressor?"

The Regent smiled. "Not a very good start to discussions, however, I will overlook the rudeness and lack of diplomatic language. I have just returned from Vienna and I have to tell you that the French and the Austrians have reached an agreement."

"About what?"

"About the future of Venice."

"What about its future?"

"It hasn't got one!"

"Guards, arrest these men and throw them in the New Prison!"

Even as the four guards with halberds moved from the door I was on my feet and had my sword at the throat of Carlo Abruzzi. Jean had drawn his pistols to cover the armed guards. They looked at the two guns and I suspect their barrels looked to be as big as cannons. Venice had not been to war for many years.

The guards were overweight and lacked experience. The Regent held his hands up for restraint but continued to smile and talk in a quiet voice. "As you can see my young companions do not wish that to happen." He shrugged, "To be frank nor do I. Let me finish what I was about to say before I was so rudely interrupted. Even as we speak General Napoleon Bonaparte is heading for Venice from Mantua. He may even be in the outskirts already. Now this army of the French has defeated every Austrian army sent to defeat it. Will your," he pointed at the halberdiers, "antiquated army be able to stand against them? I think not." He pensively tapped a finger against his chin. "Perhaps an ally will come to your aid, Austria perhaps? But no, they are quite happy to stand and watch."

The council members were all white with shock. It matched their wigs. Signor Abruzzi blustered, "This is outrageous. You cannot do this."

"The point, gentlemen, is that I am not doing this. I am merely the diplomatic envoy of the man who is. As far as I can see you can do little. Venice is a beautiful city. Would you have its buildings destroyed by French cannon? I have seen them at work and they are deadly." He turned to me, "You may lower your sword. I would not have our host have an accident." I lowered my weapon but I did not sheathe it and I kept watch on the four guards. I had no doubt that if they attempted anything, I could easily disarm them. A halberd is no use in a confined space.

"If you wish you can send a rider towards Mantua to confirm my words. I was sent here to avoid needless deaths and destruction."

The members of the council remained silent. I could see the internal debate but none had the power to take a decision."

"You have my word that you will not become part of France. The general has assured me that the model of Genoa and the Netherlands will be the one he chooses. There will be a republic run by the people." He smiled, "It will function much as it does now."

A silence fell in the room. "We will have to discuss this with the full council."

"Of course. If you could send in some refreshments, we have had a long journey and..."

The looks on their faces were those of pure hatred but twenty minutes after they had left food and drink was brought in. The two footmen who brought in the food placed it on the table.

"Excellent and, before you leave gentlemen, would you be so good as to taste each plate of food and jug of wine?" Although he smiled it was a thin-lipped smile and he gave a subtle nod to Jean and his guns. The two men looked at each other and did as he asked. When they had tasted everything the Regent said, "Now you may go."

Jean placed his pistols on the table while he ate. I did the same with my sword. The Regent ate for a while and then said. "An impetuous gesture, Roberto, but an effective one. You are fast with that blade. When this is over there will always be a place for you in San Marino, should you tire of this life. You and your friend will be more than welcome for you are quite resourceful." My mouth full I shook my head. "Ah well. Your general is a lucky man to have such servants."

It was getting on for dark when the council members returned. They looked defeated. "You are correct. What terms does the general offer?"

"No terms. Unconditional surrender."

There was a collective gasp from the Venetians. "But that is unreasonable."

"Were you not listening before? The Venetian Republic will remain but its organisation and boundaries will be set by General Bonaparte. You are in his hands. You now know the size of the army which faces you. You know you have no friends and therefore no help. You have no choice."

In a resigned voice, Abruzzi said, "What do we do then?"

"Tonight, you lower all of your flags and tomorrow morning you open your gates. I will send one of my servants to ask the general not to open fire. You will give a pass to my man to allow him free passage."

"But we have agreed."

"And how does the general know this? He does not. He will come here to destroy your city unless I send him word that peace has been agreed. I will send a servant. We, of course, will need accommodation. There are rooms here?"

"You wish to stay here?"

"Why not? We are civilised men. This is not war, it is diplomacy. The wounds we suffer are less life threatening I have found."

As rooms were found and a pass secured, Antonio turned to me. "You will ride to the general."

"What about your safety?"

"Send Cesar and Michael to me that will be more than adequate." He gestured at the guards. "Do you think they will pose a problem?"

"No." I grinned at Jean, "Enjoy the food!"

Tiny and Charles were waiting at the entrance to the palace. "Where are our horses?"

"We found an inn and stables close to the Rialto Bridge. What is going on? After we arrived it was as though a wasp's nest had been broken. There were men racing all over."

"The general is coming and I have been sent to meet him. After I have my horse you two are to join Jean with the Regent. You are sleeping in a palace."

I went back with the two of them to the palace and told the guards that they were to be sent to the Regent. One looked truculent and so I flashed my pass. He reluctantly allowed them in. I rode west towards Mantua. I had no idea how far I would have to travel but I was pleased to be given such an important task. I was no more than two miles from the city when there was the sharp crack of a musket and my horse staggered. I saw the blood and knew she had been hit. I kicked my feet from my stirrups, pleased that I had no spurs on, and I jumped clear of the dying horse. I rolled as I hit the ground but, as I hit the bole of a tree the wind was knocked from me. I closed my eyes with the pain. When I opened them there were two swords at my throat and one of them was mine but in the hands of a stranger.

The two men were Austrian. I could tell that from their dress and their accents. "So, Frenchman you escaped our little trap in Graz but we have you now."

"We are now allies. I have met Count von Cobenzl."

"He is a traitor. We do not serve him. We serve Austria and we have heard of your general's plan. When you do not arrive, he will assume that the Venetians wish to fight and he will destroy the city. My countrymen will not stand for such an action and the peace treaty will be destroyed. I will take great pleasure in killing you."

As he pulled his sword back, I grabbed my sword by the blade, my gauntlets giving me some protection. At the same time, I slipped my stiletto out of my boot. I pulled the man holding my sword across my body and he fell in front of his companion who could not complete his blow. I stabbed him in the neck and wrenched my sword from his hand. The first man stabbed at me and I barely had time to move my head. The razor-sharp sword slid along my cheek cutting it open to the bone.

I was on my feet in an instant. I beat away the second blow with my stiletto. We were quite close and I could not swing my blade. Instead, I punched him in the face with my pommel. One of the handguards slipped into his eye and there was a scream as it ruptured the ball. He became angry then and that is always a mistake. He swung at my head with such force that when I ducked, he overbalanced and I thrust my sword under his left arm and pierced his heart. He fell dead at my feet.

I grabbed his cravat and held it to my cheek to stop the bleeding. I quickly checked for any other assassins and there was no sign of any. I sheathed my sword and quickly searched them. They had papers which had an Imperial seal upon them. I could not read Austrian and I stuck them in my jacket. After I had found their horses, I retrieved my pass, mounted and carried on my journey. After a mile or so the bleeding had stopped and I was able to remove my temporary bandage. Charles would be impressed with the scar.

I had not travelled more than five miles from the ambush when I was suddenly surrounded by horsemen, chasseurs. I heard a familiar voice say, in very bad Italian, "Put your hands up now!"

"Is that any way to talk to a superior officer, lieutenant?"

As soon as I spoke, they all recognised me and they thronged around me with dozens of questions. When they saw the wound, they looked around for an assailant as the wound was still fresh. "The two of them are dead about five miles up the road. I have to speak with the general urgently!"

Pierre nodded. "Trooper Vallois. Escort the lieutenant to the general." He grinned at me. I can see you have some interesting stories which might make up for the fact that I have been in the dark for the past three weeks!"

Bessières was at the head of the column surrounding Bonaparte and he expedited my journey. The general beamed all over his face. "Ah, my resilient little Scotsman you have returned and with a scar to impress the girls eh." Then he became serious. "What news?"

"The Regent has the letters from the Austrians. They agree and the Venetians have surrendered. You need not to attack."

He leaned into me. "Confidentially I had no intention of attacking. Who would attack a city where the roads are made of water? I am not stupid. If I can win a war by diplomacy, then so much the better. These letters with the Imperial seal will be useful in any future bargains with Austria too. Now you go and see the surgeon. You have done well for me, again!"

I was soon stitched together again and I rode back to the head of the column. I did not want to be alone. My comrades were the vanguard and I would join them. I passed through the infantry battalions who looked at this Italian dandy riding through their columns. I heard their disparaging comments and smiled. I noted their regiment. I would return when in uniform and embarrass them. I caught up with the colonel. He looked genuinely pleased to see me but a little concerned that I was alone.

"Don't worry sir, the other three are safe and guests in the

Doge's palace. They are all living well."

"I know the general thinks highly of you and Jean but I prefer my men with me. It is generally safer with the regiment than performing well… I don't actually know what you have been up to." He looked at me expectantly.

"And we can't really say, sir. What I will say is that the results of our adventure are that not one of the soldiers in this column will die today in a battle to take Venice."

For the first time since I had ridden Killer, I saw a look of surprise on Albert's face. "Then I salute you, Scotsman. That is an achievement worthy of the highest medal."

The general halted us outside the city. He and his Guides rode in to accept the formal surrender of the city. It was the middle of May and the war looked to be over. There were no enemies left to fight.

CHAPTER 15

We spent the summer close to Golfe Juan. I think General Bonaparte rewarded the regiment for what we had done. No-one complained; Pierre least of all. The beautiful little port just across the bay from Les Ils de Marguerite was as perfect a spot as you could wish for. We used the sea to condition our horses and bring them back to full health after two years of constant campaigning. Killer had had a month off but he still benefited. It also enabled us to train our new recruits. We now had three squadrons and could muster five hundred men. It was a long way from the dark days of the Netherlands three years earlier. We had promotions too. Captain Roux had died and so the three captains were Jean, Claude, and, most surprising of all, me. I heard that Bonaparte had insisted but the colonel told me confidentially that he was more than happy to do so. With Francois and Charles promoted to sergeant and Sous-lieutenant respectively, the general had rewarded, at no cost to himself, the four men who had made him such a hero of the Directory. He could do as he wished. We heard, as we enjoyed the warm Mediterranean climate, that he had become a Consul. We did not know then what it meant but we were told it meant he had more power. I wondered what effect that would have on the man who seemed to crave power and glory.

Our sojourn ended in October when we made our way back into Italy and thence to the Venetian Republic and Campo Formio where the peace treaty was to be signed. We had been chosen because we were the closest cavalry regiment and Bonaparte liked the symmetry of it. We had been there at the start of the negotiations and we were to be there at the end. We received new uniforms before we left with the new style shako. My pigtails and queue had regrown and I felt quite dashing in a new captain's uniform riding at the head of my squadron. All the way through the new republics we were greeted as heroes. Girls would throw flowers at the troopers in an attempt to lure them down for a kiss. The colonel had no time for such nonsense and we rode with straight backs and serious demeanour. It seemed to enhance our attraction.

Once we reached Venetian land it changed. There were no smiles and only scowls. Food and drink became in short supply and we were treated like lepers. I could understand it. They had given in without a fight. The red-blooded Venetians would not suffer that disgrace.

When we reached the town of Campo Formio, we could see Austrian Dragoons as well as infantry. They too were dressed for a parade. After we had camped Jean and I were summoned to Bonaparte's headquarters where we met the count and the Regent again. It was a private meeting and was a measure of the respect Bonaparte had for the other two.

"These two gentlemen insisted that you be present. They both tell me that without your intervention and resourcefulness we would have had a war to fight." He pointed at my healed scar. "That was well earned."

The count came to shake our hands. "I am sorry I was not able to stop the attempts on your lives from my countrymen but I fear it was they who should have been afraid. Your skills belie your age."

We both nodded. It is hard to take compliments, especially when you do not feel that you have earned them.

The general said, "This is a great day for our three countries. It guarantees peace in Europe and you two young men had a great deal to do with that. As a reward, I am issuing the two of you a month-long furlough. You have deserved it."

Jean shook his head. "No General Bonaparte, we just did our duty."

"Nonetheless I insist that you take the furlough as I have plans for next year and you two, as well as the rest of your regiment, are key components." He was still smiling but there was steel beneath the words. He would not take no for an answer.

"In that case, we will take our leave."

As we left, I asked, "Where will we go?"

He shrugged, "I don't know. Let us sleep on it."

The colonel and the others were envious of our furlough. "It is not fair," I said, "Tiny and Charles took the same chances as we did but they have not been rewarded."

Albert shook his head, "As it was you two who had your lives threatened three times, I believe it was you who were in the greatest danger. Besides the two young men would not begrudge you a leave. Where will you take it?"

"We don't know."

In the end, our destination was decided for us, by Napoleon himself. He arrived the next day in his carriage. He sought us both out. "Why have you not obeyed my orders? This is no place for a furlough."

Jean then made one of the few mistakes I can ever recall him making; he spoke the truth. "I am sorry sir, we haven't decided where we will go."

"Good then you will come to me in my carriage and we will go to Paris." He waved his hands at our faces. "I think this is a wonderful idea. We can talk on the way and you will enjoy Paris at this time of year. Besides, it will allow me to show you off to some of the old men of politics who never leave Paris. It will do them good to see real heroes for a change."

Our chests were loaded aboard his carriage and we sat with the general. He looked up from his writings. "I work when we travel. Amuse yourselves!"

He did just that. As the carriage raced through France, with regular changes of horses, the tireless general read, wrote and contemplated the whole way. It did not bother Jean or me. We watched out of the window or we slept. There were no stops, we just kept on going. The occasional stops for food or our toilet were brief and functional. We did not mind. We had not expected the journey but now that we were on it, we would enjoy it.

When we reached Paris, just after dawn on a damp October morning the general said, "There are rooms for you arranged. The coach will take you there. Let the hotel know where you will be for if I need you then I expect you to be on hand."

This was not so much a furlough as a tour with the new Consul of France. The hotel was close to the Rue St Honore and the Place de La Revolution but time had softened the raw wound of my father's death. We left the hotel to find some food. The whole city was filled with a Napoleonic fervour. The new treaty and his successes in Italy had made him something like a god. If the crown was an elective then he would have been crowned king, that much was obvious. We wandered over to the Sorbonne and the left bank. Whilst being fervently left wing it had some lively restaurants serving good food at a reasonable price.

We were just crossing the Pont Neuf when we heard a voice, "Sir! Is it you?"

We looked down. Julian, the son of the gardener from my father's estate was staring at Jean. He had no legs and was a beggar. Jean knelt down. "Julian! What happened?"

"It was Rivoli sir. We charged some guns and I was hit by a cannonball. More of my fellows would have died if it were not for you and your brave chasseurs. Your charge saved many lives. Thank you."

"But not you."

"Is this the way the Revolution treats its heroes?" I was angry.

Julian said, "Ssh. There are many more like me." He smiled at me. "You have the same compassion your mother had. My father and I adored her." Suddenly he slapped his forehead. "I would forget my own head. When I went through my father's papers, I found this, it is a letter to you from Madame Lefondre." He handed me a crudely written letter. While I read it, Jean

188

counted out a large number of coins and handed them to Julian. I heard him try to refuse them but I did not take the words in. The content of the letter was too shocking.

'Robbie,

I have kept this secret until now and I fear for my life. Guiscard is the only one I can trust to get this letter to you. Your mother was murdered by Mama Tusson. She slowly fed her poison and made your mother's end painful.

It took me some time to work it out and when I confronted her with it, she threatened me. God forgive me but she threatened to have you killed. I knew she was capable of such a thing for she is truly evil and I kept my mouth shut. I should not and I will rot in hell for that. I wanted to tell you after your mother died but I was afraid for she had a hold on the count and he would do whatever she wanted.

After your mother died, I made sure that she had no chance to hurt you. I cooked all your food and watched to see that the witch came nowhere near it.

I am writing this letter as I fear for my life. Beware the black witch. She is evil.

I am sorry Robbie, I let you down and your dear mother. May God forgive me.

Jeanne Lefondre'

Jean saw my face and I handed the letter to him. He read it and then put his arm around me. "She killed them all. The evil bitch."

I became cold. I knew she had killed my mother but it had been hearsay before now and here was the proof in my hand. After all this time it was somehow even more shocking. Jean was right and all of the innocents she had killed must be avenged but first I had to deal with the living. I reached into my money belt and took out two gold coins. I gave them to Julian. "Buy yourself an inn. We will be going to Breteuil. There will be one there."

"Sir, I cannot take more money. The captain has given me more than enough."

"Soldier of France, would you disobey an order from a superior officer? Take the money."

He hesitated and then wrapped his fingers around the coins. Jean nodded his approval and then said, "We will need a wagon." He knelt down and picked up the crippled soldier. "Tonight, you stay with us."

He stayed in our rooms but we were not with him. When we reached the hotel there was a messenger from Bonaparte. There was a soiree at the Palais de Luxembourg and our presence was requested. Whilst we did not wish to go, we could not afford to offend the little general. We changed and attended.

The soiree was boring. They were not soldiers they were politicians living vicariously on the exploits of soldiers. We smiled and told our stories. We left enough gaps in the story of Vienna and Venice for the more intelligent to make the connections and the ones who were mentally challenged asked the others. At the end of the evening, Bonaparte congratulated us. "You did well, as I knew you would."

"And now, general, we must beg leave to finish our furlough in Breteuil. Events have come to light which necessitates our presence there."

His keen eyes bored into us and then he nodded, "Very well. Take care. I have plans for you."

We almost ran from the Palais, glad to be away from that nest of vipers. Once back in the hotel we packed and began to make plans. We had twenty-seven days of our furlough left. We were under no illusions. If we did not return then we would be shot as deserters. We had to avenge the dead.

We had plenty of money. Bonaparte had been generous with his expenses and we had been frugal. We hired guards, drivers and a wagon as we headed north. Julian was not happy that we had given him so much money. I clambered in the back of the wagon and gave Killer a rest.

"Julian, I have lost many comrades and seen others who have been severely wounded as you have. We are giving the money to you as a symbol of all of the wounded and the dead. Use the money wisely and emerge from this tragedy stronger. You are what the revolution is all about. And if not for that, then for the kindness shown to me, by your father, and Madame Lefondre. I can do little for them but I can for you."

He seemed satisfied and I could concentrate on deciding what we would do once we reached Breteuil. We stayed some miles from the chateau in the small hamlet of Frossy. We found rooms in the inn; in the old days, it had been a popular stopping off point between Calais and Paris. We sent the drivers and guards back to Paris and set off for the town and estate we knew so well, Breteuil. We were chasseurs and we would scout. We had time aplenty to get the lie of the land. We also felt honour bound to do something for Julian.

The nearest large town was Amiens and, leaving Julian in the inn chatting to the owner about the pitfalls of owning an inn, we left to see what we could discover in the city. Both of us had visited Amiens before and knew it well. There were old soldiers around, normally begging, and they were a good source of information. It also made us feel better when we were able to give them money for the information. I suspect they felt less like beggars. A morning in the town gave us a clearer picture of life in Revolutionary France and Breteuil in particular.

Mama Tusson had become an important woman. Her lover from the Committee had mysteriously died but, as the soldier who gave us the information told us, he would have died in one of the many purges anyway. Mama Tusson had played on the Revolutionary idea of equality. She claimed she had been victimised and persecuted because of her colour. She blackened my father's name by accusing him of rape. I knew for certain that was not true. She had murdered my mother as a rival for my father's bed. She was now the representative of Breteuil and ran that small town. She had also spread her web further and had much influence ion Amiens. Some of the soldiers who spoke to us kept looking fearfully over their shoulders.

We had some food in a tavern and asked about businesses. We were directed to a young lawyer, Francois Latour. He was young and earnest. His office was Spartan and small; business could not be that good. Even as we were talking to him, I wondered how he had avoided the draft. We explained what we were looking for. He nodded sympathetically. "I think I can find one or two but not in Breteuil. If you wish to buy there then you have to go through Madame Tusson's representative, Gregor Savinsky." He lowered his voice, "He came here last year from Russia and he has become a very powerful lawyer and businessman. He handles all the business affairs of Madame Tusson. I warn you to steer clear of him. He has an office on the next street. Avoid it. He is a dangerous man. I do not do this to gain business for myself but I can see that you are soldiers of France and I would not wish harm to come to you."

Jean smiled and nodded, "We can look after ourselves."

"That may be true on the battlefield but this Savinsky has surrounded himself with a veritable army of thugs; all of them foreign. I suspect they are deserters. There are Austrians, Hanoverians even some British. Be careful."

"We will. Now we will return again tomorrow. If you could have some properties for us to examine, we would be grateful."

"It will be my pleasure. I will try to get one as close to Breteuil as possible but I am not hopeful. The spider spins her web wide these days."

As we rode back, we spoke of the problems. "This will not be as easy as we thought eh Jean?"

"I, for one, never thought that it would be easy. What is so difficult now?"

"The thugs this Russian has hired."

"They are deserters. Remember Robbie, they are the soldiers who fled before us. We are the ones they should fear."

"But there are only two of us."

"They do not know we are coming and who knows the land around here better than us? No one. We use the skills your father drilled into us and those we have learned as soldiers." He gave me an appraising look, "You have come on since we joined the army. I would gladly have you watching my back and I know that all the others in the regiment feel the same. Even Old Albert trusts your skill and judgement. It is time you did. You have inherited much from your father; his skills with weapons and his strength but from your mother, you have gained other traits equally valuable. You are clever, inventive and loyal. Believe me, the thugs would fear us if they knew that we were coming."

Julian and the innkeeper had got on like a house on fire and were firm friends. We were the only guests and Jacques, the innkeeper, joined us after we had eaten. He had been wounded in the campaign in the Low Countries but he had only lost an eye. He now had a glass one. He was a joker and when he went for some more ale, he took out the eye and left it on the table, when I asked why he joked, "To keep an eye on you."

Old soldiers have a way of mocking themselves which would put many politicians to shame. They know that life is too short to take yourself as seriously as they appeared to. When he returned with the wine he said, "I know who you two are. They have been looking for you for the past few years. There were posters offering a reward." He saw the looks on our faces. "Do not worry. Your secret is safe with me. That Madame Tusson is evil and those she wishes dead usually end up that way."

"Why does she want me dead?"

"Because you are the legitimate heir to the estate. The only other one who still lives from that time is your friend here, Jean, should the king return then you would gain the estate."

Jean nodded, "That makes sense. In fact, if you went to the courts it could well be that they might look sympathetically upon you. You were illegitimate and oppressed. You would have a good case. It seems to me that this spider and her web are fragile. She controls Breteuil but so long as you are alive then you would be the wind to destroy her world."

"Julian tells me that you know this General Bonaparte. What

is he like? We heard he brought order to Paris last year and he is undefeated in Italy."

Jean looked at me, "Go on Robbie, you are the one with the words. What is he like?"

"He appears to be a small man but when you speak with him it is you who feels small. He is tireless. We travelled from the south of France to Paris and I never saw him sleep. He is totally ruthless and yet the soldiers love him." I looked at Julian. "You fought under him is it not true?"

"It is. Before he came to the army, we thought we would be defeated each time we fought. He gave us belief and we all fought harder for him. He was always visible on the battlefield and you knew where he was."

"That is true. But he is ambitious. He is now in Paris and if I were the other members of the Directory, I would be afraid. He will not be content with life as a mere general. He wants the world."

We returned the next day to Amiens and our young lawyer had found a tavern in Marseille-en-Beauvaisis. It was just five miles from Breteuil. We gave the money to the lawyer and left the negotiation in his hands. He did issue a warning however, "The Russian wanted this tavern too. Fortunately, I knew the owner. He was a friend of my father's and he was happier to sell to us rather than the Black Widow."

"The Black Widow?"

He smiled. "It is the nickname of Madame Tusson. Her mates have a habit of dying quite soon after they meet her. There is a tropical spider which has the same habit. It seems appropriate. If you return tomorrow, I should have the deeds and the bill of sale."

Jean shook his hand. "Thank you and be careful. We would not like you to fall foul of this Russian."

"That is thoughtful but I can look after myself."

"It is time to find our new enemy Robbie. We will go to the centre of Amiens and approach this Savinsky from the other direction. Just in case they are watching our young friend. The walk enabled us to familiarise ourselves with the geography of the town. As we approached the office of the Russian, we could see the man stationed on the street corner to watch for strangers. It identified the office quite clearly. On the opposite side was a boulangerie. We crossed the street and went in. While I bought two baguettes Jean checked out the office.

As I paid Jean said, "Is there a lawyer close by? We are keen to buy some property in the area."

The baker said, "There is one across the street but I would avoid him. It is far better to go around the corner to young Francois Latour. He is young but honest."

"Meaning the one across the street is not."

"I did not say that and I would be grateful if you did not give voice to your suspicions on the street. I have to live here and those three men you can see across the street all work for him."

We both looked at the four men and stored their faces in our memory. We would know them again. "Thank you, sir and we will be as silent as the grave."

We left and walked down the street, assiduously avoiding all glances across the road. We could feel the eyes of the sentries staring after us. As we rode back to Frossy we detoured to pass close by Breteuil. We could pass the front gates which led to the main house. It was another way to get to Frossy and we would appear to be normal travellers. As we passed the gates, we saw another two guards. They had the look of violent men and they stared malevolently at us as we passed. We tipped our hats as we rode by and were rewarded with a scowl. When we were out of earshot Jean said, "That is at least six men. We can assume there will be replacements for the evening and others inside. I would estimate there are twelve men for us to deal with."

"And how will we deal with them?"

In answer, Jean posed me a problem, "Suppose we were hunting a boar. How would we achieve that?"

"The first thing would be to isolate it from the rest and lure it into a trap."

"And that is how we will deal with these deserters. We will

tackle them one by one."

"Won't that make them suspicious?"

"Yes, and worried; all of which will give us the advantage. We need them to close up around their leader. We want them to think it is the Russian we target and not the Black Widow. Once they are looking close to him it will enable us to get close to her."

When we returned with Julian to the lawyer's office all the paperwork was done. Francois gave us the money he had not used. "You did take your fee?"

Francois smiled, "Of course. I am a business albeit an honest one. Did you visit the baker on the next street yesterday?"

"Yes, why? Some of Savinsky's thugs paid him a visit and asked what you had wanted. They visited me later on and asked had I two new clients who were new to Amiens. Be careful. He knows of you now and he will be wondering about you. I would avoid that street in future."

I detected some criticism in his voice. Jean did too. "I am sorry for the attention but we had to find out who his men were. Now we know we can begin to plan." He leaned forward and lowered his voice. "If it is any consolation, I believe that his power will begin to wane soon."

"Listen my friends I should warn you. The Russian and his woman are suspected of many crimes. People have disappeared. Bodies have appeared. Young girls and boys are taken to his house and... well, it beggars belief. I implore you to be careful and do not underestimate either of them. The world would be better off without them but they have the power around here and they cannot be hurt."

I shook him by the hand, "Thank you for your concern but we know what we are doing. Trust us."

We hired a cart and left for the inn. On the way, we used the excess money to stock up with food and wines. We also managed to buy a wheelchair. Julian had used crutches but the wheelchair would be more comfortable. Julian had learned from his new friend at Frossy where he could acquire a regular source of good ale. The land to the north, the land of the Belgians was noted for its beer and now that it was the Batavian Republic, they were keen to do business with the French Republic.

The tavern had a good position on the main street. The man next door was expecting us and he had been paid by the owner to keep an eye on the place. He was pleased that there were new owners. "We have had some very suspicious looking men eyeing up the place. They looked like deserters to me."

So, the Russian's men had been scouting too. It was a warning to us to keep our eyes open. The tavern was dusty but it was furnished. That had been a worry. We spent the morning dusting and cleaning. Soldiers learn to keep their barracks spotless and we were three old soldiers. The wheelchair enabled Julian to move around much easier. We found a living room at the back next to the kitchen and Jean and I brought the old bed down from upstairs. Julian was in a positive mood, "When I hire some workers, I can use the rooms upstairs for customers."

The stables at the back were in good condition and we could see that we had managed to get a bargain. "What about a name?"

The lopsided sign hanging forlornly from the front wall was faded but it showed that it had been called 'The Grapes'. "Will it be 'The Grapes' again?"

"No, I thought 'The Chasseur'. It sounds classier and is a thank you to you two."

That pleased us. We stayed the night with Julian. "We are about our business now. We will not return here until our business is done. We would not embroil you any further."

"But I am involved."

"Yes, we know but you cannot evade danger as we can. Have you any help coming?"

"Aye, the man next door knows of a couple of girls in the village who are looking for work. I will be fine." He grinned, "I lost only my legs, not my remarkably good looks!"

As we left, I was confident that Guiscard's son would survive. Many others would have allowed the loss of legs to deprive them of a normal life. To Julian, they were an inconvenience and would not prevent him from living life to the full.

CHAPTER 16

We returned the cart to Amiens and then began to set our plan in motion. We changed our appearance by wearing working clothes rather than the fine ones we had hitherto. Francois let us leave our good clothes and effects in his office. Jean had worked out that the deserters and guards would drink and eat close to the office and they would choose somewhere they felt comfortable. We found the bar almost immediately. We went in and bought the cheapest wine they had. It was rough and it was potent. We sat in the corner and Jean smoked a pipe. We waited. Eventually, two of the guards came in and ordered food and ale. They sat close by as the bar had filled up. As they began to speak, I suddenly realised that they were English. It should have been obvious as their accents when they spoke French, were abysmal.

After their food arrived and Jean and I spoke French they relaxed and began to open up to each other. "I thought we would have made more money than we have Jack."

"Listen, mate, this is early days yet. We have only been here for six months. We eat, we drink, and we get to kick lumps out of the Russian's enemies so relax. It's better than being back with the Old Duke of York. There are no sergeant majors flogging us and we don't sleep in a field."

"Yeah I know but we haven't seen much coin have we?"

"True but we can always go into business for ourselves. The frog, Andre, he spotted those two toffs in the street yesterday;

he reckoned they looked soft as. Now there must be a load like that. When we are off duty tonight, we will wander the streets. We find a couple of likely victims and rob them blind. Old Andre might like to come along too. He knows the town."

The other one brightened up at the prospect of becoming robbers. "Aye all right."

After they had gone, I told Jean what they had said. He had picked up some of the words but their accent was not one which facilitated understanding by someone who was not fluent. We discussed what we ought to do. "If we could get rid of three of his men it would make things easier for us. These are his town guards, obviously."

"But, Jean, there are three of them."

"I know. I had hoped it would just be two but we need to take our opportunities when they arise. We only have two or three more weeks and that includes the journey back to Golfe Juan."

"I'm game. How do we play this?"

"We use you as bait. If they think you are alone it will make them more confident. Hopefully, it will make them overconfident. We just need to find a nice little place for an ambush."

We found a quiet street off the Rue Conde and close to the cathedral. At night time the cathedral grounds were empty. The beggars and the worshippers had left. It was also the route to the bridge across the river. Jean could wait in the shadow of the cathedral. It was where I would ambush someone if I was a criminal.

I returned to Francois' office alone and changed into my fine clothes. He was curious but he said nothing save, "Be careful. These are dangerous men."

"Do not worry Francois; we have met men far more dangerous than these men. If they were worth worrying about, they would have stayed in the army. They deserted and that shows that they are afraid. Jean and I are not."

He nodded, "Good luck, my friend."

Jean was waiting close to a better quality inn just along from the Russian's office. I had acquired a cane with a metal head.

It was the sort of thing a young man about town would have and it helped my disguise. I walked slowly along the street and marched deliberately towards the clutch of men on the street. I knew that they were guards but the character I was playing did not and so, I passed them I tipped my hat and said, "Good afternoon." They touched their caps but I saw two of the men from the tavern and saw the voracious grins which appeared. They were nibbling the bait. I continued to walk down the road, quite slowly. I paused at the end of the street as though trying to get my bearings but, in reality, checking to see if I was being followed. It was the one called Jack. When he had spoken in the bar, I got the impression that he was the leader.

I played the part of a young man about time who was bored and rich. As we entered a slightly more prosperous part of town I went into a couple of expensive shops. I did not buy but I made a point of holding my purse in my hand. I then walked back towards the tavern we had chosen. It was a street away from the Russian's office. Jean was lounging by the street corner smoking a pipe. I ignored him. I studied the menu; it was expensive. Then I entered. I took a table by the window so that Jean could see me and I could see Jack. I ordered a bottle of wine and then studied the menu. I saw my follower watch for a moment and then disappear. He was going for help. I took my time eating the meal. I only drank half of the wine but I made sure the bottle was almost empty by pouring some of it down my jacket. I was sure the waiter would finish the rest. I wanted them to think I was drunk.

As the light faded and dusk fell, I saw Jack and his two companions reappear. They spread themselves out to cover all the exits. Jean had become invisible to them for he had not moved. When I paid the bill, he disappeared. It was our signal. Now it depended upon me and my ability to make them follow me.

I thanked the owner and then stepped somewhat unsteadily into the street. I made good use of the stick. I wanted them to think that I was drunk. I staggered one way, away from the cathedral and then stopped as though I had realised, I was going the wrong way. I turned around and almost bumped into them. They looked startled but I smiled and gave my apologies. They would have smelled the alcohol on my jacket and thought that it was a sign of my drunkenness. I lead them circuitously through well-populated streets until I came to the cathedral. It looked dark and sinister and it was deserted. I, of course, knew where Jean waited and I headed for the cathedral door as though I was going to enter. When I reached it, I tried the door and then turned left to walk next to the medieval building. I could hear their steps crunching on the gravel as they closed with me. I passed Jean in the shadows and then leaned against the wall as though I was going to be sick. The one called Jack had got ahead of me and he stood with a short sword in his hand. I recognised the blade as the type issued to artillerymen. That was a good sign. He would not be competent with it.

His French had not improved since lunchtime. "Hand over your purse and you might live."

"How dare you!" I raised myself to my full height. He did not notice that I had turned the stick so that the ferrule end was in my hand. "Out of my way, ruffian!"

Just then the one called Andre spoke behind me. "There are three of us and we don't mind slitting your throat. But we would rather let you live and then sell your clothes."

Jean stepped out and stabbed Andre through the heart. I swung the stick at the surprised Jack and smacked him on the head making him stagger backwards. The second Englishman must have had a club for I was struck hard from behind and I fell forwards. As I stumbled, I reached into my boot and pulled my stiletto out. The one called Jack shook his head to clear it and then roared as he leapt at me. I used the stick to deflect the sword which was aimed at my throat and then stabbed upwards with the knife. It slid into his gut and he groaned as he slid to the ground. Behind me, I heard the death gasp as Jack finished off the man who had clubbed me.

"You alright Robbie?"

Yes. He just winded me and I will have a bruise in the morning.

Nothing to worry about."

The one called Jack was still alive. "Question him, Robbie. Find out how many other men he has."

I spoke in English and his eyes popped open as I did so. "You are dying. Is there anyone you want me to tell?"

"You're a Jock!"

"Yes, I am Scottish."

"You spoke like a frog!"

"I know. Is there anyone?"

He wheezed. "No, there's no one bothered about me." He coughed a little blood up. "You are quick, I'll give you that."

"How many more men does the Russian have?"

Even in his pain, his mind was working, "So that's your little game eh? You want to rob the Russian. Well, good luck to you." He had a spasm of coughing and I thought for a moment that he had expired but he opened his eyes. "No skin off my nose. He's a tight bastard. There are twelve of us." He suddenly laughed and more blood came out. "There were twelve including him. There's just nine now." He shook his head and his eyes closed. "The bastard better watch..." and then he died.

I stood, "We had better get out of here before someone comes." As we fled the scene I said, "There are nine left, including the Russian."

Jean nodded, "Slightly better odds than I had hoped. We will have to find another ruse to lower the odds." We had worked out that there were six plus the Russian in Amiens; that left five at the chateau.

We were up early the next day in our working clothes rather than our fine clothes. My jacket smelled like a vinery and would have to be cleaned before I could wear it again. We walked down the street and entered the boulangerie. This time we pretended to be working men and asked for one baguette. It was a woman serving and she paid us no mind. As we left, I could see that there were no guards but I could see shapes in the upstairs room and there sounded to be a heated argument. We took ourselves down the street and divided the baguette. We each ate half as though we had not eaten for a week. A few moments later three guards came out of the office. One stood at the end of the corner while a second lounged on the pavement. The third disappeared down the street.

My stomach told me it was midday when the third man returned with two other men. I recognised one from the chateau. "We have him worried Robbie. Now it is our turn to do the stalking. We will follow them tonight and see where they live. If we take out another two then he will be forced to bring most of his men from the chateau. We will eat where those men ate yesterday. We may be lucky."

As it turned out we were not lucky. They did not eat there. Towards dusk, we returned to the office and waited. The light in the upstairs room was doused and the Russian came out. Flanked by his five men they marched down the street. Anyone who got in their way was pushed aside and they stared at all those who approached them as potential attackers. We had them worried. Their belligerent attitude helped us as they never looked behind them. They crossed the bridge and went to a large house standing alone. The Russian went in after speaking to the men. Three went in with him while the other two walked back towards us. We followed them at a distance. Once they had crossed the bridge we sped up and soon caught them as they passed an alleyway close to the cathedral. We went to overtake them but one of them grabbed Jean's arms as we passed them.

"What is your game? I have seen you before." Jean was dragged into the alley.

I saw that there was no one near and, as the second man tried to grab me, I head-butted him. He fell against his companion and they fell, along with Jean to the ground. I saw the man who had grabbed Jean pull a long knife from his boot. It looked wickedly sharp. I kicked at it. Although he retained hold of it, I knew that I had numbed his arm. The second man pulled his knife. It was too narrow a space to evade him and I grabbed my stiletto just as he stabbed at me. That was a mistake. My weapon could only stab but he could have used his knife like a sabre and slashed at me. I grabbed his hand and stabbed at his throat with my blade. He grabbed my hand and we fell over Jean and the other man who were grappling on the floor. I looked into the man's eyes and saw fear. He thought I could beat him and that gave me extra strength. I pushed harder. I had the advantage now as my blade had a better point. He tried to push me but my left hand is as strong as my right. I kept pushing and I saw the fear fill his face. He began to mutter, "No, please! Please!"

He should have concentrated on holding me for suddenly his resistance ended and the stiletto went through his eye and into his brain. He died without a sound and without any blood. I stood and looked for Jean. He too was standing. "Let us get out of here. I think our time in Amiens is done."

We went back to the hotel and packed, paid our bill and left. We rode straight for Julian and his inn. I suspected that there might be a hue and cry after another two deaths on top of the first three. The inn was in darkness. We knocked on the door. I saw a light from under the door. Jean said, "Julian, it is us; Jean and Robbie."

I heard a mumbled conversation and then the bolts on the door opened and a young woman with a sheet around her shoulders stood there. She smiled and said, "Julian said you are friends. I am Monique. Put your horses in the stable."

"Off you go Robbie. I will open the back door."

I walked through the arch which led to the yard. I could see that Julian had been busy. It was swept clean and the stables now had a working door. I took off the saddles, rubbed the horses down and fed them. I then went to the back door which was open. Jean met me. "We can go straight to our room." He grinned, "Julian is a little occupied."

As we prepared for bed, he told me of his conversation with Julian. Monique, it turned out, was an orphan and was happy to be a live-in servant. However, the mutual attraction meant that that arrangement lasted less than a night. It looked like fate was smiling at last on our friend.

We put on working clothes and took our weapons as we

headed for Breteuil. We reached there as dawn broke and we waited in the hedgerow opposite the main gate. There were two men on guard and they had a brazier going to keep them warm. We had been there for some time when he heard the galloping of hooves and four riders approached. It was the Russian and his men. They paused at the gate and then entered. The two guards suddenly looked more vigilant.

We backed into the woods. "I think we were too successful. We have frightened him to the arms of the Black Widow."

"So, we have failed?"

"No. We merely have to change direction. We know the estate and we know where the guards are. If we were on campaign when would we attack an enemy who was camped?"

"I would do it just before they change guards when they are tired and ready for their bed."

"Which is what we will do. We will head back to Julian's and we will prepare for tonight."

Our swords would be of no use at night and so we made small clubs and took knives. We also took some hanks of rope. We tied the horses to a tree in the woods and made our way towards the gate. We went to the right of the gate and slipped out where the road curved and we were hidden from view. The fire was burning low which was a sure sign that their shift was almost over. They would not do the work of the others. If they were chasseurs then they would as we were all on the same side. These were deserters with no allegiance to each other at all. They were in it for the money. It was that type of greed which had caused three of their colleagues to die already.

We made our way along the wall. Trees overhung it and the leaves had not all fallen. The undergrowth also afforded us cover. The two men made it easy for us as they huddled around the warmth of the brazier. They were oblivious to all behind them. I could almost hear their conversation. They would be wondering what they would be eating. They would be anticipating a drink. They would be looking forward to a warm fire.

We could both move silently when we wished. We crept up

behind them and struck them both a blow on the back of the head. We were not gentle and they collapsed in a heap. We disarmed them and trussed them up like a piece of meat. We took off their breeches and their shoes and put them in the fire. A man without breeches is less brave. They had a pistol each and we added them to the brace we carried. By our reckoning, there should just be the Russian and five men inside the chateau. We were entering a building we knew like the back of our hands.

Once through the gates, we ran towards the house. Any sign of a sudden light would alert us to someone coming out but no-one did. We halted next to the climbing rose which clambered up the wall close to the back door. Suddenly we heard the noise of a door opening. "Don't forget to relieve us early tomorrow. This is a long shift! We did one yesterday."

"Well it's not my fault that the others got themselves killed is it?"

"Yeah well, there is someone out there with a grudge against the boss that is for certain."

Two of the voices had a Germanic accent but we had no time for further thought as the light went out and we heard the crunch of footsteps on the gravel as the two guards came from the servant's entrance. We were dressed in dark clothing and pressed against the wall as they came along. We were almost invisible. One of them must have sensed something as he half turned. Our clubs were ready and the two of them crashed to the gravel. We did the same as with the other two guards and pocketed two more pistols. We were now well endowed with pistols.

We crept to the back window and peered in. There were no men but there were four women there. One looked to be crying. In one movement we stepped in and held our fingers to our lips.

"We mean you no harm. Would you like to leave?"

The one crying said, "We would love to but we will be beaten if we do."

Jean shook his head, "No, you will not. The guards are taken care of." He took out the handful of coins we had taken from the guards. "Here take this as payment. There are better places to earn a living."

As they began to leave, I asked, "How many more servants are there and how many guards?"

"Two guards in the house and no other servants. They all left or they were..." The one crying held a cloth to her mouth and fled.

There were no more innocents left in the house and we each took out two pistols and left the kitchen. I assumed that the other two guards would not be in the grander quarters but there was a small servant's hall with a fire and a range. We headed for it. Our luck had held until then but it ended when one of the two guards decided to leave the hall. Jean and I were framed in the hallway. The man was quick and he pulled at his pistol. Jean fired both of his guns and the guard flew back into the hall. The second man fired blindly through the door and a splinter from the door struck Jean on the cheek. I kicked the door open and fired both barrels as soon as I saw the figure advancing with the musketoon. I kicked the lifeless body to make sure he was dead.

"What's that?" The accent was Russian. We discarded the pistols and took two more from our belts. The Russian appeared at the top of the stairs. Behind him was Mama Tusson. The Russian carried a brace of pistols.

"What are you doing in my house?"

"I think you will find the house belongs to my young friend here. He is the son of the Count of Breteuil."

Suddenly Mama Tusson spat out, "Kill them, Gregor! They are the ones who killed your men!"

Jean said, "We killed your men when they attacked us. Your guards are trussed up outside. We had no quarrel with you. Take your men and go. Leave Amiens and find somewhere else to ply your trade. You have damaged enough lives here."

He smiled, "I think you overestimate your own abilities. Besides this is now my home and I do not intend to flee because a couple of nobodies ask me to." Even as he was speaking, he was bringing his guns up and squeezing the triggers. Had we not been soldiers then his speedy action might have succeeded but we had quick reactions and we both moved to the side, firing our own weapons as we did so. The smoke from six pistols made a fog so thick that you could see nothing. It made us both cough. The discharges in the confined space had been so loud that my ears were ringing. I looked around for Jean and saw him standing on the stairs reloading one of his pistols. I did the same. By the time we were reloaded the smoke had cleared and the Russian lay on the stairs his chest ripped open by the force of the balls. Mama Tusson lay at a strange angle behind him. We slowly mounted the stairs. One ball appeared to have gone through the Russian and struck her in the heart. As it had become flattened during its journey it had made a large hole and killed the Black Widow instantly.

We lit candles and began to search the house. We found many papers which told the story of the greed of the two of them. There were deeds to many properties in Breteuil. We also found boxes of jewellery. The Black Widow had obviously been something of a magpie taking pretty things from those that they abused. We placed the papers and the jewels in boxes; we had plans for those. I also found my father's signet ring. It was the one he used to seal documents. I suppose it was returned after he had been executed. The French Revolutionary bureaucrats could be quite proper at times.

We took the two bodies to the rear of the house. Dawn was beginning to break. We searched the house and the grounds. The most upsetting sight we discovered were the bodies of two young women. They did not look to be more than fourteen. From the state of their bodies, they had been used most foully before they had died. I had not regretted the killings but now my heart hardened and I regretted that the deaths had been so swift.

With loaded pistols, we went back to the four guards who had shivered into consciousness. While Jean covered them, I cut the tethers on their legs and we led the four of them to the bodies. Jean pointed to the dead girls. "Who did this?"

There was ice in his voice. The Hanoverian almost broke into tears. "It wasn't us I swear. The Russian he liked young girls and she liked to watch him."

"There were others?"

He nodded and pointed to a blackened area where a bonfire had been. "He had us burn their bodies."

"Where did he get the girls from?" I thought we might be able to find their parents.

He looked at the ground shamefaced. "The Russian had their parents killed and he took their property. They were all accused of being disloyal to France."

"By Mama Tusson?" The four of them nodded. "And you killed them." It was not a question but a statement.

"We had no choice."

I saw Jean's fingers tightening on the triggers. "Jean, they had been soldiers. They were obeying orders."

"But Robbie, killing unarmed civilians and letting," he pointed at the pathetic bodies unable to speak the words, "this happen; it is not right."

"I know but I for one have had enough of killing and I will not shoot four unarmed men."

The Hanoverian sobbed, "Thank you, sir."

"I do not do it for you, deserter and if we ever see you again then I will kill you on sight."

Jean looked at me and nodded. "You four get some wood we will burn these four bodies and then we can leave this charnel house."

We would have buried the girls but there would have been no one to visit the grave and neither of us could face the prospect of the bodies being dug up by foxes and further desecrated. We had buried comrades before and Jean said the right words as the two girl's bodies were consumed.

When the fire was dying down Jean faced the four men. "Find yourselves shoes and breeches. We will be leaving here in an hour. If we see you again, we will kill you." The coldness in his voice left them in no doubt of his intentions. Get as far away from here as you can."

They ran, still with their hands tied, towards the gate. "What do you think they will do Jean?"

"I think they are rats and they will find their own level. They will continue to do what they have done but they will find bigger rats who will consume them." He shrugged. "I suspect they will go back to the home and office of their former employer. I think he would have secreted money there." He pointed at the chests. "We will take these to Francois and let the lawyer deal with them."

We took the horses from the stables and hitched them to a wagon we found. We loaded my father's bed and a couple of chairs upon it. Julian could have the use from it. We went to the inn where he was delighted with his bounty. "If you wish to take anything else from the house then feel free. I think Robbie here is the rightful owner but I have no confidence that the courts would look favourably on him so we would prefer our friends to benefit. The cart and the horses are yours, a gift."

Francois read the letters and the papers. He sat back in his chair and his young face suddenly looked careworn. "This is a travesty. The two of them were evil, I knew that but their perfidy knows no bounds. They have used the Revolution as a tool to satisfy their own greedy ends." He pointed to the jewels. "What would you have me do with these?"

Jean spread his arms, "There is blood on them and we wish no part of them. We are soldiers and we go back to war. Use them as you see fit for, we both think you are a good man. Now that Gregor has gone there should be more clients for you. I would like you to make a claim on the estate for Robbie here."

"That could take years to go through the courts."

"I know but I suspect this war will go on for years and he is a young man. Soldiers only need money when they are old soldiers and of no use to anyone. Robbie is a long way shy of that."

"Good, just so long as you know. We will begin the paperwork now establishing Robbie's claim. I will have to use you for a witness." He looked at my hand. "Is that the ring of the De Breteuil's?"

"Yes. We found it in the chateau."

"Good, then you can use that to seal letters to me. I will know it is from you." He took a piece of parchment and began to write. Suddenly he looked up. "Did you know that five of the Russian's men were found dead in the town?"

Jean's face was impassive, "I did not know that Amiens had such an efficient rat catcher."

Francois gave a wry smile, "I am afraid that the rat catchers have finished their work but most citizens of Amiens are pleased with their efforts. Now let us get the names of all the parties correct, French courts are very particular."

When all was done and the papers signed and I had used my signet ring for the first time Francois leaned back. "Where can I contact you?"

"We will be returning to the army in Golfe Juan. Our furlough is up in ten days. We are with the 17th Chasseurs and General Bonaparte."

He looked impressed, "Then you should be easy to find." He held out his hand. "I am pleased to have met you and I will keep an eye on your friend the innkeeper. If he is a friend of yours then he is worth cultivating."

As we headed for Paris, I felt happier knowing that Julian was no longer alone. He had Monique, his innkeeper friend and Francois. He would be a beggar no longer. We could not help every old soldier but we had given one some hope at least.

CHAPTER 17

We had taken some coins from the chest to pay for our journey south. If we hired a small coach, we could make the journey as quickly south as we head north. We would also be able to sell our horses in Paris and leave us with money to spare. We reached Paris as dusk was descending upon the city. We stayed in a small hotel off the Rue St Honore. We had stayed there before and it was comfortable. After we had eaten, we strolled across the Seine to the Champ de Mars and Ecole Militaire. We were back in uniform now. We had discovered that, with the mass conscription, any healthy young man not in uniform risked questions from the police. It was a pleasant evening and we sat in one of the bars which overlooked the academy. We were joined by some Hussars in their gaudy red uniforms. They recognised ours and had heard of our success.

"You are lucky to have been with Bonaparte. We have been cooling our heels here in Paris while you have had all the glory in Italy."

I thought of Julian with no legs and the dead comrades we had left littering the battlefields of northern Italy but I said nothing. "Well, we are all at peace now. There is only Britain who is an enemy and until we have a fleet which can match them then we will have no more wars to fight."

"Ah yes but you and your regiment are, at least close to a potential enemy. Who do we get to fight in Paris? The mob when they turn ugly/"

"Yes, we heard that our general sorted the mob out on his last visit."

The lieutenant of hussars gave a wry laugh, "And even then, he used his cannons to disperse them."

His companion said, "It was effective. They did leave."

We laughed. We enjoyed the company of the two officers. We rarely got the opportunity to speak with other cavalrymen. As the eyes and ears of Bonaparte's army, we worked either with infantry or by ourselves. The two officers promised that they would look us up should they ever receive a posting to the south. Jean and I knew that it was unlikely that we would ever meet again.

We returned to our hotel. We would have to be up early the next day and seek a carriage to take us south. After our breakfast, we headed for the commercial side of the city where we negotiated a reasonable price for a carriage to take us home. When we returned to the hotel there were four policemen waiting for us.

Major Jean Bartiaux, Captain Robert Macgregor, you are under arrest. Come with us."

"What is the charge?" Jean was far calmer than I was feeling.

"The disappearance of Madame Tusson of Breteuil."

"And where are you taking us?"

The officer grinned, "To the Conciergerie!"

Even I had heard of this place; it was called the antechamber to the guillotine. Jean nodded calmly, "Before we go, we would like to pay our bill and make use of pen and paper. Do you object?"

I think the calmness of Jean took the officer by surprise and he stammered, "No, so long as you are quick."

He smiled and took the pen and paper. "Of course. Robbie, please pay the bill." He wrote two quick letters. "Have you some wax?" The man handed it over and Jean put a blob on each letter. "Robbie, your ring." I sealed the two letters. I saw that one was addressed to Francois and the other to General Bonaparte. He handed them to the hotel owner and gave him some coins. "Could you have these delivered, please? When we are released, I will bring the same amount. You have my word as an officer."

The owner gave him a sly look. "But what if you do not survive? It is the Conciergerie you go to is it not?"

Jean pointed to the name on the letter, "We have important friends. But if you do not send them then you will not receive the rest of the money. It is your choice. Please store our belongings until we return."

As we were led away my heart sank to my boots. I was not as confident as Jean. Once in the carriage, I turned to speak with him but he pressed his fingers to his lips and pointed to the two policemen sat opposite. He smiled at the officer, "How did you know where to find us?"

He smiled a reptilian smile. "Since the Revolution, every hotel has to send a list of its guests on a daily basis. When the warrant for your arrest arrived last night, we knew exactly where to look. This is not a country ruled by aristocrats any longer." He cast a disparaging look at my ring. "We now promote people for their ability and we have an efficient police force!"

The prison we were being taken to was the one they had used for all the important prisoners during the Terror. Marie Antoinette had spent her last days as a guest there. It was one of the oldest buildings in Paris and had been used as a barracks for the king's guards in times past. Since the Bastille had been demolished it had become the most secure prison in France.

Jean asked, "Does the prison governor still make his money from the prisoners."

"Yes, captain. I hope that you have kept enough money for your accommodation. The poorer sections are filled with lice-ridden paupers with more diseases than a hospital." His smile showed that he cared not a jot what our fate was to be. Jean just smiled at me.

When we reached the prison, I was struck by its solidity and its darkness. As soon as we left the street it was as though we had been plunged into a dark cavern. The prison governor did not appear quite as callous as the policemen. I suppose it is policemen all over the world. They have a little power and they like to use it to make up for other shortcomings. Had they been real men they would have been in the army and not skulking in Paris.

"I am sorry to see two officers of such a fine regiment placed in this position. Have you a lawyer?"

"We have sent word to our lawyer but he is in Amiens."

"Good." He gave an apologetic look. "Do you have money? If not..."

Jean had the money already. He placed fifteen livres on the table. "I assume the rate is still the same?"

"You wish to share a room?"

"My friend and I have shared many things on campaign. We will endure this hardship together."

He seemed pleased with the answer. He turned to the policeman. "You may leave us Inspector Javert." The policeman looked disappointed as he left. I don't know if he expected a cut from the governor. "An odious little man. I cannot bear to be in the same room as him." He nodded to the guard, "This guard will take you to your cell. He will explain the arrangements for food and other things." He smiled brightly, "Perhaps your stay here will be brief."

Jean smiled back. "You never know we may be innocent."

"I hope so but it makes no difference to me."

As we were taken down into the depths of the prison it felt like we were descending into hell. As we went lower, we heard moans, groans and tears. The two guards who escorted us kept their pistols cocked and ready. Had we wanted to escape we could not. The cell had two straw mattresses and a bucket.

"We let one of you out each morning to empty the bucket. When that it is emptied you can buy your first meal of the day. The last meal is in the evening."

"And how much does that cost?"

The older guard laughed, "It depends upon your purse, my friend."

When the door was closed, we just had the light from one cheap candle. Jean saw my despondent look. "This is not the end of the world Robbie. It is a setback. I am sure that Francois will be able to secure our freedom."

"But we are guilty!"

"Keep your voice down. The only ones who can prove our guilt are the deserters and they have more crimes on their conscience than we do."

"Then how did they know to arrest us?"

"The servants; they would have told others of their liberation and when the chateau was found empty then the local committee would have put two and two together. Remember Mama Tusson was part of the local committee. It is logical that she would have had friends and I daresay she shared her profits with them. With the two deaths then the Breteuil committee is poorer. The burden of proof is on them."

I was not as confident as Jean. That evening we paid a few sous for some stale bread and onion soup. In truth, neither of us was that hungry but we knew we had to keep our strength up. I was the one tasked with emptying the slops. I was escorted by the guard to a drain in the courtyard. There were other prisoners there. Some of them looked to be well off but many were in rags and coughing. I suspected they were the ones we had been warned about, with the diseases. Had we not had money, then that could have been us.

Francois arrived in the late afternoon. He gave an apologetic smile as he came in and the door was slammed behind him. "I am sorry it has come to this. I have entered letters to the court detailing the actions of Gregor Savinsky and Mama Tusson. Since their disappearance," I noticed how he stressed that word, "many people have emerged to make complaints and claims against the estate. It will do our case no harm. As the men who worked for him have disappeared whilst his home and office have been ransacked the consensus amongst the reasonable citizens is that there was a falling out and the perpetrators of the crime are his men. The fact that five of his men were found dead recently has added credence to the claim." He sighed, "That is the good news. The bad news is that the local committee is annoyed that it has lost a valuable source of income. They are pursuing their demands for your deaths at the highest level. It means there will not be a speedy end to your trials. You say you have written to General Bonaparte?" Jean nodded. "Good. That cannot hurt for he is the darling of the people at the moment." He seemed to see our surroundings for the first time. "Have you enough money?"

Jean smiled, "We have paid for this sumptuous room for a month and we can afford to stay for longer but..."

"But you hope for a speedy release. I quite understand. I am also pursuing Robert's claim for the estate and that may help our case. I have depositions from others who knew the count and your mother attesting to your claim. It is looking hopeful but I am afraid, not speedy."

The guard rapped on the door. "I think the guard is telling you that your time is up Francois. Thank you for coming."

"No, it is I who should thank you. Since Savinsky's disappearance, I have had so much business that I will have to take on a partner. It is an ill wind as they say. Do not lose hope. I am confident that justice will prevail."

"I hope that is true and if so, will show the change in France!"

The next two days were desperate ones. The only enlivening part was that we talked. We talked of my mother and the people we had both known at Breteuil. We spoke of Julian and our pleasure at his new life but most of all we talked about our comrades. It was they we missed the most. Our furlough was almost up and I wondered if we would be posted as deserters. That would be adding insult to injury. Jean had shaken his head, "I would not worry about that. Albert knows we would not desert. The paperwork will be lost. If he were closer, I would have written to him. I am sure that the regiment would have found a way to extradite us from this predicament."

We had another miserable night listening to the moans, groans and tears of our fellow prisoners. It made sleep difficult, if not impossible and when we awoke from a fitful sleep again, we were both red-eyed. When the guard rapped on the door Jean stood with the bucket but when the door was opened it was the governor. He was smiling, "It seems my friends that you have friends in high places. You have been released and the charges dropped. There is a carriage awaiting you outside." He stood aside for us to leave. We left as quickly as we could. When we reached his office, he shook our hands. "I can honestly say that this is the outcome I wished for. I have spoken with friends from the army and I know of the deeds you have done." He pointed to me, "For the capture of the Dutch Fleet alone you should have been pardoned. France owes you both a debt and I hope this has gone some way to paying it."

When we stepped outside there was Bessières. He shook our hands. "I am sorry this took so long but the general did not receive your letter straight away. He was not in Paris. As soon as he did, he sent me and this carriage. I am to take you to the Tuileries."

As we entered the closed carriage Jean said, "Could we stop at the Rue Honore first. We need our luggage and we have a debt to pay."

Bessières pointed to the rear of the carriage which was festooned with our equipment and luggage. I was relieved to see my sword there. "It is here."

"Nevertheless, I have a debt to pay and I gave my word."

Bessières nodded his understanding. "It is on the way anyway."

When we reached the hotel Jean and I went in. Jean took out twice the amount he had promised. He walked up to the owner and handed it to him. "Here you are, sir. A debt is paid and thank you."

We reached the palace and the carriage pulled up around the rear so that we could get out unseen by any. Bessières took us to our rooms. "I have baths ready for you gentlemen. The general is busy tonight but feel free to wander the palace. Just do not try to leave until the general has spoken with you."

"We are prisoners still then?"

Bessières shrugged, "Let us just say you are guests we would prefer not to leave."

I did not mind as the change in circumstances was more than welcome. The baths were perfect and I lay luxuriating in mine until Jean came in. "You will end up a prune. Come I wish to explore this palace. It may be the only opportunity I ever get to visit the place where the kings and queens of France lived. While you dress, I will pen a letter to Francois. I would not have him worrying about us."

I have to confess that it was worth it. The palace was everything I had heard and more. I had thought that my father had lived well but it was a hovel compared with the opulence of the palace. Many of the treasures had been removed in the fervour of the early Revolution but now it was being renovated and brought back to its former glory. I think I saw the hand of the general in all of this.

When Bessières found us, we had visited almost all of the rooms that were available to us. Guards had turned us back from one or two but we had seen the glory by then. "If you would care to join myself and some of the other Guide officers for dinner, I think we can offer you fine food and sparkling conversation."

He was right about the food and the wine but the conversation was dull. It was when we were halfway through the meal when I realised that we had been invited to enliven the meal without tales. Bonaparte's Guides were with their general but they did not see action. I watched their eyes light up as Jean retold tales of our beloved 17th. From the dark days of the Low Countries to the glory of the campaign in Italy, they sat enraptured.

In a brief moment of silence, I asked, "Do you not have glory too then?"

The silence was so awkward that I deeply regretted my question. Bessières answered. "We have chosen to protect the general rather than enjoying your life but that does not mean that we do not envy you. I served with you albeit briefly but I can tell you that the esprit de corps and the loyalty you enjoy is unique. We envy you."

As I lay in bed, later on, I reflected on what Bessières had said and the sadness with which he had spoken the words. The elite regiments were the ones we all aspired to but when it was right there was nothing better than a good line regiment and I suddenly wished myself back with Pierre and the others.

Napoleon Bonaparte returned the next day. We knew he had arrived from the fevered and frenetic activity of the servants and officers of the Guides. "Will we be returning to the regiment, Jean?"

"I would imagine so. I think we are an embarrassment for those in power and the sooner we are out of Paris the better but I wonder why Bonaparte has kept us here so long."

We found out in the evening when we were summoned by Bessières to Bonaparte's study. He looked serious and came straight to the point. "You have behaved foolishly in the matter of the Chateau of Breteuil. Had I known that you would use your furlough in that way then I would have forbidden you to leave Paris. That is done. The next time you stray over the line between duty and personal vendettas I will leave you to rot in prison. Is that understood?"

I nodded but Jean said, "In that case sir, send us back to the Conciergerie for I do not regret any of my actions and I do not guarantee my future conduct."

I saw Bessières' look of horror and heard his sharp intake of breath. Bonaparte remained impassive. Had Jean gone too far and would we be sent back to prison?

When Napoleon smiled, I knew we had been saved again. "I should not be surprised when the guard dog I have trained bites my hand. Both of you have spirit and you have done France a service by ridding the north of two vultures but I cannot let you off the leash; you need handling. You are mine and you will obey me. Will you agree to that?"

I held my breath and stared at Jean, willing him to agree. "We are soldiers of France and you are a general of France, quite possibly the greatest general in France at the moment. Of course, we will obey you."

The air suddenly became breathable again. "Good, for I have work for you two and your other companions." He stood and took us to a map on the wall. "Egypt is the gateway to the east and Great Britain's India. I intend to capture that land as part of the new French Empire. However, I need a base closer to Africa." He jabbed a podgy finger at a speck on the map. I had thought it was a dead fly. "Malta is the key. I intend to capture Malta but we know little about it. You will go to the island aboard one of my ships and find out what the defences are like." He stared at us.

Jean looked at the map and then he smiled. "Very well. When do we leave?"

Bonaparte nodded as though he knew the answer already. "To-night. There is a sloop waiting at Golfe Juan and your two companions are waiting for you even as we speak. You will go in my carriage and as soon as you arrive you will depart for the island. Everything has been arranged. You will have a week on the island to discover its strengths and weaknesses. I will be waiting in Golfe Juan for your report. You may go."

As we hurtled down the heart of France, I asked Jean, "You took a risk. Why?"

He needed us more than we needed him. He would have gained nothing by throwing us back in prison. I wanted to see his resolve and how much he values us. We can ask for the moon and he will try to give it to us for he believes we can give him the sun."

The journey down passed as quickly as the one north had. The general had power and there were changes of horses and drivers at regular intervals. We slept and made up for the sleep lost whilst in prison. We did not need to speak. Those days and nights in the Conciergerie had left us with little else to discover about each other. We did not need to fill the silence with meaningless babble.

We reached Golfe Juan as the sun was setting over the beautiful sea. The golden rays of the sun belied the cool of the November water. We had little time for warm welcomes and talks about the furlough. The colonel was there with Tiny, Michael and Pierre. The latter was a surprise. Albert explained, "When our new lieutenant discovered that you would be off on another

Bonaparte adventure, he begged me to allow him to accompany you. To shut him up I agreed but if you wish to throw him overboard then I would be just as happy."

"I thought it was time that someone came on one of these expeditions who understands what to bring back."

The young captain of the sloop coughed. "We have little time sir, to achieve our aims. Malta is not just around the corner. We need to board and sail."

"Very well. We packed what we would need in one chest. Have you our muskets?"

"Of course."

"Then we are ready."

"Take care, Jean. I think our general is using your luck up at a prodigious rate."

I looked at Jean, if only he knew about the prison, he would have confirmation. "Goodbye, sir. Tell my squadron I will be back soon."

We went down to the quay and saw the Carillon for the first time. She had four small guns on each side and three masts. She looked tiny and I shivered a little as I stepped aboard for my first voyage on a ship.

CHAPTER 18

The three-masted sloop ghosted out of the small harbour. The lights of the bars around the port soon faded into pinpricks and we were lost in the dark waters of the Mediterranean. We left the young lieutenant to his task of navigating to Malta and we retired to the mess we had been allocated. Conditions were cramped but we were soldiers and we could put up with it. We briefed our three companions. They had been told little save that we would be scouting out a potential battlefield and we would be behind enemy lines.

"We will be landing on the Island of Malta. It is ruled by the Knights of St. John. We have no intelligence at all about the forces that might face us when we land. I will find out where the captain will land us but the island is small and we could walk it all in one day. We will travel in civilian clothes. Pierre you will have to be the dumb one as you don't speak Italian." He looked put out. "You wanted to be in on this so deal with it. I only intend to spend a couple of days on the island. The general wants us back sooner rather than later. You all know how quickly he moves, well the thirty thousand men he has marked out for this invasion are heading for the ports along the south coast right now."

"Why the hurry sir?" I felt I had to ask the question which was on everyone's minds.

"Well I am not privy to the general's thoughts but I would guess that as we have no continental enemies to fight, he is thinking about Egypt. The Royal Navy is no longer in the Medi-terranean as they have no bases and so he has a free rein but make no mistake the British will be back and so speed is of the essence."

"Well, it will be warmer in Africa at any rate. I wonder what the wine will be like."

Jean shook his head, "You always bring it down to the basics don't you Pierre?"

He shrugged and grinned, "At the end of the day that is all that life is about isn't it sir; the basics?" He was of course right. He had that annoying habit of always being right.

The Carillon was a fast, little ship and three days later we arrived off the south coast of Malta. The young lieutenant had timed it to arrive after dusk on the loneliest part of the heavily populated island. He pointed to the towers we could see. "They have the towers to watch for corsairs and pirates but they use Xebecs. When they spot us, they should take us for a smuggler. If you speak French, they will assume you are a smuggler."

Jean shook his head, "We need to play Italians as we need infor-mation. We will pretend that we are here to buy supplies for the ship."

"Then why did we not land in Valetta?"

The lieutenant was young but he had a head on his shoulders. "We have damaged the hull and you are repairing the ship." Jean waved vaguely up the coast. "Somewhere up there."

The lieutenant smiled and nodded, "Sounds plausible. Say we have sprung some planks and need pitch. We will be back here each night after dark. Shine a light three times. Count to thirty then three more times. Keep doing that until we reply. I will send a boat in for you. Good luck."

We descended into the skiff and the two sailors rowed us towards the darkened beach. After we waded ashore and the sailors returned to the sloop, I felt very lonely. Here there was no quick way home.

We scrambled up the bank to get our bearings. We could see pinpricks of lights showing houses but, in the distance, we could see the larger glow which had to be Valetta. Jean waved us closer, "We will split up and find out as much as we can. Pierre and Michael, you reconnoitre the walls around the port. Are they old or have they been improved? We need to know if they will stand up to cannon. Robbie, you take Tiny and go into the town. I want you two to listen to conversations in the bars. Find out the mood. I will go to the citadel. We meet back here at sunset. Hide your muskets in the undergrowth here. We should be able to carry pistols and swords as long as we are discreet. We will only need the muskets if we are pursued and the boat is late. Tiny, make sure the lamp for signalling is secure. If that gets broken then we are in trouble. Any questions?"

Pierre said, "Well with all due respect sir I think I am best suited to getting information from bars."

"Normally Pierre that would be true but as you don't speak Italian..."

He nodded, "Point taken. Education eh? What a wonderful thing."

"Come on Tiny. Let's secure that lamp and the muskets." There were many rocks around and we moved some to make a shallow grave. We jammed the lamp between our muskets with cloth wrapped around it and then carefully replaced the rocks above them. Safe that it was secure we set off across the fields. Although the fields were uneven, they were neither muddy nor dangerous. I was relieved when we reached a rough road which appeared to lead to the town.

As we tramped down, I went over our story. "You are Cesar, again and I am Roberto. We come from Naples and our ship is the Santa Maria. She is beached around the headland with a leaking hull and we need to buy some pitch."

"And where were we going, sir?"

"Good point. We were heading for Gibraltar. We had despatches for the British."

He nodded. "I'm glad I improved my Italian sir. I would hate to be Pierre and not understand a word."

"I think Pierre can understand some Italian but he cannot

speak it."

As we approached the walls, I saw that the gate was open and there were men with weapons lounging there. We approached cautiously. Would we even get into the city? As we neared them, I could smell the wine. They were drinking. Closing with them they waved and carried on with their conversation. Within three yards we were within the walls of Valetta. I took the opportunity of turning to look at the men and their weapons. Even in the dim light of their brazier, I could see that the muskets were old and not in good condition. They were using their short swords to toast some bread and the blades looked rusty and dull. Their uniforms were patched and worn. Perhaps the real army was better prepared but the ones at the gate were not soldiers.

We headed down the hill to the port. There would be many people there and we would be more likely to find out what we needed. I was also aware that we would have the opportunity for a night in a bed. Poor Michael and Pierre might be sleeping rough. I sought a tavern with rooms. As residents, we would be more anonymous. As we walked down to the port, I observed that there were few soldiers around. The walls had sentries but they were so far apart that they served no purpose whatsoever.

We reached the port which was quiet now that night had descended. We headed for a substantial looking hotel and entered. It was a hot, smoky room filled with the people who worked and lived around the harbour. There were sailors and fishermen along with those burly labourers who would unload the ships. As one would expect there were the ladies of the night who serviced the workers but the atmosphere contrasted sharply with the tavern in Amiens where Jean and I had watched the deserters. This was not a town at war. This was a prosperous port with contented citizens.

I went to the quiet end of the bar. "Have you a room for the night?"

The barman signalled an older man over, obviously the owner and spoke briefly to him. "You want a room?" I nodded. He leaned over suspiciously, "Luggage?"

"We haven't got any. Our ship sprang a leak on the south side of the island. The captain sent us to get some pitch to repair it but the journey took too long. We don't fancy going back in the dark and besides, we couldn't find any pitch."

He nodded, seemingly satisfied and named a price, "In advance." Obviously, he had been cheated before. As I handed over the coins, I noticed the sign advertising the prices and we had paid over the odds. I said nothing but it was a warning about the owner. "Do you want food?"

"And some wine."

He looked around the room and saw a table occupied by two whores. There were no drinks on the table. He wandered over and said sharply, "These gentlemen have money and want food so shift!"

They did not seem put out but smiled, "After you have had food if you want more comforts then we will be over there." They pointed to the corner of the bar we had just vacated.

Remembering my role as a sailor I winked and said, "I always like my comforts. We'll be along later."

The jug of rough wine appeared and we sat back. Our job was to listen and not to talk. I poured the wine and eavesdropped on the conversations. Occasionally, I said something trivial to Tiny, just to keep up appearances but I generally just listened. The food came. It was hot and it was filling; that was all. The men around our table appeared to be quite happy that, while the rest of Europe was embroiled in war, they were benefiting by supplying services for the ships of the combatants. I heard talk of the knights and got the impression that they were a throwback to the days of chivalry and quests. They seemed to be held in high regard by the men in the bar, mainly because they kept the island prosperous.

Tiny stood to go out of the back and I listened to other conversations. A couple of new men arrived and sat close to me at a recently vacated table. When they spoke, I discovered they were English. They kept their conversation limited to the menu until the waiter had gone.

Tiny returned and grinned at me, "They think we are smugglers or pirates. I heard the boss talking to the whores. They intend to rob us blind by charging over the odds."

I laughed, "That suits us; just so long as they don't guess our identities." Just then the English sailors began to speak and I put my finger to my lips.

"I've had enough of that captain. How about we jump ship? This seems a nice place."

"Nah. He's Italian and they are thick as thieves with this lot. Besides I heard that Nelson is coming back into the Med. The last thing we need is to jump ship and be press-ganged. I had enough the first time I was in."

"I heard they were fighting the Spanish?"

"They are but I was talking to an East Indiaman in Gib and he said they were coming back to Naples. No, we'll jump ship in Alexandria. There are more ships for us to choose there."

The rest of the conversation involved the two whores who would be enjoying the company of the two English sailors before us. I waved the waiter over, ostensibly to order more wine but in reality, to play on the fact that they thought we were smugglers. "Does this island have a navy then?"

The waiter gave me a shrewd look. "We don't need one. The fort is solid enough. We beat off the Turks a hundred years or so ago. This is a peaceful little place."

"Yeah, but we saw soldiers when we came in the city."

He laughed, "Those old soaks? The knights like to parade them every so often to make them all feel like soldiers but I am not sure they have even fired their guns this year. No, Malta is a little piece of paradise."

He brought us our overpriced wine and we watched the Englishmen disappear upstairs with the whores. I nodded to Tiny, "Let's finish our drinks and we will have an early start in the morning eh? I think we have found out all we need to here."

We were still soldiers and we laid our pistols within easy reach and our swords. We took our jackets off but retained our boots, breeches and shirts. We would be ready for action in an instant. We moved my bed so that it stuck out a thumb's width. If the door was opened then it would scrape the bed. We had found we slept much easier knowing that we would be awakened by intruders.

"Sir?"

"Yes Tiny?"

"Why doesn't the general use those Guides of his for this sort of thing? Why does he always use us?"

"Are you tiring of it? You can always refuse."

"Oh no, sir. I enjoy the work and we always make a few livres from it. It's just that they are supposed to be the elite, the best so why to use us?"

"I think that is the reason. They may be the elite on the battle-field but we are real soldiers and we can get the job done. I also think that we are expendable. I suspect he thinks that we might not come back and so it's no loss to him."

"That doesn't sound right sir."

"Tiny, the man is ruthless and ambitious. Don't get me wrong I think he would regret us not returning but that is only because he would have to find someone else to do the dirty jobs."

"Now that makes sense. Good night sir."

"Goodnight Tiny."

The wine had made me sleepy and I soon dropped off to sleep. Of course, the wine also made me need to pee and I wriggled in the bed as I debated whether to go and use the bucket or wait until morning. The indecision was a godsend as I felt the door move against the bed. My left hand slipped down to my stiletto and my right grabbed a handful of jacket and dragged the bar-man through the door. Tiny was up in an instant and, as I sat astride the barman with my blade to his throat Tiny had his pis-tol aimed at the hotel owner.

"Now where we come from if you break into a man's room at night then your life is forfeit." I pushed the tip so that it pierced the skin and a tendril of blood ran down his neck.

"No please sir. Let my son live. We mean no harm."

I stared at the man. He had a short sword in his hand. "You come here in the middle of the night and you are armed and yet you mean us no harm. For that lie alone I should cut your son's throat."

"No please!"

I stood and in one movement ripped his breeches down and placed the blade beneath his manhood. "Or perhaps make it so that you have no grandchildren. What should I do?"

The son was now weeping. "Please, we will do anything!"

"What do you think Cesar? Should we let the worthless creatures live?"

"Considering they have overcharged us since we arrived and they have tried to rob us not to mention making us lose sleep, I think that they deserve to lose a limb."

"I am inclined to agree but I think we will give them one more chance." I put the blade to the tip of the barman's nose. "You will stand guard outside our room all night. If anyone comes near..." I lowered the tip. "Is that satisfactory?"

I saw the relief on both their faces. "Yes, thank you, sir!"

"And tomorrow we will discuss compensation eh?"

Needless to say, our sleep remained unbroken. The relief on their faces when we left was that of men given a reprieve from death row. They returned us all the money we had spent and a gold piece as well. When I said we would not be returning I think they were on the point of weeping with gratitude.

We spent the morning exploring the walls around the town. The mortar between the stones was old and crumbling. There was ivy growing in parts and the stairs leading to the ramparts were broken in places. We did not get close to the cannon but they looked to be museum pieces. The balls looked to be four pounders and there were a couple of eight-pounders too but they were so old that I doubt they had any accuracy. The balls themselves were speckled with rust. We were passing the palace when we saw six of the Knights of St. John sitting outside. They were playing chess. When I saw how old they were I wondered if there was a hospital nearby. One of them saw my sword and called me over.

"Young man would you let us look at your blade. It seems to me a fine sword for one so young and if you do not mind me saying so, so poor."

"Of course, not sir. I am a visitor on your island. It would be rude to refuse."

I handed it over to him and he held it and balanced it feeling the weight as he turned it in the air. I could see that he had had some skill with a sword. When he returned it to me, I asked. "Where do the knights live sir?"

He pointed to a hall close to the palace. "We all live there. We are the last of the Crusader knights and we hold that honour dear."

"Do you have a king sir?"

"No, we elect a Grand Master."

One of the other knights gestured to see the sword. As he held it, he said, "Tell me, young man, this sword has seen war. Have you?"

I could not lie nor did I wish to. These were all gentlemen. I imagined them being similar to my great grandfather. I showed the respect of the truth. "Yes, sir. I have fought in wars. I was a horseman."

They nodded their approval. The one who had the sword asked, "Tell me how they fight these days. Our enemies come in pirate ships and not in armies." He handed me back my sword and gestured for us to sit.

"The Austrians and the French like to fight by using light infantry spread out in a thin line followed by a column of men."

"A column you say? How big?"

"It varies but fifty to a hundred men wide and a hundred men deep. They fire volleys from their muskets and then charge with the bayonet. Of course, their cannons are blasting ahead of them as they go as well."

"And the horsemen, like yourself, how did you fight?"

I tapped my pistol. "Sometimes we used these and sometimes a musket. The sword we use when we are out of musket balls."

They all looked sad. "That is not the kind of warfare we would like."

"No young man. I am pleased that we will not have to fight an enemy like that. Malta is suddenly a more attractive home than it was before you stopped by. Thank you for your honesty." The oldest looking knight held out his hand to shake mine, "I am Grand Master von Hompesch and that palace is my home. These" he gestured with his arm, "are the five best knights on the island."

If they were the best then what were the rest like? "In that case sir, it is me who is honoured. Thank you for allowing me to talk with you. It is rare to find gentlemen such as yourselves these days."

We took our leave and I decided that we would head towards the rendezvous point but go by the coastal path and the watch-tower. We bought some hot bread with tomatoes and cheese to eat for our meal and set off for the coast. "Would you have whipped that lad's balls off sir?"

"He believed I would and that was all that counted. But no, I had no intention of hurting them. They were not bad men, merely greedy men. They thought we had money and they could get their hands on it easily. They have learned a lesson."

The tower, when we reached it, was in an even worse condition that the walls of Valetta. The wooden ladder leading to the top was so old I would not trust it to take my weight. It was a pleasant spot and we ate our meal there.

"Look, sir! It's the ship!"

Tiny was right, out at sea we could see the sloop about two miles offshore. It looked like the lieutenant was sailing up and down the coast. I realised then that he must have been given instructions from Napoleon Bonaparte to find suitable landing places. The general was certainly thorough. I wondered how he could be so driven. He was the most single-minded person I had ever met.

We made our way down to the rocks where we had hidden the guns. I was keen to find them in daylight. I felt guilty that we were the first back but we had succeeded. I hoped the others would be along soon. We recovered the guns and the signal lamp. Tiny made sure it still worked while I loaded the muskets. We needed to be ready for anything.

I saw Jean well before he saw us. I could see him constantly checking to see he was not being followed whilst looking for the rendezvous point. I stood and waved when he was forty yards away. He quickly made his way down to us. "Any problems?"

I grinned at Tiny, "None we couldn't handle sir and you?"

"That was probably the easiest scouting mission I have ever had." He shook his head. "They are stuck in the middle ages. I wish the general would leave them there."

"Me too. I was talking with some of their knights and the Grand Master. They do not want a war. They want to see their years out in peace and the old way of life."

"Yes, but the general has heard of their treasure. When the King of France wanted money, he killed all of the Knights Templar and stole their money. That was almost five hundred years ago. The Knights of St John have been gathering the money ever since. They will be even richer. Our general is from Corsica and has more than a little of the bandit in him."

It was beginning to get dark. "Better get the light lit Tiny."

"We saw the sloop before. She is just sailing up and down."

"Good, when it is lit then give the signal."

"What about the other two? "

"Hopefully they will get here in time, otherwise we will return tomorrow."

"Ready sir."

"Right. Three flashes. Count to thirty and then three more."

The ship answered almost immediately. "Right stop the signalling. Robbie, you wait here for the other two and Tiny and I will get down to the beach." The night seemed suddenly lonely and quiet as they left me.

It must have been half an hour before Tiny returned. "Sir? The captain says you can go back to the ship and I will wait. The lieutenant is keen to sail."

"I will wait with you. It is a little..." Just then we heard the pop of a musket. We both grabbed and cocked our weapons. We could hear the sounds of men running. I took a chance. It had to be Pierre. I shouted in French, "Over here!"

The white faces of our companions suddenly appeared and I could see a mob behind them. "Tiny, as soon as our lads are close fire over the heads of the mob. Let's try to scare them."

Pierre and Michael slithered down the rocks to us and I shouted, "Fire!"

The two guns together sounded unnaturally loud and the mob dropped to the ground. "Quick! Get down to the boat!" They needed no urging and they scrambled down the rocky slope. I took out my two pistols and fired them too and then I followed the three of them to the boat. The sailors pushed off even as I was clambering aboard and they began to row out to the dark ship; invisible in the moonless sea.

My two companions were trying to catch their breath as the sailors hauled on the oars. "I can see an interesting story here." Michael shot a murderous glare at Pierre who managed an embarrassed shrug.

We scrambled up the side and the sloop slid silently into the night. Jean just gave a questioning look at the two of them. I said, "Well Michael, what did he do?"

"He only tried it on with the farmer's daughter. The farmer did not take kindly to his intentions and we had to run."

"I'm sorry. I thought she was happy about my attentions."

Jean said, "Perhaps this is the reason we do not take you on these missions, Pierre. You are a good soldier just as long as you are in a battle. Enough of this. Let us go below decks and share our information."

We all had similar experiences. Michael and Pierre felt the same about the Maltese as Jean and I. They should be left alone in their little backwater. The modern world was not theirs and I envied them their values. The old knights I had seen would not know how to fight in a modern battle.

CHAPTER 19

When we reached Golfe Juan the general had not arrived and it gave us the opportunity to be reunited with our horses and our comrades. The troopers who had the responsibility of the stables were grateful to see me. "That horse of yours is well named. He is the most ill-tempered horse we have ever had to care for."

I walked up to him and he nuzzled me. "He seems fine now."

They collectively shook their heads and went about their business. I knew what they meant. He could be bad tempered but when I was around, he seemed calmer. It had been some time since we had been together, I suspected it would be some time before we would get to ride again. I wondered how he and the other regimental horses would cope with a sea voyage to Africa.

The general arrived a few days later and Jean and I were summoned into his presence. "Well?"

Jean looked at me and sighed, "General you could ride in there with your Guides and capture it all without a shot being fired. They have no cavalry at all. Their cannons are a hundred years old. Their army is like the National Guard with older weapons and they would struggle to muster five thousand men. The knights themselves are an anachronism. They belong in the crusades, not a modern war."

"Good, excellent. This will be a swift campaign."

"General do you still intend to invade?"

"Of course."

"It will be like taking cannon to kill a fly."

He laughed, "This is why you are captains and I am a general. I need the troops to invade Egypt. I do not want my men on the ships all the way to Egypt. By fighting a little war in Malta, they will recover their legs and gain confidence. I do not care if the Maltese fight or do not fight. The result will be the same. Egypt is the prize Malta is but a step to achieving that prize." He shook our hands, firmly, "I do appreciate your efforts. You have, once again, done valuable service to France. I ask you again, would you care to join the Guides? I know that Bessières would relish the chance to serve with you again."

"As we said before general, we still have work to do with the 17th but we thank you for the offer."

We were dismissed with a disappointed wave. Bessières accompanied us to our horses, "He is right I would enjoy serving with you again but beware the general. You can only reject his offers so many times before he begins to resent you."

"Thank you Bessières and we mean no insult to your Guides but we prefer the 17th."

We spent the next days making sure that we would have all that we needed for a campaign in another country. Pierre gathered a collection of sausages and jugs of wine. Now that he was an officer, he had more power and could ensure that he ate and drank well. Jean and I made sure that we had essentials like spare flints, plenty of musket balls. I had acquired a mould and it was as precious to me as my sword. I procured a number of apples; Killer would be as well served as I was and would enjoy his treats.

We began to embark a week later. Our horses were loaded aboard a transport. The quay at Golfe Juan was dwarfed by the ship but at least they did not need to be slung aboard like bales of hay. A wide gangplank was used and they were led aboard by their riders. We securely tethered them in their stalls, relieved that it had been so easy. We were issued hammocks and the sailors showed us how to sling them. They did not tell us how to get into them and I know that they were looking forward to our first efforts. At least five of us knew how to do this. The crew would not derive as much pleasure as they hoped when the troopers first tried to clamber into shifting and treacherous canvas.

The journey south was much slower in the ponderous transport than it had been in the speedy sloop. It was made worse by the fact that we had to wait for all the ships to join us from Toulon, Genoa and all the other ports. It was a huge fleet which gathered. There were thirty thousand men embarked on a variety of vessels. There were few cavalry on the transports. We heard that the remainder of the cavalry would join us at Alexandria and I hoped that they would be there when we reached Africa. The fact that we had just our regiment and the Guides as cavalry was worrying. I knew this would not be a problem in Malta but Egypt struck me as a different proposition.

The closer we came to the little island the more depressed I became. I wished that I had never met the knights, for now, they just reminded me of a great grandfather I had never seen. Jean sympathised with me but he told me to put them from my mind. "They will not put up a good fight and I do not think they relish a war. They are old men and I think they will surrender. They will look at what happened to Venice, a much bigger country, and they will accept it. At least we are not the Turks who would impose their religion on them. We are Christian as they are. Their way of life will continue."

Since I had been away, we had received replacements and I now had sous-lieutenant under Pierre. He was a very studious young man who had recently left University. He was called Pierre-François Bouchard and he was desperate to impress all of us. He was a little too refined for Pierre but I found him an affable young man. He was almost the same age as me but, of course, his last four years had been at the Sorbonne whilst my university had been the battlefield. We got on as I had someone other than Jean with which to play chess. I enjoyed talking to him. Had I grown up as the son of a Scottish noble then I might have attended university. He had a great knowledge of the past for he had studied history. He gave me a great deal of information about the land of Egypt. He made a tedious voyage go quickly.

While we sailed south, we received our orders from the general; Albert opened the sealed orders once we had sailed. As I had expected we were not to be used as cavalry on the island; we were to fight dismounted. The five of us who had been scouts on the island were each assigned to a brigade to ensure that they advanced safely. Tiny and I were to be with General Lannes. Jean and the others were with General Desaix.

We landed in the second week of June. We advanced in two columns towards Valetta. As I had dreaded and expected the Maltese who opposed us were no opposition. They marched fearfully from the town and faced us across an open piece of ground. The general was so confident he had not even unloaded his precious cannon. It was as he had told us. This was to brush the cobwebs away and make the army literally fighting fit.

We stood with Lannes just behind the two battalions of infantry and the light infantry. The best troops in Malta faced us, the Royal Regiment of Malta. They bravely stood in their three lines and awaited our assault. I saw four of the knights with them. I hoped none of the men I had spoken to was amongst them. The light infantry advanced and the Maltese made the classic mistake of firing volleys. They wasted their ammunition as they hit no-one and they blinded themselves to the advancing light infantry who closed up and began to kill the officers and sergeants. When the two battalions fired and charged the terrified Maltese fled for the safety of Valetta. As we knew this was false security as the walls would not stand up to the artillery we could summon from the ships if it was needed. The port itself was blockaded by our fleet of warships and their guns could reduce the walls to rubble if necessary. I suspected our little general would prefer to save his powder and ball for more worthy enemies and opponents. We camped beneath the walls of the capital.

General Bonaparte sought me out. "You say you met the Grand

Master?"

"I spoke with him briefly, yes."

"You will know him then. I want you to go to the walls under a flag of truce and ask for the surrender of the island. Bessières will accompany you."

"What if he refuses?"

"Then tell him I will reduce the walls to rubble and slaughter his men." He smiled, "Be persuasive."

The next morning the two of us walked towards the city. The walls bristled with men and guns. I hoped that they would respect the white flag. I looked at Bessières and saw that he was even more nervous than I was. I realised that it had been some time since he had been in action. He sweated a little and kept rubbing his hands. "Will they respect the flag then Robert?"

"They struck me as old-fashioned honourable men but there may be some on the walls who are afraid and will fire first and be reprimanded later."

"You do not inspire confidence, my friend."

"If it is a single man who fires then we should survive. They do not have good weapons."

We walked towards the walls and I could see the movement along the top. We were a hundred and fifty paces from the walls when one soldier fired his musket. The ball went well wide but I did not miss a step. Bessières next to me did. "Come along sir. He missed by a country mile."

When I was within fifty yards I halted and shouted, in Italian, "Do you not respect the flag of truce?"

One of the knights leaned over. "I apologise for that, Frenchman, it was an impetuous youth. What do you want?"

"I am here to speak with the Grand Master."

"And who are you?"

"I am Captain Robert Macgregor. I met the Grand Master once."

He nodded and spoke with the man next to him. The guns were still aimed at us. I turned to Bessières who ran a finger along his collar. "How can you be so cool? Any of those muskets could go off."

"True and they could miss. If they hit me, I will know nothing so why worry about that. If they miss then the musketeer will be impressed by my courage and fear to face me." I saw him shake his head. It was late morning and the sun was getting hotter. Eventually, two knights appeared. I recognised them as two of the knights I had spoken with but neither was the Grand Master.

"The Grand Master is indisposed but I will speak for him. I recognise you. You are the young man who spoke with us. I see you did not lie to us. You are a soldier."

"Then let me plead with you. I was not lying when I described the effect of our army. Your soldiers fled, leaving their dead on the field. We lost none." I pointed behind me beyond the low rise. "General Bonaparte is there with thirty thousand men. We can reduce your walls to rubble in under an hour. Do you want your civilians to suffer? If you fight us you will only delay the inevitable and you will lose many men as well as others who do not fight."

"I must consult with the Grand Master."

"I will give you an hour. My general is not a patient man."

After they had gone, I told Bessières what I had said. "You are a remarkably confident soldier for one so young. Your voice was so calm when you spoke, I wondered what you were saying."

"I have learned that what works with horses works with men. If you speak in an excited way then that animal becomes more excited and unpredictable. It is the same with men. If you scream at a trooper because he has made a mistake, he is more likely to make another. Besides when you get excited yourself you often say things you regret. It is far better to measure your words."

He laughed and clapped me on the shoulder, "What a common sense approach."

An hour later the gate opened and the two knights approached me. "We surrender."

Bessières said, "I will go and tell the general."

The two knights stood with me for a moment and then one of

them said, "Come. We will get out of the sun." He looked at me seriously for a moment, "Will your general keep his word?"

I nodded, not that I thought that Bonaparte was a truthful man but he needed every soldier he could get if he was to conquer Egypt. "He will come with just those soldiers he needs for his position as general and no more."

I was taken through the gate. The soldiers stared at me, most of them with undisguised hate, others with a curious gaze. We went into the palace where there was a table with cool drinks and fresh fruit. "Will the Grand Master be joining us?"

"As I said, he is indisposed. This is all a little too much for him. He thought, as we all did that, we, the Knights of St John would continue our existence as we have for almost seven hundred years but it is not to be."

He held out his hand, "My name is Sir John and I, like the Grand Master, had hoped to see out my days here."

I felt sorry for the old man who seemed gentle. "Perhaps the general will allow you to stay."

Sir John laughed, "We are old here but not yet senile. Your general will want us off the island. Firstly, we would be seen as a focus of rebellion for the Maltese but, more importantly, he wants our treasure."

I leaned forward, "He is not here yet and you have time. Secure some of the treasure. I know that he has no idea of the quantity. You could, at least, live in comfort."

"That is a kind and selfless thought but it is not honourable and when you get to our age all you have left is honour. I have enough to get by and I will take the ship. Perhaps I will return home."

"Home, I thought that this was your home?"

"No, my home is in Britain. In the land, they call the Borders."

I suddenly spoke in English, "My mother was of Scottish parents. I am Robbie Macgregor."

For the first time, the old man looked non-plussed and surprised. "Well Robbie, we may well be related for I am a MacAlpin and we are related to the Macgregors." He stroked his beard. "I

242

wonder if this is a sign." He appeared to make a decision and suddenly rose. "Come with me!" He grabbed a lantern from a table.

The other knights had shown no surprise when we spoke English and they showed none now as we hurriedly left the hall and descended into the bowels of the palace. I think they were all preoccupied with their bleak future. There were guards everywhere but the appearance of the knight caused them to stand to attention and they allowed us to pass. Sir John said quietly, "These are the vaults your general will wish to see. These are the treasure rooms." He nodded to the guard at one room and the man opened the door. Sir John closed it behind us.

"When I first came here, I was interested in the treasures as all young men are and I examined them. You can imagine my surprise when I found this." He held up a seal with a bloodstone on it and a signet attached. "This is the seal and signet of the clan. I know not how it came to be here but I come down once a week to look at it." He handed it to me.

It was beautiful and it was inscribed,

'Triogal Ma Dh'ream
Een dhn bait spair nocht'.

"What does this mean, Sir John?"

"I am of royal descent,
Slay and spare not"

I went to hand it back. He shook his head. "No, it is fate that has brought you here. You must return it to the clan home."

"But we are at war with Britain. You should take it."

"No Robbie, Something beyond our ken has brought you here and you must do all in your power to return this to its home. Swear it so."

I felt the power of the old man as he placed my hands on the seal. I felt a shiver run down my spine. I could, at last, do something for the great grandfather and grandfather I had never met. "I so swear."

He nodded, "Good." He reached, seemingly at random, into a chest and drew out a purse of coins. "Take this. You may need it and it is payment for your honesty." I hesitated, "Take it as a kinsman then." I nodded and took it. "The sentry will remember that you came down here so tell your general where the treasure is. He would find it anyway and this way no one will suspect you."

The old man was certainly sharp and knew what he was about. I felt sad that I had known him so briefly. "We have much in common Robert Macgregor. I was five when my father was killed at Culloden and my mother might have suffered the same fate as yours had my uncle, her brother, not taken us both to Sicily where I was trained to be a knight. That is how I ended my days here. I suppose I will go back to Sicily. It is easier than trying to return to Britain and my cousins still live there, I believe. We had better revert to Italian now."

When we reached the main hall there was much anxiety as General Bonaparte and his Guides had entered the citadel. I went to the door with Sir John and we awaited the arrival of the conqueror of Valetta. I saw the brief look of surprise on Sir John's face as he saw the diminutive size of the general but he covered it well. He stepped forward and bowed. "I am Sir John. The Grand Master is indisposed but I am here to formally surrender to you." He pointed to me. "Your representative here has been most courteous and I would like to express my appreciation."

Bonaparte smiled, "He is one of my lucky stars. Well done Scotsman." His tone became more serious. "I will require the presence of all of the knights here within the hour when I will give my judgement on their future. If the Grand Master is still indisposed then he will have to learn his fate from one of you."

Sir John nodded. "I will make the arrangements." He turned to me and shook me by the hand. "Farewell Robert Macgregor. We may not have the opportunity to speak again so God speed and I hope you enjoy a happy and successful life." He squeezed my hand as he shook it and gave me a smile.

After he had left Bonaparte turned to me. "I did not know you had diplomacy as a skill. Well done." He turned to Bessières. "We will have to find where the treasure is. Get a couple of guards and interrogate them…"

"Sir, I know where the treasure is. Sir John took me there. He seemed to think it would make things easier for the knights."

His eyes narrowed, "He is a shrewd one. Lead on my young friend."

We went down the stairs accompanied by Bessières and some of his Guides. The guards looked at us warily. I said, "You saw me before with Sir John. The Knights have surrendered. This is the new ruler General Bonaparte." The man saw the wisdom in compliance and stepped aside.

By the time we had left the rooms filled with treasure General Bonaparte's eyes were sparkling. "Well done Scotsman. Once again you have done me a great service." He turned to Bessières, "I think we will deal leniently with the knights but the Grand Master is another matter. You had better order Vaubois to occupy the town."

Before we could speak with the knights Sir John burst into the room, quite distressed. "I tried to get all of the knights as you requested but a mob heard we had surrendered and they have killed some of my brothers in the streets!"

Bonaparte knew how to handle mobs. "Bessières, take my Guides and clear the streets. Hang any looters and recover those bodies." As his commander left Bonaparte said, "I am sorry that your knights suffered. Your people should know that you acted wisely to save lives." He clapped me on the shoulder. "And you should rejoin your comrades. Bessières has another task for you."

As I left, I saw Sir John nod at me. It was the last time I saw the old man. It was a sad moment.

The army was camped just outside of the city. Not all of the thirty thousand men had been put ashore. The 17th was still aboard the transport. The others were there however and Pierre had managed to acquire us a mess tent all to ourselves. He grinned as he told me, "I pulled rank with a sergeant. First time I have done that and it felt good."

I told them what had transpired but not Sir John's conversation with me. I might tell Jean but it was private and I wanted to keep it that way. Jean was amazed, "We conquered the whole island and lost no-one. A few men with cuts and bruises and that is all."

"Well, the Knights suffered. The mob got to them."

Pierre shook his head, "Stupid! Typical civilians. They don't do any fighting but always get annoyed when the fighting men don't protect them as they think they should."

We heard the popping of muskets, "Well they are learning now. Bessières has taken his Guides to give the populace a lesson in democracy."

They all looked at me in surprise for there had been venom in my voice. "This is not like you Robbie. You sound almost political."

I lowered my voice. "Perhaps I am realising that the ones who lead us are not doing it for the right reasons." I told them of the treasure I had seen. "You can bet we will not see any of that and who will?"

Jean poured me a mug of rough wine, "And it has been the same since the dawn of time. The soldiers who fought at Troy did not get the treasure. It was Menelaus and Agamemnon. It was Alexander the Great who reaped the rewards of his men's blood and Julius Caesar gained riches and power on the backs of his legionaries. We have to accept it."

I remained silent and thought of the seal I had concealed beneath my jacket. Soon it would be joining my other treasures and I would begin to plan how to fulfil my oath to Sir John.

Some days later we were summoned, along with a major of grenadiers, to the palace. We had heard before we left for the palace that the Grand Master was to be exiled to Trieste but the others were allowed to leave freely. General Bonaparte was no fool and he knew the debt he owed the men who had handed the island and the treasure to him. Sir John and most of the knights had already sailed when we marched through the gates of the palace now topped by a huge tricolour. I hoped he would find peace in Sicily.

The little general was seated at a table surrounded with maps. I noticed Francois, the captain of the Carillon standing to the side. He smiled when he saw us and joined Jean and me. The general beamed. He greeted the young major. "Ah Major Lefevre, I am pleased to meet you. General Lannes speaks highly of you." He pointed to the five of us. "These six men do little jobs for me now and again and I thought it time to put the two of you together."

He rubbed his hands as he pointed to the map. "Tomorrow the fleet sails for Egypt. We will soon conquer that country for the glory of France. But tonight, you will go, along with a company of grenadiers and sail on the Carillon to Alexandria. I need the port making secure. That is the mission you will undertake. You will sail under the flag of Malta. You will enter the harbour and capture any guns so that we can sail in unmolested."

I was bereft of words. How would we achieve that? The general seemed to almost read my mind. "Many Maltese ships had fled there in the last couple of days." He gave a sly smile. "Some of the knights have gone there on their way to the Holy Land." He had thought all of this through. "You will need to hold the port for no more than twelve hours. I am sure you can manage that." The major nodded confidently, as for me, I was not too sure.

CHAPTER 20

As we walked through the town down to the port, I asked Francois. "Is it possible?"

"Do you mean can I sail into the harbour under a Maltese flag? Of course. Can you capture and hold the port? That I am not too sure of."

Jean asked the major, "Have your men done this before?"

I saw the flicker of doubt briefly cross the grenadier's face then he smiled, "We are the soldiers who attack and hold the most difficult positions. We did so at Rivoli."

"Yes, we were at Rivoli."

He seemed to notice our uniforms for the first time. "Of course, the famous 17th; I am honoured to serve with you. I wondered why he wanted cavalrymen for this mission."

"It is not for our skills as horsemen I can assure you."

The grenadiers had embarked already and our gear was on the deck. I didn't think I would spend much time below decks. I could not see where they could put a hundred and twenty men. This would be a very crowded voyage. The smell alone would make me vomit.

Jean and I were alone at the bows of the sloop. There was little enough space on the tiny vessel but few wanted to be at the bows where the spray constantly wetted you. "Well Robbie, what was so important you wanted us to catch our death of cold here at the bows?" I told him of my meeting with Sir John and my oath. After I had told him I watched his impassive face as he stared towards the distant coast of Africa. "So, you want my help to run. Is that it?"

"No, of course not. I will continue to fight for France. I would never desert. I am just telling you so that when this war is over and I leave the chasseurs I will be going to Scotland to return the Great Seal to my family."

He seemed to relax at that news. "In that case I am pleased and I promise that I will help you." The sense of relief I felt made me feel as though a massive stone had been lifted from my back. With Jean at my side, I was confident that I could carry out my sworn mission. "You cannot escape your destiny, you know that? It is in your blood and I can see your mother and her determination every time you speak."

We joined the others by the mainmast. We had discovered that we did not get in the way if we were there. The major wandered over. "You have done things like this before?"

"You mean sneak in somewhere without being seen? Yes, a couple of times." Jean pointed to the white webbing and belts on the grenadier's uniform. "You need to take those off when we go into action. If it is night, and I think the young lieutenant will try to land at night, then you need to be as dark as possible. You also need you, men, to work independently. I suspect Bonaparte sent you because you can do that but when we land your men will be spread out over a large area. I would not have done it this way."

The major looked puzzled. "No? What would you have done?"

"I would have found out before we landed where the guns were and where the defences were the strongest. This way you and your men will have to think on your feet. You will have to find the guns and disable them at the same time; that will not be easy."

His face fell. "That makes sense."

"Sir, we could still do that. Land us a mile away, perhaps in daylight. We scout it out and then the captain picks us up. It would only take a couple of hours."

Jean nodded, "That could work."

"But that is a huge risk to you is it not? You would be alone in a hostile place."

"Well major, that will happen anyway. The difference is that when the force is landed it will be fighting from the moment it lands. We will try to avoid any kind of action. It is the intelligence we discover which is vital."

"Good I will tell the lieutenant."

We had just reached him when we heard the lookout yell, "Sail Ho!" There was a pause, "Three ships. Arab Xebecs."

The lieutenant gave an apologetic shrug. "Whatever you needed of me will have to wait." He pointed to the Maltese flag flying from the taffrail. "Our general is a victim of his own success. The pirates will know that the knights are fleeing Malta and will be seeking their treasure."

The major looked perplexed. "Should I bring my men on deck?"

"Not yet they will only get in the way. They do not have a large number of guns but they do have many men. Let us keep your grenadiers as a surprise in case they close with us and try to board us."

We loaded our muskets and stood behind the helmsman watching, carefully, the Xebecs which were closing rapidly. They appeared to move like greyhounds. I had thought the sloop was swift but now that I had seen the pirate ships I knew differently. I saw that they were spreading out so that they could catch us if we headed north or south. If we continued in the same direction then they would catch us. It was inevitable. The young lieutenant looked at the masthead and then at his chart. "Number one put chain shot in the guns; we'll try to dismast one of them." He glanced over at us. "When they close, we can bring the grenadiers up. It might make a difference but each one of those has as many men on board as we do and they are used to fighting on ships. Your men are not marines. Unless we can sink two of them then we are in trouble."

He sounded calm but I knew he would be as nervous as any of us. The Barbary pirates were not known for their gentle behaviour and the best we could hope for would be slavery.

Pierre peered down his barrel as he murmured. "I've heard they make eunuchs of their slaves." He looked at Michael. "Don't let them take me alive. I couldn't live if I was a eunuch."

"It would cause less trouble if you were. Perhaps we ought to do it before they get here!"

He turned around and glared at us. "I'll feed you to the fishes if you come close."

He was so serious that we all laughed, including Jean. In some strange way, it made us more relaxed. The three ships were now half a mile away and they fired their bow chasers. They were not trying to sink us but make us change direction. I was not a sailor and even I could see that. The six cannon balls flew harmlessly overhead.

The lieutenant laughed, "They are idiots. Everyone knows your first shot is your best shot. Once the barrels get heated up the balls could go anywhere." All the time he was glancing at the wind and glancing astern. He saw us watching him. He pointed to the masthead pennant. "I am just waiting for the wind to veer a point or two then I am going to turn and try to dismast the one in the middle."

I couldn't resist asking, "Why the one in the middle?"

"If we miss to the left or the right, we could still hit one of the consorts." He must have seen something he liked for he suddenly shouted, "Hard a starboard! All guns fire as you bear at the centre ship." The 'all guns' was a little grand, he had but four on each side.

I had never seen or heard chain shot before. It was two cannon balls attached by a small chain. If it struck rigging or a mast it sliced through it. As the guns fired, we heard a strange whizzing noise as the chain shot sped and spiralled towards the xebecs. We had, of course, made ourselves a bigger target by turning and two balls crashed through the sail of the foremast. "Hard a port! Starboard guns you will get your chance in a moment."

As the smoke cleared, we all peered anxiously to see what damage had been done. The foremast of the middle ship had been damaged and there appeared to be a hole close to the water line. It was slowing down but the turn had allowed the two others to close with us.

"This time when I turn to go for the ship to the north. Larboard battery load with the ball and have grapeshot ready." He gestured to us. "There are two deck guns on each side. Load them with grape and we'll use them if they close with us."

Tiny and I raced to one gun. They were long tubes, a sort of seagoing musket but cruder and larger. We rammed the grapeshot down the barrel and poured in a handful of musket balls for good measure. Its range would only be forty yards or so but they would clear the decks if used judiciously. I saw that the major and Jean had taken another of the guns. I was not surprised; it was always better to be doing something rather than just watching

As the order was given, "Hard to larboard!" I was glad I was at the gun for it gave me something to hang on to as the ship heeled hard over. The cannons sounded the same as before and the chain shot whizzed across the water. The northern ship was closer and I saw the mast begin to crumble even above the smoke of our guns. There was a crack as it broke. When the smoke cleared, we could see that the mast had fallen in the water and dragged it around. The young lieutenant yelled, excitedly, "One more while they are broadside on. The sailors reloaded and fired as the ship heeled around. The four balls cracked into her hull and she began to sink.

We now had one damaged ship and a second one which was less than two hundred yards away and racing to get to grips with us. The first ship we had damaged was two hundred yards astern of us and trying to reach our larboard side. "Major, get your men on deck!"

The grenadiers, eager to be released from their dark prison, poured on to the deck. Their officers lined them up along the two sides so that the ship bristled with weaponry. It was too late for the pirates to avoid a collision and their captain kept his ship heading for us. The young lieutenant shouted fire and first the cannons and then Tiny and I fired our guns. I had forgotten to wrap something around my ears and the whole world became silent with the crash and the concussion. I tapped Tiny on the shoulder and we reloaded. There was too much smoke to see what damage we had caused but we needed to reload anyway. Suddenly we were almost knocked to our feet as the pirate xebec lurched into us. I pulled the lanyard and the gun belched death at the half-naked, glistening black warriors who launched themselves over the side. I felt, rather than heard, the volleys from the grenadiers.

I took out my sword and led Tiny to the fray. The grenadiers had done serious damage to the pirates but now, with their muskets as their main weapon they were at a disadvantage. I saw an Arab lift his scimitar to behead a prostrate grenadier who had slipped on the blood which ran like water on the deck. I lunged and my sword went through his silk shirt and emerged on the other side. I pulled the soldier to his feet and heard him say, "Thank you, sir." My hearing was coming back at least.

Suddenly I felt a crash as the second ship lurched into us and more pirates leapt aboard. I drew my pistol and fired at two men who were clambering aboard. I could do nothing about the other side. Pierre and Michael would have to cope. We were fighting for our lives. We had to clear this side first. Then I heard the major shout, "Grenades!" Ten of the grenadiers lobbed their fizzing grenades into the air. They must have cut the fuse as finely as they dared for the ten bombs all exploded on the xebec's deck. I could not see the effect but I imagined that it would be devastating. If nothing else the concussion would have made the pirates dizzy.

The lieutenant took advantage of the hiatus and yelled, "All guns fire!" Our cannons were almost touching the xebecs and the force of them drove the two ships away from us. We still had pirates aboard but they could not get more men on to our decks and we could begin to clear the enemy away.

Once again, I heard, "Grenades!" There was another ripple of explosions along both sides. I saw the xebec nearest us begin to drift south. I turned to head towards the other side. I saw Pierre lying on the deck, covered in blood and Michael desperately fighting against three men. I hurled myself through the air. I impaled one with my sword and crashed into a second. It did Michael no good as the third one swept his scimitar around to behead him. As I lay on the ground, I pulled my second pistol and held it to the man's stomach as I fired. I saw daylight through his middle before he collapsed.

The man I had knocked to the ground suddenly put his hands around my neck and began to squeeze. He was incredibly powerful and I began to feel myself blacking out. I reached down to my boot and felt around for my stiletto. I could sense myself slipping into the dark abyss of death when, thankfully, I found the end of the handle. I tugged it and sliced across his wrists ripping into the arteries and tearing the tendons. He gave a scream and released his grip. I stabbed forwards into his throat and was covered in arterial blood as he fell backwards. I turned to Michael. His head lay some way from his body. I sought Pierre. He lay as still as a corpse on the slippery blood covered deck. I put my hand to his neck and felt a faint pulse. I searched his body for a wound. I could see none and then I gently rolled him over and saw that he had been stabbed in the back. I took his scarf and balled it to stop the bleeding. I undid his belt and tied it as tightly as I could to hold the temporary dressing in place. It was only then, as I looked around for medical aid that I realised the battle was over. The last of the pirates were being despatched. We had won but at what a cost. One of my friends was dead and the other near to death.

I saw Jean and felt relief, at least he was alive. "Jean, it is Pierre. He is badly wounded." Jean raced to my side and I scoured the survivors for a sight of Tiny. His huge frame was helping a wounded grenadier but he still managed a wave. Jean and I lifted Pierre clear of the bodies and laid him face down on a clear part of the deck.

"Robbie, press the cloth into the wound and stop the bleeding." As I did that Jean went below decks and returned with some brandy. He gave a rueful smile, "Pierre may say I am wasting this but..." he poured some of the fiery alcohol onto the wound. I felt Pierre's body tense which I took to be a good sign. He took out a sail maker's needle, thankfully one of the smaller ones and some catgut from the medical kit. He poured the brandy on them both. "Right Robbie, take away the cloth and then hold the two ends of flesh together. We will have to stitch him. Thank God he had that blow on the head. It might just save his life."

The blood seeped over my hands but it did not gush. I hoped that meant it was not an artery which had been cut. The flesh was slippery but I managed to hold it together as Jean put four big stitches into the wound. It held the flesh together. "Right Robbie, get some sea water and you can wash the wound while I finish stitching. "

As I made my way to the side, I saw that the major had ordered the corpses of the pirates to be thrown overboard. I threw a bucket into the sea and saw the dorsal fins of the sharks which flocked to feast on the floating dead and dying. I carried the water back and saw that the dead grenadiers were being laid, reverently in a line by their comrades. There appeared to be fewer than I had feared. Tiny had joined Jean and I could see the shock on his face. Michael's corpse was a few feet away and in plain sight. We would help the dead when we could but first, we had to save the living.

Jean nodded, "Start pouring. The salt will clean the wound." I did not know how Jean could sew Pierre's flesh. I found myself squirming each time the needle entered his body but soon it was done and I could stop pouring the sea water. "Tiny get a dressing from the grenadiers and a bandage." Jean poured some more brandy over the wound.

We were just finishing the bandaging when we felt Pierre stir. "Michael, is that brandy I can smell there? Give your old pal a drink, will you?"

Jean stroked Pierre's hair. "Michael is dead Pierre. This is Jean and Robbie."

We gently rolled him over and his eyes opened. "I was a dead man and then Michael came in like some sort of whirlwind." He blinked. "He's dead?"

Jean nodded, "Robbie here got all three of them but not before they killed Michael."

We were all silent. There was nothing else to say.

After we had cleared the decks, we began the burials. Ten grenadiers had died and five of the crew. All sixteen were buried at sea. The lieutenant had done it before and knew the service. I felt slightly sick as the head and then the body of my friend were sewn into the hammock and weighed down by a cannonball. At least the sharks would not feast upon him.

As the last of the bodies were sent to the bottom, we all stood in silence. The coast of Africa was now within touching distance but this did not feel like the start of something new it felt like the end. Our luck had finally run out and one of us had died. It is strange but none of us expected to die. The fact that Pierre had almost died and Michael had, made our life more precarious and precious at the same time. Hitherto we had gone into action with the confidence of immortals. Now we knew that we were more mortal. I could still feel the hands of the pirate around my neck and I knew how close to death I had come.

Jean put his arms around Tiny and me. "Well, tomorrow we go ashore. We will have to do the work of five but we will do it in the memory of a good soldier and a good friend, Michael. We cannot afford to dwell on his death. We are going to be in Egypt for some time and I do not think that our lives will get any easier. There will be more deaths. Let us just make sure it is not us."

And so, we prepared for the adventure that would be Egypt. I felt that my life had changed that day that we were attacked by the pirates. I had much to think on; the oath to Sir John, the death of my friend and my future as a chasseur. Who knew where I would be in a year?

THE END

GLOSSARY

Fictional characters are in italics

Albert Aristide-Lieutenant later colonel of 17th Chasseurs

Brigadier-Corporal

Captain Bessières-17th Chasseurs & Napoleon's Guides

Charles Chagal -17th Chasseurs

Claude Alain-Sergeant Major

Colonel Armand-Colonel 17th Chasseurs

Count Cobenzl-Austrian Diplomat

Francois Latour-Lawyer Amiens

Gendarmerie-French military police

Gregor Savinsky-Russian criminal

Guiscard- The gardener from Breteuil

Jean-Michael Leblanc-Trooper

Julian-Ex soldier- Guiscard's son

Louis (Tiny) Barriere-17th Chasseurs

Madame Lefondre-The housekeeper at the chateau

Major Lefevre- Grenadier

Maréchal-des-logis- Sergeant

musketoon-Cavalry musket

Pierre Boucher-Trooper/Brigadier

Pierre-François Bouchard-17th Chasseurs

Sir John MacAlpin-Knight of St John

toffs-Rich young men (English slang)

von Hompesch-Grand Master of the Knights of St John

xebec-Mediterranean ship with oars and sails

HISTORICAL NOTE

The 17th Chasseurs a Cheval only existed for a year. I have used them in the same way that Bernard Cornwall uses the South Essex in the Sharpe books. They have no history and can be where I wish them to be. None of the Chasseur regiments accompanied Napoleon to Egypt but I felt he needed scouts so that the 17th can have a glorious end to their career.

The books I used for reference were:

- Napoleon's Line Chasseurs- Bukhari/Macbride
- The Napoleonic Source Book- Philip Haythornthwaite,
- The History of the Napoleonic Wars-Richard Holmes,
- The Greenhill Napoleonic Wars Data book- Digby Smith,
- The Napoleonic Wars Vol 1 & 2- Liliane and Fred Funcken
- The Napoleonic Wars- Michael Glover
- Wellington's Regiments- Ian Fletcher.

The Dutch fleet was captured by French horsemen and they did ride with French infantry hanging on to them. The Texel was frozen and it led to the end of hostilities and the establishment of the Batavian Republic. Sometimes the truth is stranger than any fiction.

Antonio Onofri was a real person and it was his intervention with Napoleon personally which allowed San Marino to continue to exist as a sovereign state. The secret negotiations between Austria and France which led to the annexation of Venice did take place between April and October in 1797. The Austrian negotiator was Count von Cobenzl. Napoleon did orchestrate the events. I have used my heroes as the glue which holds history together.

This period was the one which marked Napoleon for greatness. Whilst other armies and generals were struggling to defeat the Austrians Napoleon did it with ease. He used his success to get rid of some of the members of the Directory he did not like and then formed the Triumvirate which ran France. They were so worried about him that they endorsed his plan to invade Egypt as it sent him far away from France.

The governors of the Conciergerie did make a fortune from renting beds. The price had been over 27 livres but by the time that Jean and Robbie were incarcerated, it was down to 15 livres a month. As some of the 'guests' only had the bed for a couple of nights one could see how the governors could make their money. The prison was said to be the most expensive hotel in Paris.

Napoleon did send spies to Malta before he invaded. The aged knights posed no problem and the militia who went against him were soundly whipped. The Grand Master was exiled to Trieste and the other knights were given their freedom. The mob did react as described and killed a number of the elderly knights. The island did not remain in French hands long after the battle of the Nile and it became British. Napoleon expelled the knights and took their fortune. Unfortunately, the treasure was lost after the battle of the Nile and now rests on the sea bed off the African coast.

The rapid promotions and the young age of some of the officers are not surprising. In 1789 Napoleon himself was only 20 yet within eight years he was the leading general in France and within ten would be virtually running the country. When the Revolution came many of the officers left the army and many of the non-commissioned officers joined the Royalist cause. It left every regiment bereft of leaders. The high casualty rate meant that any leaders were rapidly promoted. Most of the French marshals were either privates or non-commissioned officers at the outbreak of hostilities. The Revolution enabled men like Napoleon to achieve ranks which would have been impossible in a Royalist army. This contrasts with the British Army where the generals were all from the landed gentry and even the middle classes found it hard to become officers.

Robbie will return in a second novel. This one will see him experience the war in Egypt and the horror of being abandoned by his general when his fleet was destroyed.

Griff Hosker October 2013

OTHER BOOKS
by
Griff Hosker

If you enjoyed reading this book, then why not
read another one by the author?
Ancient History

The Sword of Cartimandua Series (Germania
and Britannia 50 A.D. – 128 A.D.)
Ulpius Felix- Roman Warrior (prequel)
The Sword of Cartimandua
The Horse Warriors
Invasion Caledonia
Roman Retreat
Revolt of the Red Witch
Druid's Gold
Trajan's Hunters
The Last Frontier
Hero of Rome
Roman Hawk
Roman Treachery
Roman Wall
Roman Courage

The Wolf Warrior series
(Britain in the late 6th Century)
Saxon Dawn
Saxon Revenge
Saxon England

Saxon Blood
Saxon Slayer
Saxon Slaughter
Saxon Bane
Saxon Fall: Rise of the Warlord
Book 9 Saxon Throne
Book 10 Saxon Sword

The Dragon Heart Series
Viking Slave
Viking Warrior
Viking Jarl
Viking Kingdom
Viking Wolf
Viking War
Viking Sword
Viking Wrath
Viking Raid
Viking Legend
Viking Vengeance
Viking Dragon
Viking Treasure
Viking Enemy
Viking Witch
Viking Blood
Viking Weregeld
Viking Storm
Viking Warband
Viking Shadow
Viking Legacy
Viking Clan
Viking Bravery

The Norman Genesis Series
Hrolf the Viking
Horseman

The Battle for a Home
Revenge of the Franks
The Land of the Northmen
Ragnvald Hrolfsson
Brothers in Blood
Lord of Rouen
Drekar in the Seine
Duke of Normandy
The Duke and the King

New World Series
Blood on the Blade
Across the Seas
The Savage Wilderness

The Reconquista Chronicles
Castilian Knight

The Aelfraed Series
(Britain and Byzantium 1050 A.D. - 1085 A.D.)
Housecarl
Outlaw
Varangian

**The Anarchy Series England
1120-1180**
English Knight
Knight of the Empress
Northern Knight
Baron of the North
Earl
King Henry's Champion
The King is Dead
Warlord of the North
Enemy at the Gate
The Fallen Crown
Warlord's War

Kingmaker
Henry II
Crusader
The Welsh Marches
Irish War
Poisonous Plots
The Princes' Revolt
Earl Marshal

Border Knight
1182-1300
Sword for Hire
Return of the Knight
Baron's War
Magna Carta
Welsh Wars
Henry III
The Bloody Border
Baron's Crusade

Lord Edward's Archer
Lord Edward's Archer
King in Waiting (December 2019)

Struggle for a Crown
1360- 1485
Blood on the Crown
To Murder A King
The Throne
King Henry IV

Modern History

The Napoleonic Horseman Series
Chasseur a Cheval
Napoleon's Guard
British Light Dragoon
Soldier Spy

1808: The Road to Coruña
Talavera
Waterloo

The Lucky Jack American Civil War series
Rebel Raiders
Confederate Rangers
The Road to Gettysburg

The British Ace Series
1914
1915 Fokker Scourge
1916 Angels over the Somme
1917 Eagles Fall
1918 We will remember them
From Arctic Snow to Desert Sand
Wings over Persia

Combined Operations series
1940-1945
Commando
Raider
Behind Enemy Lines
Dieppe
Toehold in Europe
Sword Beach
Breakout
The Battle for Antwerp
King Tiger
Beyond the Rhine
Korea
Korean Winter

Other Books
Great Granny's Ghost (Aimed at 9-14-year-old young people)

For more information on all of the books then please

visit the author's web site at www.griffhosker.com where there is a link to contact him.

The opening pages of the next novel
in the series Napoleon's Guards.

CHAPTER 1

I had no time to mourn for my friend Michael. He had been beheaded by the pirates even as we were edging close to Egypt. General Bonaparte had sent five chasseurs and a company of grenadiers to secure the harbour of Alexandria. We had to make the port safe for the invasion fleet of the charismatic French general. Now we would have to do it with just three chasseurs and grenadiers depleted in the pirate attack. I am Captain Robert Macgregor of the 17th Chasseurs à Cheval. I had campaigned through Ital with the general and, with Major Jean Bartiaux, my friend and mentor we had acted as spies and scouts many times. This last one was the first in which we had lost men. Michael was dead and Sous-lieutenant Pierre Boucher was seriously wounded.

"Robbie! Snap out of it!" We had just passed the entrance of Alexandria harbour and soon we would be landing. "Get rid of the hat and the jacket."

"Sorry, sir. You are right."

"Sergeant Major, go and get the spare pistols from Pierre and Michael they may come in handy." As I did as ordered he came closer, "I know you are upset but Michael would not wish you to lose your life, too would he?"

He was right and we all knew how parlous our existence was. A blade could come from nowhere, as it had for Michael or a volley of musket balls. This was a war which took no pity on those involved.

The captain of the sloop edged us to a small beach some two miles from the port. We had seen the flags, the guards and the guns but the Maltese flag meant that we sailed unmolested. We too our swords and a brace of pistols each. We had to find where the cannons where so that, when we landed, after dark Major Lefevre and his grenadiers could disable the guns and hold the entrance until the fleet arrived.

Francois, the captain of the sloop came down to see us. "I will sail out to sea and be back here in four hours. I will not be able to hang around."

Jean smiled, "We know and we have done this before."

"These are not the Maltese so be careful. To these people, you are the infidel. They trade with the Maltese but if you step ashore then you become fair game."

We descended into the rowboat. The last time we had done this there had been five of us and this time it was not so crowded. I wished it was. We leapt ashore and raced towards the line of palm trees. It was not much cover but it was better than standing on the beach. When we turned around the two sailors were pulling as hard as they could to reach the sloop.

We knew which direction in which to travel and we also knew that we were conspicuous. We had white faces and there were not many of those. We did not speak the language and, if we had to run, then our means of escape was four hours away. The prospects did not look good. It was close to noon and unbearably hot. As Jean had said that gave us our only chance for most people would be indoors. Who would be foolish enough to walk in the full sun? We began to pass small mud huts. The only creatures stirring were the cats and the dogs and they were just seeking shade. We had travelled a mile when we saw our first gun. There was a small stone wall and behind it was one old cannon. We had not seen it from the sea and it surprised us. Jean took out his crude map and drew an x where it was. The gun crew were nowhere to be seen.

Made in the USA
Middletown, DE
21 February 2020

85131584R00161